THE GHOSTS OF
MAYFIELD COURT

July, 1894. When Maximilian Paget inherits Mayfield Court, he and his niece Catherine find it to be half-ruined and haunted by the wraith of a murdered child. Catherine discovers a child's skeleton, bringing rural Detective Inspector Jackson and his bibulous but shrewd sergeant, Herbert Bottomley, to investigate. Once returned to London, neither uncle nor niece can shake off the baleful influence of Mayfield. And when Uncle Max is murdered by a deranged killer who, Jackson discovers, has left a trail of corpses in an attempt to secure a hidden fortune, Catherine herself faces imminent death, and a monstrous betrayal . . .

D0230211

Books by *Norman Russell*
Published by *The House of Ulverscroft:*

THE DRIED-UP MAN
THE DARK KINGDOM
THE HANSA PROTOCOL
WEB OF DISCORD
THE AQUILA PROJECT
DEPTHS OF DECEIT
THE DORSET HOUSE AFFAIR
THE CALTON PAPERS

NORMAN RUSSELL

◆

THE GHOSTS OF MAYFIELD COURT

Complete and Unabridged

ULVERSCROFT
Leicester

First published in Great Britain in 2013 by
Robert Hale Limited
London

First Large Print Edition
published 2014
by arrangement with
Robert Hale Limited
London

The moral right of the author has been asserted

Copyright © 2013 by Norman Russell
All rights reserved

A catalogue record for this book is available
from the British Library.

ISBN 978–1–4448–2075–1

TOWER HAMLETS LIBRARIES	
C001661844	
ULVERSCROFT	17 JULY 2014
F	£16.99
THISWH	

Contents

1

Catherine's Narrative:
The Spirit-Child

It was on Tuesday, 17 July, 1894, a hot and languid day, that I first heard of Mayfield Court. Uncle Max had received a visitor at our house in Saxony Square that morning, a heavy, taciturn man who had acknowledged my presence with a curt nod before being ushered into Uncle's study. It would never have occurred to me to ask what their business was: Uncle did not invite that kind of question.

I passed the morning in my little sitting-room, discussing the latest wonders of spiritualism with my friend Marguerite. Uncle and the taciturn man were closeted together for over two hours, and then the visitor had left as hurriedly as he had arrived. Marguerite left soon afterwards and, when Uncle Max came out of the study, he suggested that we take a walk in the garden. He contrived to look as sober as ever, but I could sense that he was controlling some inner excitement.

'Catherine,' he said, when we were out of earshot of the house, 'that man was an old acquaintance of my late brother, a solicitor, living in a little town in Warwickshire. He came to tell me that I've inherited an estate somewhere in that county — no, don't get so excited about it, girl! It's a broken-down old place, half ruinous, apparently. It's called Mayfield Court. My brother Hector lived there for a while thirty years or more ago.'

'Mayfield Court?' I cried. 'What will you do with it, Uncle? Surely you won't leave our house here in London to live in the country. Will you sell it? How much — ?'

'Hush, girl,' he said, while a humorous smile played about his lips, 'you must give me time to think. After all, I've only just been told the news myself. I think it would be a very good idea if I went down to this place — Mayfield, in Warwickshire — and stayed there for a few days, or perhaps a week, so that I could come to a decision about what to do with the property.'

'But we're not leaving Saxony Square?' I persisted.

'Well, no, though money has become short of late because of some failed investments — but never mind that: it's none of your concern. I shall do as I said, and go down to Mayfield at the end of the month. You can

2

stay here, if you like, with Milsom to look after you, or ask one of your friends to invite you to stay with them. Was that Marguerite you had in your sitting-room? Well, don't ask *her*. She has a bad influence on you with her tales of ghosts and spirits. At her age, she should know better. Ask Maisie Grossman if she'll have you. She's a nice, sensible girl, and nearer to you in age.'

'You've never mentioned this house, this Mayfield Court, before, Uncle,' I said. 'Did you know about it, or did it come as a surprise?'

Uncle Max frowned, and his lips tightened in a disapproving line.

'You're asking too many questions, little Miss Prying Paget,' he said. 'All you need to know is that this property has come my way in some convoluted fashion, and that I intend to go and view it. Perhaps — yes, why not? — you will come with me? If you see the place yourself, perhaps you'll stop asking all these impertinent questions.'

I knew then that I must not probe further. The ruinous house in Warwickshire was clearly yet another secret about which Uncle had no wish to enlighten me.

It is quite possible that these words of mine will one day appear in print, considering the nature of the appalling events that were to befall my family, so I had better give some details now about my uncle and myself, and our family background.

My uncle, Maximilian Paget, was a man well over seventy, a retired City solicitor, who had been my support and stay ever since his great-niece, my mother Emily, had died soon after giving birth to me. I regret to say that Emily was little more than a name. The convolutions of the Paget family tree were such that I had never really known how my mother had fitted in to it, or what had been her exact relationship to Uncle Max.

Nor did I have any recollection of my father, who had remarried only weeks after his wife's funeral, and had moved away from London. It was thought that he and his new wife had emigrated to Australia, but nothing was known for certain and, as the years passed, I lost the will to enquire further. My world, my security and my well-being, revolved around Uncle Max, the man who had reared me, loved me after his fashion, and protected me from the time of my infancy.

Uncle Max was often gruff and crusty in his manner, much given to growling and muttering when things didn't go his way, but he was always kindly and generous to me, in a cautious sort of way. There were times when he would relapse into gloomy silence for hours on end, and if I asked what was on his mind, he would shake his head, and angrily wave me away. I respected these moods of his, without understanding them, and so we got on very well together.

During the fortnight following our conversation in the garden, Uncle was much preoccupied in writing letters and in replying to a number that he received concerning his proposed visit to this mysterious house called Mayfield Court. I found it very difficult to contain my impatience, as London is very tiring during the summer, and a sojourn in the country would be very welcome.

It was the custom in our house to leave letters for posting on a brass tray in the hall, where Milsom would collect them when she was free from her duties, and take them down to the post box on the corner of Brandenburg Street. Sometimes I would idly sift through these letters, to see who Uncle was writing to. Mostly, his correspondents were fellow solicitors, but just over a week after our talk, I saw one letter that intrigued me, because it was addressed to a titled lady. I can recall it now:

Lady Carteret, Providence Hall, Upton Carteret, Warwickshire.

I heard the study door opening, and hastily

thrust the letter back among the pile, and made myself scarce. Yes, I was intrigued, but knew that it would be dangerous folly to question Uncle Max about it.

★　★　★

We arrived at the hamlet of Mayfield on the last day in July, after a tiresome journey from London which had involved two changes of train. At Warwick, we had been able to hire a pony and trap with a driver, and it was in this vehicle that we had been conveyed across a stretch of heathland and so into a secluded wooded valley. Here, we had been driven up to the rusted iron gates of Mayfield Court.

There was a ruined, roofless lodge beside the gates, and beyond them a wilderness of tangled grass, weeds, and stunted trees. The driver agreed to forge a passage through this undergrowth, just enough for us to walk; there could be no question of trying to force pony and trap through that rotting wilderness.

It was a truly depressing sight, and all my romantic notions about a grand country estate vanished in an instant!

The house, a three-storey Jacobean grange built of red brick, was almost certainly beyond repair. Sections of the roof had collapsed, and parasite weeds and bushes could be seen clinging on crazily to parapets and ledges. The top floor had lost the glass from all its windows, and encrustations of ancient soot around some of the casements showed that the building had at one time been set alight. I discovered later that some rooms on the first floor were habitable but unfurnished, and several of them had breaches in the walls. The floors up there were littered with debris.

The ground floor, however, was still habitable, and we made shift to settle ourselves in four large and decently furnished rooms, which had been made ready for us by a woman from the village, who had been engaged for us, apparently, by the taciturn man who had visited Uncle on the seventeenth.

'I think, Catherine,' Uncle Max had said, grimly, 'that we will camp out in this place just long enough for me to make an estimate of its value as building-land, and to sift through the bundles of old deeds and letters that came with the place, and then we'll return post haste to good old London. As for the house itself, I'll have it knocked down.'

And so we 'camped out' in Mayfield Court, attended by 'that old peasant woman' as Uncle insisted on calling Mrs Doake, the kindly soul who came in daily from the hamlet of Mayfield, which lay out of sight on the far side of the overgrown gardens of the house. I helped her in the dilapidated kitchen, preparing the main meal of the day, which was luncheon at one o'clock. Chattering all the while, she brought some life and cheer to the abandoned place.

It was Mrs Doake who told me about Helen, the Pale Child of Mayfield, an unquiet entity which was sometimes seen in the house. She was a spirit-child, who wandered the rooms by day, seeking some kind of undefined justice. Some folk had seen her, said Mrs Doake, a forlorn little figure in a muslin dress. Others had glimpsed her in the overgrown garden. At times she had seemed to speak, but no sound ever issued from the phantom lips.

'I've never seen anything myself, miss,' she'd said, 'but there are others who swear they've seen the Pale Child flitting about here, in the house, or out there, in that wilderness of a garden. Rector tells us to set no store by ghosts, but you never know, do you?'

'Does anyone know who she is?' I asked. 'Helen, I mean?'

'Nobody round here knows anything about her except for her name, miss. They do say that she came here to stay with a family who lived here thirty years or more ago, and that she was seen arriving at the house, but never seen leaving it. Mayfield Court was never lived in by gentry, miss.'

'So Mayfield Court was never properly inhabited?' I'd asked.

'Oh, no, miss,' Mrs Doake replied. 'Not by gentry, I mean. It had been left untenanted for years, and different people came to live here, so they say. People from London. None of them ever stayed long. Maybe the ghost frightened them away. Rector says there's no such things as ghosts, but you never know.'

★ ★ ★

No, I thought, you never know. We had been at Mayfield Court only a couple of days when I had my first sighting of the wraith of the little girl, standing motionless at the head of the first-floor landing. The child had looked at me intently, and had then pointed along the passage at the head of the stairs. A moment later, the spirit placed a finger to its lips. I found myself trembling with fright, and had closed my eyes. When I opened them again, the spirit-child had gone.

Uncle Max didn't believe in such things, but Marguerite and I both knew that the spirit world actually existed: we had seen wonderful apparitions of spirit babies in the London séances that we'd attended, and on one occasion the phantom of a dead sailor had appeared, and played us a tune on a concertina.

* * *

One morning, when we had been at Mayfield Court for some days, Uncle and I were sitting in the room where we spent our waking hours, I, engaged in some sewing tasks, and he, sitting at a table on the far side of the room, engrossed in sifting through the bundles of yellowing letters and papers that he had inherited. Perhaps I should elaborate here about their provenance.

Almost as soon as we had arrived at Mayfield, Uncle had made his way to a dark corner of the hall behind the staircase and, with the aid of a crowbar, had pulled away a section of panelling. I can still hear the violent protest of ancient nails as he did so. An alcove was revealed, containing a large, rusting, iron chest, which Uncle dragged into our living-room. Using a jemmy, he forced it open, and I saw that it contained a mass of old and yellowing papers, deeds and letters of all kinds.

How had he known that they were hidden there? I dared not ask him, as he well knew.

So, on that particular morning, Uncle Max continued his sifting and searching of these old papers. Occasionally he frowned, or made a little growl of contempt, tossing any offending document into a wicker basket beside the table. Then he would untie a further bundle, coughing at the cloud of dust rising from the musty, yellowing paper.

I could see the gleam of his white teeth where his lips had drawn back from the gums as he concentrated on his task. That unconscious habit of his, together with his luxuriant black beard contrasting with his shock of unkemt white hair, gave him a decidedly sinister appearance, though to me, there was nothing sinister about irascible old Uncle Max.

Uncle strongly disapproved of my interest in the supernatural, but things had happened to me since we had arrived at Mayfield, things that I felt I had a right to share with others. The first sighting of the spirit-child had been fearful enough, but I had seen her again, and it was not right or just that I should bear the burden of what I had seen alone. Should I tell him, and risk his wrath? By an effort of will I had kept my own counsel, but now it was time to speak.

11

'Uncle,' I said, laying down my sewing, 'I saw the spirit of that little girl again yesterday. It was in that small bedroom off the second-floor landing — '

Uncle Max threw down the letter he was reading and drew in his breath sharply. His keen blue eyes exhibited a sudden flash of anger, and I winced in spite of myself. Evidently I had chosen the wrong moment to share this bizarre confidence with my old uncle.

'Confound it, Catherine,' he shouted, 'I thought you'd forgotten that bout of silliness! We've been here for only a week, hardly time for us to make an inventory of what this wretched house contains, but already you've allowed yourself to be swayed by the gossip that that old peasant woman from the village retails, because she's nothing else to do to brighten her drab life. This wreck of a house lay virtually derelict for years, so the village folk peopled it with spooks and monstrosities. Forget it, do you hear me?'

'But, Uncle, how can I forget something that really happened — ?'

'It didn't, damn it!' Uncle Max rose from the table, his work forgotten. For one chilling moment — chilling to me — he looked at me as though I were a stranger. I watched him in some trepidation as he crossed to the window

12

which overlooked the desolate, overgrown gardens of Mayfield Court.

'Yes, I thought you'd forgotten it,' he repeated in a low voice. 'If you saw anything at all, it was because you'd nodded off, and had a daydream. No, don't contradict me, Catherine! If you persist in this silliness, I will take you to an alienist in Harley Street, and have your brain examined.'

I thought that it was only in novels that men stamped their foot with rage, but Uncle did it at that moment, and motes of dust rose from the floor.

'It was the same in London — the sanest place on earth — where that silly friend of yours, Marguerite — What kind of a name is that for an English girl? What was I saying? That girl, that Marguerite, took you off to séances, where your head was filled with crazed notions . . . '

Uncle Max paused for breath. I was startled, and rather frightened, to see how pale he'd gone. There was an expression in his eyes almost akin to fear. Fear? Fear of what?

'I forbade you to visit spiritualists,' he continued, 'and I'm glad to say that you did as you were told for your own good. But now you are *willing* yourself to see 'ghosts'. There are no such things. Are you trying to frighten

13

me? Well, I'll not be frightened, do you hear? My only fear, Catherine, is that you'll drive yourself insane with this unhealthy nonsense.'

Uncle Max stopped speaking, and his shoulders sagged as though he were suddenly aware of the imposition of some great burden. When he spoke again, I heard with alarm a kind of controlled desperation behind his words.

'You and I — we have both been cast adrift in the courses of our lives. You were more or less an orphan from birth, and I lost my wife to consumption when you were only eighteen months old. We had only each other, I with no wife, you with no good aunt to advise and admonish. Yes, we were both set adrift. And that's why we must both strive to meet the realities of this world with practical common sense. I am not frightened of your fantasies, but I am frightened for your sanity — your sense of balance. Think over what I've said. I paid for you to receive a first-class education, and yet you choose to behave like an ignorant peasant girl.'

Uncle Max rose from the table and walked heavily out of the room.

To my surprise, I found that I was experiencing a rising resentment of my own. He was treating me as though I was a little girl, afraid of bogies. He had said my second psychic experience was a dream. But it was not a dream.

That unpleasant scene with my uncle occurred on Monday, 6 August. The afternoon of the previous day had been still and oppressive. Uncle had been engaged all that morning in sifting through correspondence, scarcely acknowledging my presence, so I decided to explore the first floor of the house. Mayfield Court, being half-derelict, was in parts unsafe, but I had not lost the spirit of adventure that had made my childhood so full of dramatic incidents, some dangerous, others wildly funny.

When I was very young, Uncle Max had been less minatory, and very tolerant of my youthful antics. We lived in what is still my home, a fine old house in Saxony Square, a quiet secluded kind of place near Upper Berkeley Street, on the fringes of Mayfair. There was a large walled garden, where, as a child, I spent hours playing by myself. Uncle Max, then still practising law, had viewed my antics with amused tolerance. He had become a man darker in spirit, more withdrawn, but no less dear to me than he had been in the halcyon days of my childhood.

As I have said, Uncle had decided to spend Sunday engrossed with his musty papers, and

I had thought to seek amusement by exploring the first floor of the house. Accordingly, I mounted the rickety stairs and pushed open the door of a bedroom where Mrs Doake had told me that the spirit-child sometimes appeared.

The room was bathed in quiet sunlight, but held no sinister atmosphere. It was simply a small room with a single window, a collapsed iron bedstead, a chair, and a tallboy from which the drawers had been removed and stacked up in a corner, near a number of planks standing upright against the wall.

I smiled to myself — what had I expected to see? — and turned to go back on to the landing. Uncle Max would think me mad, maybe not without reason! As I mentioned, I had fancied that I'd glimpsed the little girl a week earlier, soon after we had arrived at Mayfield. Little more than a shadow, it had flitted across the head of the first-floor landing, and had then been lost in the gloom. I blush even now when I recall that I had been too frightened to investigate further.

It was as I stepped out of the little bedroom and on to the landing that a change in the light behind me made me turn round. I stood transfixed on the threshold of the room, quite unable to move. The somnolent rays of the afternoon sun lay across the chamber, revealing tiny motes of dust hovering in the air. Beside the iron bedstead I saw the figure of a young girl, perhaps ten or eleven years old. The child's face was pale and expressionless, though her dark eyes seemed to be fixed earnestly on mine.

The blood pounded in my ears, and I remained motionless and totally consumed by supernatural dread. The child was wearing an ankle-length frock of faded muslin, and her dark hair fell down over her shoulders. She made no sound of any kind. *You're supposed to speak first*, a little voice somewhere deep in my consciousness told me, *otherwise they can't speak*. My voice, when eventually I found it, sounded thin and reedy.

'Who are you? What do you want?'

The figure of the girl pointed to the bed. Her lips moved, but no sound came to my ears. I kept my eyes riveted on the child's mouth, and fancied that she had said the word 'Helen'. The figure pointed once more to the bed, and placed a finger to its lips.

I closed my eyes in dread, at the same time feeling for the frame of the door for support. Was this silent wraith really the spirit of the child who had once stayed in this house, long years ago? What had happened to her, that her spirit could not rest until some hidden truth were known? What was she trying to say, as she ventured for a while into this world from the world unseen? I opened my eyes again to find that the figure had gone.

* * *

On the Tuesday following, Uncle Max declared that he would spend the morning finishing his reading of the letters that he had inherited with the house.

'Another couple of days, Catherine,' he said, 'and we shall be able to leave this benighted place and return to London. We've been here too long already.'

He settled himself at the table in what had become our common living room, and I decided that I would fetch a straw basket from the kitchen, and go out into the overgrown rear garden to pick some of the ripe raspberries that I knew were growing there.

There was a romantic stillness and peace about the gardens of Mayfield Court that appealed to me. Wild nature had taken up residence there, so that clumps of brilliant yellow poppies, and wild purple geranium sprang up defiantly from the sallow tangles of dock and bindweed covering what had once been the paths and beds of a kitchen garden. Behind some banks of dying rhododendron the stark roofless walls of an old washhouse had long ago yielded to the advance of the invincible ivy. I had never explored as far as the containing wall of the rear garden, but I could glimpse sections of it through the bushes.

I pushed my way through the tall weeds and made my way into that part of the garden where a number of raspberry bushes, covered in enticing fruit, were to be found. I spent some time picking raspberries, and placing them in the straw basket, at the same time enjoying the warm sun, and the sense of being apart from the mundane concerns of Mayfield Court.

Quite suddenly, a cloud obscured the sun and, at the same time, I was conscious of something moving near the ivy-clad ruin of the washhouse. I turned sharply to my right, and saw once again the child revenant who had mouthed the name 'Helen' when I had asked her her name.

I found myself utterly deprived of the will to move. My fear was such that I scarcely noticed that the sun had come out from behind the cloud, so that the silent visitor was now bathed in light. She was wearing the same faded muslin frock, and her dark hair fell freely over her frail shoulders. I could see now that she was barefoot. Her little round face, devoid of expression, was turned to face me and, as our eyes met, she began to speak, but no sound issued from her lips.

What did she want? Why had she come back to haunt me?

The figure moved nearer to the ruin, and pointed to a particular spot close to the ground. The lips moved again, but no sound came. Then she placed her hands over her eyes for a moment, and seemed to move aside behind the bushes. I found that the spell had been broken, and that I no longer felt afraid. The little ghost had been trying to tell me something, but the words echoed in a world beyond this.

I picked up the basket in which the succulent raspberries reposed, and walked slowly towards the washhouse beyond the sprawling rhododendron bushes. With the disappearance of the apparition the garden had reassumed an air of encouraging normality. Even as I picked my way through the brambles one part of my mind was registering the fact that the fruits that I had just picked had come from the descendants of cultivated plants: they were too large and well-formed to be from wild stock.

When I came to the ruins I recalled the reappearance of the silent ghost-child. She had pointed to a spot in a partly-collapsed wall near where I was now standing. Had she

come with a message? Had the spirit material-
ized to reveal some long-concealed crime or
enormity?

I crouched down near the foot of the wall,
and saw that there was a v-shaped fissure
between the bricks, beyond which something
white gleamed where a little beam of sunlight
rested. I spread a handkerchief on the ground
and knelt down, so that I could get a better
view through the cleft in the bricks.

Delicate and beautiful, looking for all the
world as though it had been sculpted from
marble by a renowned artist, a skeletal hand
and the bones of an arm were revealed to my
appalled sight. I had no grounding in
anatomy, but I knew at once that these were
the bones of a child, and it was these pathetic
remnants that the child-ghost had yearned to
be revealed to the world.

I had experienced enough horrors for one
day. I walked unsteadily back on to the
tangled path, willing my legs to carry me
where I wished to go. I would soon be back in
the safety of the house, and Uncle, or Mrs
Doake, would rouse someone in this sleepy,
deadly hamlet to send for a policeman.

I glanced back involuntarily towards the
secret tomb, and saw once again the phantasm of the dead child, standing near a tree,
and pointing with a kind of silent accusation

21

at the spot where her mortal remains had been concealed. Would this haunting never end? It was then that I fainted, as though my mind willed my body to banish the denizens of another world from my consciousness.

★ ★ ★

'My niece has always seen things, Doctor. Ever since she was a little girl. Things that no one else sees, I mean. It's due, I suppose, to a heightened imagination. She used to consort with mediums, lured into doing so by a giddy woman acquaintance of hers, someone who's years older than she is, and ought to know better than encourage a young girl of twenty. But I soon put a stop to that after I found out about it. And now, Doctor, she's frightened herself into a fainting-fit. It's too bad. I shall take her back to London immediately.'

I lay on the sofa in our living room, watching my uncle through half-closed lashes. How long had I been unconscious? Long enough for Uncle Max to send Mrs Doake for a doctor. He was a man in his fifties, with a kindly face and shrewd eyes. He still held my wrist, measuring the progress of my pulse, while listening to Uncle Max's dismissive words.

I was suddenly overcome with a surge of

indignation — the beginning of a rebellion against my uncle's assumption that he could override anything that I said or thought as though I was a silly creature of no consequence. If I did not say something *now* in my defence, this doctor would prescribe a draught of some sort and leave the house. I opened my eyes, and fixed them earnestly on the doctor's face.

'I saw a skeleton — ' I began, but was interrupted immediately by Uncle Max. I glanced almost despairingly in his direction, and was shocked to see how his face had been suddenly drained of all colour.

'You see, Dr Tracy?' he cried. 'She wilfully persists in these wild assertions. I shall take her to Harley Street. You foolish girl. You saw no skeleton.'

'Oh, but she did, Mr Paget,' said Dr Tracy. 'When she fainted, the good woman who helps here — Mrs Doake, isn't it? — found her lying in the grass, and she, too, saw the skeletal remains, hidden in a ruined wall. She had the good sense to send a lad for me out at Thornton Heath, and when I came in the back way into your garden, I saw the skeleton too.'

At last! I was to be vindicated. Whoever this Dr Tracy was, my heart warmed to him. He turned then to address me directly.

'There,' he said, 'your colour is returning. You will be quite all right, now. Mr Paget, ask someone to bring your niece a cup of well-sweetened tea.'

Uncle Max made no move to accede to the doctor's request. He seemed dazed, as though talk of the skeleton had robbed him of the will to act.

'This skeleton,' he said at last, 'what's to be done? *Must* anything be done?'

The doctor drew a watch from his waistcoat pocket and consulted it.

'Oh, yes, Mr Paget,' he said, 'something must certainly be done. It's just after eleven o'clock. I have already sent a note to a neighbour of mine at Thornton Heath, and he should be here by twelve. He was working on his smallholding when I left, and I know he'll call in to the Volunteer for a glass of gin before setting off for his work in Warwick. But when he gets my note, he'll come here.'

While the doctor was talking, Uncle Max had regained control of himself. I saw the beginnings of a sardonic smile hovering about his lips.

'And this gin-drinking smallholder,' he enquired, 'is he an authority on skeletons?'

'Well, yes, he is,' said the doctor, smiling in his turn. 'I'll leave you, now. My neighbour will be here within the half-hour.'

2

Catherine's Narrative: Laying the Ghost

'There's somebody making his way through that wilderness of a carriage drive,' said Uncle Max. 'Probably a fellow yokel come to call on the peasant woman.'

It was just over half an hour after Dr Tracy had left. I joined my uncle at the window, and saw a heavy, thickset man approaching the front door of Mayfield Court. Despite the summer heat, he was clad in a buff overcoat which he wore open, so that it flapped about him as he walked. Beneath the overcoat he wore a dark moleskin suit, the trouser legs tied around his ankles with string.

The man held a riding crop, which he used to beat a way through the tangled weeds growing over the path. As he neared the door, I could see that he had a clean-shaven face, which was flushed either with exertion, or with what Uncle would have called 'ardent spirits'.

There was a brisk knock on the door, and presently Mrs Doake came into the room.

She gave a little bob of a curtsy in Uncle's direction, and told us that Mr Bottomley had ridden over from Thornton Heath to see us. In a moment, the man called Bottomley came into the room.

'Mr Paget?' he asked. His voice held the pleasant accents of a Warwickshire man. 'I'm Detective Sergeant Bottomley of the Warwickshire Constabulary.' He fumbled in one of the pockets of his overcoat, and produced a rather grimy warrant-card. I noticed that there was soil beneath his fingernails.

'You'd better go out into the garden straight away,' said Uncle Max. 'I have no desire to see this skeleton myself, and it would not be fitting for my niece to do so a second time. The woman who looks after us here will show you the way.'

Our rustic visitor treated Uncle Max to an amiable lopsided smile.

'Yes, sir,' he said, 'I'll be looking at the skeleton in a little while — but not just yet.' His face became suddenly grave, and he turned to look at me from a pair of fine, shrewd grey eyes.

'I'm told by Mrs Doake that you are Miss Catherine Paget,' he said, 'and that you are the young lady who has been seeing ghosts.' There was no mockery lurking behind his words, and when he asked me to give an account of what I had seen, I had no difficulty in confiding in him. Uncle, I noticed, had fallen silent. Leaving him to his own devices, I bade Mr Bottomley follow me into the kitchen, where I told him of my three encounters with the spirit-child. He listened with what I can only describe as becoming gravity. It was a novelty, as I was accustomed to all my accounts of ghosts and spirits being met with derision.

'A very interesting account, miss,' said Mr Bottomley, when I had finished. 'The Pale Child of Mayfield. Would you care to show me the room where you saw this phantom?'

The first-floor bedroom was just as I had seen it when the spirit called Helen had appeared to me. I watched as Mr Bottomley leant down, his hands on his knees, and peered at the uneven floorboards. He made an inarticulate sound of satisfaction, and then moved slowly around the room. When he reached the corner where the drawers from the chest had been placed, he carefully moved them aside, and it seemed that he looked at the wall in the dark corner for minutes before straightening up and treating me to a gentle smile.

'I don't suppose you like it here much, do you, miss?' he said. 'You'd rather be back in Birmingham, I expect.'

'Not Birmingham, Mr Bottomley,' I corrected him. 'Uncle and I are from London.'

'Oh, London,' he said, the suggestion of a smile playing about his lips. 'London. I see. So you won't like it out here much, will you? Here in the parish of Mayfield, in the hundred of Yeadon Vale, and in the county of Warwick, within walking distance of the hamlet of the same name?'

'What a strange man you are, Sergeant!' I laughed in spite of myself, and realized that it was the first time I had done so since the pathetic little haunting had begun. 'Why won't you go out to see the skeleton?'

'I will, miss, cross my heart; but the skeleton will stay where it is until I come, whereas ghosts and suchlike lead us a lively dance — or a deadly dance, I should say. When the spirit-child, this Helen, put her finger to her lips, did she do it like this?'

He placed the edge of his index finger to his lips, and held the pose until I became aware that Helen's action had been different. Mr Bottomley read this realization in my eyes, and slowly turned his finger until the front of it touched his lips. I could see his fingernail gleaming in the morning light. It had been the same with Helen.

'That's right, Sergeant!' I cried. 'That's how Helen did it. But how did you know?

28

Have you, too, seen her?'

'Oh, no, Miss Catherine,' said Mr Bottomley. 'I've heard tell of her, but I've never seen her. But now that I know how she held her finger to her lips, I reckon I know all about her. So it's time for me to examine the skeleton.'

The amiable half-smile suddenly faded from his homely face, to be replaced by an expression approaching bleak despair. I suddenly felt in awe of this man, who looked like a farm labourer, but who was, in fact, a police detective.

'I will examine the skeleton alone, miss,' he said, 'but there'd be no harm in Mr Paget and yourself watching me from one of the windows on the garden side of the house. As soon as I've finished my examination, I'll come back and tell you both what my conclusions are.'

★ ★ ★

From a window on the first-floor landing I watched Sergeant Bottomley as he went to work. Uncle Max had refused to join me, pleading more work on examining the bundles of letters. I suspected that he had no stomach for the macabre.

I saw Mr Bottomley, still wielding his

riding-crop, thresh his way through the wilderness of the rear garden until he reached the crumbling wall where I had found the ghastly remains. Once again, this rural detective did not behave predictably. He stood for a while staring fixedly up at the wooded hill that rose above the unseen hamlet. Then he turned slowly towards the south, and seemed to sniff the air like an eager hound. He suddenly plunged through the choking wall of rhododendrons to his left, and did not appear again for ten minutes.

When he came back from wherever he had been there was a jauntiness in his step that intrigued me. Indeed, everything that this burly man did intrigued me, perhaps because I have always been attracted to the unpredictable. At last I saw him kneel down beside the breach in the old ruined wall. He remained motionless for so long that I wondered whether he was not, in fact, kneeling in prayer. He made no effort to remove the pathetic bones of the dead child, but after what seemed an age he rose slowly to his feet.

Seating himself on part of the ruined wall, he rummaged in his pocket and produced what looked like a half-smoked cheroot. Retrieving a box of wax vestas from the same pocket, he lit the cheroot, and puffed away delicately for a while. When he had finished smoking, he dropped the butt into the grass, and ground it vigorously with his heel. He stood up, glanced briefly back at the house, and then disappeared once more into the bank of overgrown and rank rhododendrons.

I remained looking out on to the quiet, sunlit garden, where I had encountered the child-spirit known only as Helen. I felt mesmerized by the scene, the lack of animation, the illusion that no sound emanated from any kind of woodland life in that tangled wilderness. It was a strange, darkly enchanted place, a place where this world and the hidden world of the afterlife met and acknowledged each other.

After what seemed an age, Sergeant Bottomley reappeared, and to my heightened imagination he seemed to be a denizen of that enchanted garden. And then my heart gave a leap of fear and disbelief as I saw that the burly police sergeant was not alone.

The spirit-child Helen walked beside him, *and she was holding his hand.*

*   *   *

'This little girl, Miss Catherine,' said Herbert Bottomley, 'is Hannah Price, and she is a Romany child.'

When Mr Bottomley came back into the

house, he sat down on an upright chair near the table in the living room. Of Uncle there was no sign. The little girl stood beside the sergeant, leaning rather timorously against his right arm. I could see by her stance that Hannah Price knew instinctively, as children often do, that this was a man whom she could trust.

'I'm not one to belittle belief in spirits, Miss Catherine,' Mr Bottomley continued, 'but as a local man I knew about this tumbledown old house, and how easy it was for curious folk to gain entrance. When you showed me that little bedroom, I saw that there was a cavity in the far wall, which someone had tried to cover up with some old drawers. Well, I could see quite clearly that if you crawled through that hole you'd come out on to a stone staircase, leading down to the kitchen yard. That's how little Hannah got into the house and out again.'

'But why should she come here?' I asked. 'She knew where that poor skeleton had been concealed, and she knew that the little room on the first floor was where Helen had been lodged. She flitted about like a ghost, talking silently — '

'Yes, miss, and that's when I suspected that an afflicted child had been wandering about here. When I asked you how she laid her

32

finger on her lips, and you told me, I was almost certain. She'd been told always to do that in order to let people know that she couldn't speak.'

Bottomley suddenly encircled the child with his arm, hugging her towards him. He looked at her with a kind of grave compassion.

'How old are you, Hannah?' he asked.

The girl spoke, and I saw her lips form the word 'ten', though no sound came from her mouth. Immediately, she placed the front of a finger against her lips.

'You see, miss?' said Mr Bottomley gently. 'Hannah's telling you that she's dumb. She's also something else, Miss Catherine. I went looking for her in the gypsy encampment, because I knew there was no girl child of her age in the village. And there I found her, sitting on the ground in front of a caravan with her aunt. I sat down with them, all comfortable, like, and her aunt told me all about Hannah — another little orphan, like Helen. This little girl's not only dumb, she's 'lacking', as we say — not daft, miss, if you'll pardon the coarse word, but not always knowing what's right behaviour and what isn't. That's how she came to be wandering about in your house and garden — Hannah wouldn't understand the meaning of 'trespass'.'

'But she knew where Helen's remains were

concealed. She knew that Helen had slept in that bed — '

'I know, miss, and that's a mystery in its own right, but it's no good me questioning this little waif of a gypsy girl about it. However, her aunt told me that there was someone in their camp who knew a lot about Helen, and it was from this 'somebody' that Hannah learnt about that iron bedstead in the room on the first floor, and the whole legend of the little ghost. What we had here was one little girl looking for another little girl, and it was while she was doing that, that she discovered the skeleton. In her muddled way she kept her own counsel, miss, until she saw you. She must have liked you, and decided to share her secret with you.'

The door opened, and Mrs Doake bustled into the room, wiping her hands on her pinafore.

'Oh, Mr Bottomley,' she cried, 'is this the little mite that's been frightening us all? Well, Hannah, if you'll come with me to the kitchen, I'll give you a glass of buttermilk, and a big jam sandwich. Would you like that?'

For the first time since I had seen her, the little girl's face was lit up by a brilliant smile. She mouthed the word 'yes' in reply to Mrs Doake's question, and immediately placed her finger to her lips. Evidently the action had become an almost unconscious reflex. The kindly woman took Hannah Price by the hand, and led her from the room.

I looked at the rural policeman, who had begun to scribble a few notes into a minute notebook that he had produced from an inner pocket. His lips quietly formed words which he then wrote down; occasionally he licked the tip of the stub of pencil that he was using. He seemed to be a friendly, kind-hearted sort of man, but one who evidently kept his own counsel. I was anxious to know what he had discovered about the pathetic remains of the dead child concealed beneath the ruins of the washhouse. I thought: should I ask him outright?

Mr Bottomley stopped writing, and returned notebook and pencil to his pocket. He looked speculatively at me for a moment, and then spoke.

'I don't think your uncle, Mr Maximilian Paget, likes skeletons, miss,' he said, 'which is why he isn't here to listen to what I have to say. So I'll let you know what's going forward, and you can tell him later. The skeleton, as I think you realized, is that of a child. Until the police surgeon has seen it, there's no way of telling how long it has lain in its hidden tomb.'

'Poor little thing!' I cried. 'What kind of

people would murder a little girl? Poor little Helen — '

'Steady, miss!' Mr Bottomley held up a large hand as though to stem the tide of my indignation. 'Let's not confuse fact with fantasy! First of all, we don't know yet whether it was a girl or a boy. All that we know is that it's obviously the skeleton of a child. 'Helen' may be nothing more than a name belonging to an old folk legend told in these parts. Don't confuse our little skeleton with young Hannah Price, the Romany child.'

It was from that moment, I think, that I stopped regarding Sergeant Bottomley as a mere rustic policeman, presumably more at home with poachers and drunks than with murders. He was clearly a man with an agile brain, and a knack of clear thinking that, I realized ruefully, I myself lacked.

'And then, Miss Catherine,' he continued, 'we don't know for certain that it's murder, do we? The child may have died of an illness, or as the result of an accident, and been buried secretly for some family reason — an inheritance, perhaps. Such things do happen, miss. It's far too early to talk about murder.'

'You're right, Sergeant,' I said, 'and I must plead guilty to jumping to conclusions. I'll be more cautious in future. So what will you do now?'

'I'll walk back up the hill, Miss Paget, and talk further to an old man in the gypsy encampment.' He looked at me for a moment, and then added, 'Would you care to come with me, Miss Catherine? After all, you've been in this business from the beginning. Your uncle, Mr Maximilian Paget, seems to have no stomach for this kind of affair. So would you like to come? I promise to bring you back safely when we're done.'

I needed no second invitation. I was so used to Uncle keeping even mundane matters from me, as though ignorance was a virtue, that I was flattered to be considered an adult. I eagerly assented to Mr Bottomley's invitation.

'In that case, miss,' he said, 'we'll go up Piper's Hill — that's what it's called — by way of the old carriage road, which means we won't have to go through the gardens. That way, we won't disturb anyone who may be hiding there.'

I knew that he was referring indirectly to my uncle, so I said nothing, although the word 'hiding' struck me as being unpleasantly near the truth. Uncle Max, normally an assertive man, had been obviously unwilling to be involved in the investigation of a mysterious death.

★   ★   ★

Sergeant Bottomley and I climbed the long winding path through the tall beeches of Piper's Wood until we came to a clearing amidst the trees. Far below, half hidden in its own plantation of gnarled oaks, we could see the lichen-covered roofs and tottering chimneys of Mayfield Court. There was a smell of drifting woodsmoke, the occasional murmur of voices, and the sporadic barking of dogs. A single caravan, painted a faded green, stood in the shelter of the beeches, and presently an old man emerged from it.

'Solomon Williams is my name, master,' he said. He spoke with a pronounced Welsh accent, and his voice was thin and reedy, suggesting damaged lungs.

'My name is Herbert Bottomley,' said the sergeant. 'And this young lady is Miss Paget — '

'Ah! So that's who they be,' said the old man. 'More Pagets. I wondered whether that might be so. Well, master, you'll have come up here — you and the young lady — to hear about Helen, the little ghost. Leastways, that's what little Hannah's aunty told me. It seems that Helen's skeleton has come to light, proving that it was murder, right enough. I always suspected that someone had made away with that poor little girl.'

I looked at the old man, who had sat down on a wooden bench, motioning to us to do the same. Solomon Williams was a man clearly above eighty, with a skin tanned and wrinkled by constant exposure to the elements, and with faded blue eyes. He was clad in an old suit of black serge, and with a red kerchief about his neck. Before I was enlightened by Mr Bottomley, Solomon Williams had jumped to the conclusion that the skeleton was that of a child called Helen, and that the child had been murdered. This was not the occasion to argue the old man out of his beliefs.

'It was long years ago, Mr Bottomley, and you, Miss Paget,' Solomon Williams began, 'and memory becomes uncertain with the passage of the years. But yes, I remember that little mite coming to Mayfield Court. I can't tell you the year now, but it was on a black and rainy October night that the child called Helen came to that ill-fated house.

'We'd set up our camp here in Piper's Wood in September, which is something that we do most years. We stay until the end of October, when we travel back to our camp in Wales for the winter months. This wood belongs to the De Boulter family, who have always been well disposed to us — by which I mean, they do nothing *for* us, but they do nothing *against* us, either.'

The old man paused, and produced a short clay pipe from a pocket. He filled it with tobacco from a pouch, and lit it with an old-fashioned tinder box. For a while he puffed away in silence, his mind harking back thirty years. Mr Bottomley was evidently content to wait.

'Yes,' Solomon Williams continued, 'I was out that wet night — I remember the year now, it was 1864. I was looking to see whether any rabbits had been caught in the traps I'd laid that morning. Well, the rain was pouring down in torrents. I sheltered under some trees which overlooked the lodge gates of Mayfield Court. A closed carriage had stopped there, and I could see the driver in his gabardine cape and hood, banging on the gates to be let in. The lodge keeper came out of his little house, a piece of sacking thrown over his head, and dragged the gates open.

'As the carriage passed on to the drive I caught a glimpse of the little girl peering out of the carriage window.'

'And did you know who this little girl was, Mr Williams?' asked Mr Bottomley.

'Oh, yes, we all knew who she was, because the woman who worked as a servant at Mayfield Court had told one of our womenfolk that a Miss Helen was coming to stay. She was the niece, or great-niece, or maybe it was second cousin, of the master's, so she said. Something like that. The cousin had died, and this little Helen was coming to live with them — the master and his wife, I mean.'

'This master — can you remember his name? I know it's a long time ago.'

'His name was Hector. I never actually saw him, as I remember. He was a very withdrawn kind of a man, so they said. And *she* was called Arabella. She was younger than Hector. They weren't gentry; they just lived there. They've been gone for years — dead, for all I know — and the house has been shut up, set on fire, and neglected until that man and his niece — the young lady there — came to stay.'

'Hector and Arabella: I don't suppose you can remember their surname?'

'Well, of course I can. I'm not that old that I can't remember a man's name. Paget. That was their name. Mr Hector Paget and Mrs Arabella Paget. And the little girl was Helen Paget.'

I was learning more about my family from this old gypsy man than I had ever gleaned from my taciturn uncle. Who were those shadowy people, Hector and Arabella? What kin were they of mine? And if what old Solomon said was true, then the little girl called Helen was kin of mine as well.

The old gypsy was eyeing Mr Bottomley speculatively, waiting for him to ask a question.

'And what do you think happened to this little girl, this Helen?'

'Well, Mr Bottomley, the woman who worked as a servant at Mayfield Court — Rose Potter, her name was — told one of our women that a coach had pulled up on the Warwick road behind the old mansion, on the very night that Miss Helen arrived there, and that the child was roused from bed and taken away to live at a school for young ladies somewhere across the shire, a long way from these parts.'

The old man permitted himself a brief smile.

'Rose Potter! She was a goodly soul, with a kind heart. She'd once been a schoolmistress in one of the National Schools, so I heard, but had fallen on evil times. Perhaps she knew what really happened to the child, because she spent a lot of time sneaking along passages and hanging about on staircases. More handy with gossip than a duster, was Rose, so they told me.'

'So you don't think it was true — about

Miss Helen going off in the night to a school for girls?' asked Bottomley.

'I *know* it wasn't true, though I expect Rose Potter had been fed some tale or other by her master, or more likely her mistress. Listen, Mr Bottomley: I was out in the fields surrounding Mayfield Court all that night, setting traps, and suchlike, and I can swear that no coach stopped on the Warwick road, and no little girl was brought out to get into it. That child — Helen, her name was — was swallowed up into Mayfield Court, and never came out of it again.'

The old man's pipe had gone out, and he knocked out the ashes on the side of the bench.

'I used to tell our people what I thought,' he continued. 'Some believed me, others didn't. That's how the story of the ghost began, people elaborating on what I'd told them, weaving tales to tell at night by the camp fires. That's why poor little dumb Hannah wandered around the place, pointing to things, and trying to tell the story herself. Poor little thing, she's lacking, Mr Bottomley, and knows no fear of strangers. And now that you've found Helen's bones, you'll be able to find out what really happened to that poor child, and bring her murderers to justice.'

★ ★ ★

We retraced our steps to the house, and went into the kitchen. It was a hot day, and I suggested that we should have a pot of tea, but the sergeant said that a cup of water would be fine for him. As I worked the hand-pump over the brownstone sink, I was conscious of Sergeant Bottomley's eyes appraising me. Ever since his visit to Mayfield Court he had addressed most of his remarks to me, realizing, I suppose, that Uncle was not prepared to interest himself in the business of the skeleton.

I gave him the cup of water, which he set on the kitchen table. He explored a deep pocket in the tails of his coat and produced a battered silver hipflask, from which he poured a quantity of gin into his cup of water. He downed the whole libation in a single gulp, and sighed with evident satisfaction. He never took his eyes off me, and there was something about his expression, partly curious and partly compassionate, that made me feel vaguely unsettled. Then he spoke.

'Didn't I hear your uncle say that you're keeping company with a young man called Jabez? Or was it Theodore? I expect you'll be glad to see him again, when you get back to London.'

In spite of myself I blushed. Whatever had possessed Uncle Max to talk about my private life to a comparative stranger?

'His name's Michael,' I said, and from the little smile that played about Mr Bottomley's mouth I realized that he had tricked me into admitting that I had an admirer. Really, it was a rather impertinent trick. Whatever had prompted this kindly, shrewd man to act in that way? As though in answer to my unspoken query, Mr Bottomley provided an answer.

'Well, miss,' Bottomley continued, 'I hope you'll tell your friend Michael about what's come to light here today, about the bones of a child hidden away in the over-grown garden of a broken-down old manor house. Secrets of that kind are best shared with someone outside the family. Tell your Michael all about it.'

He spoke with such quiet, deliberate earnestness that for a moment I felt quite unnerved. What lay behind this enigmatic man's words?

'I'm riding across to Warwick, now, miss,' he said, 'to give an account of today's doings to my guvnor, Detective Inspector Jackson. He'll come out here tomorrow morning, and he'll bring the police surgeon with him. That poor little child lay concealed in that wall for well on thirty years; but if it's murder, then we'll not rest until we've tracked the killer down.'

I saw that fleeting expression of despair and sorrow that I had observed earlier pass across

45

the burly sergeant's face as he talked about the skeleton, and wondered whether he had children of his own.

'I expect that your uncle and you will be returning to London soon,' he continued, 'leaving this local mystery for us to investigate. But this is a Paget affair, miss, and its ramifications may follow you back home.'

He drew a pocket book from an inner pocket, and extracted a calling card, which he handed to me.

'If ever you need someone to confide in, Miss Paget,' he said, 'you can rely upon me to listen. You'll find my address there, on that card. I'll leave you now, and make my way to Warwick.'

Before I could frame a reply, Sergeant Bottomley had left the kitchen.

I looked at the card that he had given me:

Detective Sergeant H. Bottomley
Warwickshire Constabulary

On the reverse, written in a bold cursive hand, were the words: 'Dekker's Field Farm, Thornton Heath, Warks.' Evidently, the sergeant wanted me to have access to his private address. I wondered why.

* * *

Michael Danvers was the elder brother of my friend Marguerite. Mr Bottomley had called him 'your young man', but Michael was, in fact, thirty-five. He was a strong, fair-haired fellow, a junior doctor, at that time walking the wards at St Thomas's Hospital. Marguerite was two years younger than he, but still very 'girlish'.

I had been friends with the brother and sister for some time. I first met them in the Army and Navy Stores, when Michael had tripped and fallen against me, sending my collection of small parcels to the floor. His gracious apology had been seconded by that of his sister, who had insisted that I took luncheon with them in the restaurant. I used to think what a curious coincidence it had been that a chance encounter should have led to what some of my fellow novelists are calling a 'romance'.

Marguerite proved to have the same kind of exploratory interest in Spiritualism as I had myself, and it did not take long for all three of us to become firm friends. We enjoyed days out on the river, or matinées at one or other of the London theatres. Michael liked to regard himself as our chaperon and protector, as he was the oldest of the three.

I decided to take Mr Bottomley's advice and tell Michael the whole story, but I had reservations about doing the same with

Marguerite: she was, I knew, utterly incapable of keeping any kind of secret!

I left the kitchen and went into the living room. I glanced in the dim, fly-blown mirror above the fireplace, and considered the young woman looking out at me: even features, glossy black hair cut in the new shorter fashion made popular by Princess Mary of Teck, Duchess of York, wide blue eyes which revealed, perhaps, too much innocence — no, not innocence, it was credulity: I had always tended to believe whatever I was told. I had not dressed for the country, and was wearing a businesslike black crêpe dress, relieved at cuffs and collar with trimmings of white lace. Of course, I had younger, more fashionable clothes at home, including a number of dresses from Liberty's.

I suddenly wished that Michael was with me, here in Mayfield Court. I was weary of this decaying ruin, and horrified at what lay hidden from sight in the tangled garden. But that was not the case. Michael was in London, and knew nothing of this dismal place. But when I got back to Saxony Square, I would follow Sergeant Bottomley's advice. 'Secrets of that kind are best shared with someone outside the family. Tell your Michael all about it.'

I turned from the mirror and set about

finding Uncle Max. Wherever could he be? He had done little more than speak a few words to Sergeant Bottomley, and had apparently thought it of no consequence that the detective should leave Mayfield Court without having seen him.

Uncle was nowhere to be found in the house. A sudden fear gripped me. Maybe he had gone out into the garden after all when Mr Bottomley and I were safely out of the way on Piper's Hill, and perhaps he had fallen ill. He had suffered a slight stroke early in 1893 and, although he had made a full recovery, I was always anxious about his well-being. I hurried out into the garden.

Behind the old house there was a line of ruined stables and outhouses, mostly roofless, and beyond these, elevated some feet above the level of the garden, lay the road to Warwick. I discovered Uncle Max standing in front of one of the dilapidated outhouses, where a cast-iron incinerator stood amidst a hillock of old clotted ashes. I saw that he had lit a fire of dried wood and paper, and was standing, grimly silent, waiting for it to take hold. Beside him stood a wooden crate, piled high with the bundles of letters and papers that had so preoccupied him ever since our arrival at Mayfield Court. There was something so forbidding about his expression that

49

I held back in the shadow of one of the trees. What was he doing?

Once the fire was burning healthily, Uncle began to throw the bundles of letters and papers on to it. The incinerator was raised from the ground on slender iron legs, so that the blaze soon took hold. A pall of smoke began to rise towards the tops of the sheltering trees. His features were twisted in what seemed to be an expression of ungovernable rage. His eyes glowed with anger, and I could hear his breath coming in harsh, stertorous bursts of sound. For a moment he stopped his work of destroying the pile of documents to glance up at the sky, and shake his fist defiantly.

And then, as he seized yet another time-stained bundle of letters to consign to the flames he gave a sudden shout of triumph, clutched it to his chest for a moment, and then thrust it into one of the pockets of his frock coat.

'That's it! That's it!' he cried aloud, all trace of his terrifying anger having disappeared from his face and mien. 'And to think I nearly burnt it with all the rubbish! The harpy will be pleased — maybe she will take her claws out of me once I have given her that elusive deed!'

My heart pounding with fear, I made my

way cautiously back to the house. How long would we have to remain in this hateful, haunted place? What was the matter with Uncle Max, that he should behave like a man demented? As though in reply, I saw in my mind's eye the figure of little Hannah Price, mouthing the name 'Helen', and solemnly holding a finger to her silent lips.

3

Fleshing Out the Bones

Sergeant Bottomley sat on a fallen tree in the overgrown garden behind the old house. A few feet away from him was the ruined wall with its deep fissure in the brickwork that had constituted the tomb of an unknown child — unknown to the law, whatever stories may have been woven about a little girl called Helen. He pulled a dented silver watch from his waistcoat pocket, and opened the cover. Five past eleven.

He heard the sound of a carriage coming to a halt on the raised road behind the house and, after a little while, Detective Inspector Jackson and Dr James Venner, who was carrying a Gladstone bag, appeared on the path leading into the garden. Bottomley watched them.

The guvnor was dressed in his usual brown serge suit, with its ample waistcoat displaying a gold watch-chain and medals. Today he'd chosen to wear his dark-brown overcoat and tall-crowned blocker, so that to the uninitiated he looked like a gamekeeper in his Sunday best, or a coroner's officer dressed to call at the house of a circuit judge.

Doctor Venner had once said that Jackson did not look a bit like a detective. Well, that was all to the guvnor's advantage: one crafty embezzler, who had thought that Jackson was a marine chandler, had passed him a dud note, and had paid for his mistake with eight years' hard labour. Another wretch, convinced that Inspector Jackson was a wholesale corn factor, had tried to recruit him into an eclectic gang of assassins, and had ended up on the gallows.

Doctor Venner was a distinguished, grey-headed gentleman in his early sixties, for many years physician to some of the leading families in the county. Rubbing shoulders with the gentry may have given him his penchant for meticulously elegant attire: today, he was wearing a black frock coat with striped trousers, and a tall silk hat worn ever so slightly rakishly, its brim tilted over his left eye. He was sporting the lilac gloves that he favoured for day wear.

To Bottomley's way of thinking, Dandy Jim was one of the most elegantly foppish men that he had ever seen. He was also a brilliant police surgeon, with an immense knowledge of forensic medicine. The three men had worked together for many years.

'So, Bottomley,' said Dr Venner, 'what have

you got for me this time?'

He deposited his Gladstone bag on a clear patch of grass near the wall and, unfastening the five 'doctor's buttons' on the sleeves of his frock coat, turned back the cuffs. He placed his silk hat carefully on a section of the ruined wall, and deposited his gloves inside it.

'I'm not quite sure yet, sir,' Bottomley replied, 'but I'm inclined to think it's murder most foul — and the foulest of all, in my book: child-murder.'

'Hmm . . . Well, it's a fine, dry day, so we can examine the remains out here in the garden, where we can be reasonably private. Can you find a bed sheet, or a horse blanket — something that I can use to place the bones upon? Then, Jackson, perhaps you'll assist me in removing the skeleton from the cavity?'

★ ★ ★

The bones of the skeleton lay gleaming white under the August sun. They had been removed piecemeal from the cavity in the wall, and Jackson had been obliged to grope around in a mulch of dried leaves and soil in order to retrieve the leg bones.

Sergeant Bottomley had withdrawn a few feet from the spot, and Jackson joined him.

54

Together, the two policemen watched their colleague go to work.

Dr Venner spent a long time articulating the skeleton, carefully arranging the bones in their correct order. Then he removed a magnifying glass from his bag, and knelt down on the edge of the linen sheet that Bottomley had procured from the house. He examined every bone, and lifted the skull, so that he could scrutinize it before putting it back in its place. Then he selected three small bones from the mournful pile, and laid them out carefully on the grass.

'There, gentlemen,' he said, 'you can see the ilium, the ischium, and the pubis. After puberty, these three bones are fused into one, which we call the innominate bone, but in the child they are the three separate bones that you can see here. This is the skeleton of a child, and the contour of the pelvis shows it to have been a female child.'

Venner rose to his feet, and dusted the knees of his trousers carefully with a hand-kerchief. 'It was a little girl, you understand, aged ten or eleven. There is no way of ascertaining the cause of death. If she died by violence, then whatever force was used was not sufficient to break or damage any of her bones.'

He looked away from the two officers, as

though suddenly ashamed of what he was about to say. 'All the bones have been gnawed by rats, and it is conceivable that the body was consumed by rodents over a period of some months after entombment. She has lain there about thirty years. Twenty-five to thirty years.'

'The bones seem unusually clean,' said Jackson. 'I'd have thought that they would have become discoloured after so many years unburied.'

'It's a very dry location, and the skeleton had been gradually covered by leaves and other desiccated vegetable debris. I think that accounts for the pristine state of the bones — that, and the gnawing by rats.'

Venner treated Jackson to a wry smile. 'I know that neither of you likes my playing detective,' he said, 'but I would see this as the illegal concealment of a dead body — a felony at law — following a natural death, or, as you have suggested, Bottomley, the coming to light after a lifetime of a wicked murder, probably for gain.'

Venner carefully adjusted his silk hat to the rakish angle that he favoured, and picked up his Gladstone bag.

'I'll go back to Warwick now, Jackson,' he said, 'and arrange for a closed van to come here to remove these remains to the police mortuary. It's a sad business, when I am called to view the mortal relics of a child. So much lost, so much potential unfulfilled. I'll send you a written report, but there's not much that I can say.'

As soon as Venner had gone, Jackson knelt down in front of the fissure and began to rake out the mulch of vegetation that had enshrouded the skeleton. He did not end his task until the cavity in the wall was completely empty. Bottomley watched him as he sifted through the dense mass of leaves and stems. He was searching for clues, but he'd find precious little of interest in that tinder-dry accumulation of withered plants.

'There's another skeleton here,' said Jackson, 'but it's only a rat. And there's this piece of cloth — a strip of something — some kind of cotton fabric. You can see fine cords on its surface, made of raised threads.'

He handed the piece of fabric to Bottomley.

'It looks like dimity to me, sir,' he said. 'This bit may have been coloured at one time, to judge from that little pinkish patch at the top. It's used for bed upholstery — and nightgowns. So maybe that little one was still wearing her nightgown when she was placed in that makeshift tomb. Poisoned, or smothered, or strangled in her bed, and carried out here in the night . . . '

Bottomley walked away into the trees, and Jackson saw him fish in the ample pockets of his overcoat until he found his battered silver flask. A swig of gin will restore his spirits, he thought. Herbert Bottomley had eight daughters, all living. Two were married, two were in service, and the four younger ones were still at home. One of them Judith, was a little girl of ten. Maybe she, too, wore a dimity nightgown . . .

It was time to confront the elusive man who was staying in the tumbledown house. Bottomley had met him, but had only exchanged a few words with him before he had flitted away. Maximilian Paget and his niece Catherine must be kin of the child called Helen Paget who had stayed for one night in that house thirty years ago. Why did he show no interest in the discovery of a skeleton in the garden of the house that he had apparently inherited?

★ ★ ★

'They've gone, sir!'

Mrs Doake, besom in hand, paused in her task of sweeping the kitchen floor to answer Inspector Jackson's question.

'They left just after twilight yesterday, the

two of them, and their luggage, sitting in the back of a cart from the village. Not what you'd expect gentlefolk to do, but he was in a tearing hurry to get away. Mr Paget, I mean. He looked very pale, and didn't say much, but he seemed to be inwardly excited, if you get my meaning. It was that sweet girl who had to see to the house, and tell me what to do as regards shutting the place up. It was Miss Catherine who paid me my due, and gave me a half-sovereign to show her appreciation, which was very generous — '

'And where did they go, Mrs Doake?' Jackson interrupted.

'They went back to London, sir. I've got the address over here, written on this bit of paper, because, of course, the gentleman wrote to me before he came down here. Here it is. 'M. Paget Esquire, 11 Saxony Square, London, W.' A bad-tempered, surly gentleman, very abrupt with his niece, especially when she fancied she'd seen the little ghost, and all the time it was a living gypsy child! There he was, out in the garden, throwing papers on to a bonfire, and shaking his fists at the heavens, which isn't right, and tempting Providence . . . I saw him, you know, but he didn't see me! Now where was I? Oh, yes, they upped sticks and went yesterday at dusk. Sam Miller took them in his cart to the Volunteer at Thornton

Heath, where they caught the evening coach to Warwick. So there you are, sir, they've gone.'

It was Bottomley's turn to ask a question. He looked at the garrulous Mrs Doake with his amiable, lopsided smile.

'Have you ever heard the name Rose Potter? She was a servant in this house all those years ago, when little Miss Helen came to stay for the night, in the October of 1864.'

'Rose Potter? No, Mr Bottomley, I don't recall any such name. We came to Mayfield twenty-two years ago, so we never knew any of the folk connected with that mystery of Miss Helen. I suppose that poor little skeleton was hers, wasn't it? Whoever could have done such a thing? Rose Potter? Why don't you go and have a talk with old Mrs Protheroe? She'll know, I expect. You'll find her in the almshouse at Overton Hollow. There's not much Agnes Protheroe doesn't know about things that went on in these parts.'

'Well, thanks very much, ma'am,' said Bottomley, 'we'll certainly have a word with this Mrs Protheroe. We can walk from here to Overton Hollow, it's not above half a mile. But first, I think we'd like to have a look at this bonfire that Mr Paget kindled. Very interesting, that sounds, to my way of thinking.'

* * *

They had come to the line of ruined stables and outhouses, mostly roofless, in front of which stood the cast-iron incinerator on its mound of ashes. It was full to the brim with burnt and charred papers, and nearby was a wooden crate containing a few old grocery bills and a tattered almanac for 1884.

Bottomley threw the incinerator on to its side and scraped the contents out on to the ground. Maximilian Paget had done a good job of destruction, but a mass of paper never burns in it's entirety: there are always scraps of unburnt paper to be found if you searched diligently enough. Eventually, Bottomley found three pieces of charred paper that contained a few coherent sequences of words. He and Jackson studied them together.

. . . Gabriel Forshaw tells everybody that he will go to Af . . .
. . . inscription on their monument in Upton Car . . .
. . . WH was not one of us. He became a missionary, and went . . .

'Gabriel Forshaw', said Jackson. 'Whoever he is or was, our Mr Paget evidently thought him worthy of being burnt up in this incinerator. He went around telling people that he was going to — Africa? Or Afghanistan?'

61

'Maybe he went to Affpuddle, in Dorset,' offered Bottomley. 'I had a cousin who went to live there after she married.'

'Well, Sergeant, if this Gabriel Forshaw went to Affpuddle, maybe you could go down there and find out what he did when he got there. You could stay with your cousin while you were investigating. Affpuddle indeed! Dear me!'

Bottomley smiled, but said nothing. Jackson considered the second fragment.

'"Upton Car . . ." is clear enough,' he said. 'That'll be Upton Carteret. It's a village on the other side of the county, miles from here. I've heard of it, but I've never been. Evidently there's a monument of some sort there. It might be an idea to visit Upton Carteret, and nose around, as they say.

'Now, let's consider this third fragment. 'WH was not one of us. He became a missionary, and went . . .' Perhaps WH was a clergyman. He was 'not one of us' — meaning, I suppose, not one of the family. Well, we'll find out in the end.'

Jackson produced a fat notebook tied with string from his overcoat pocket, and carefully stowed the three fragments of paper in it.

'Now, Sergeant,' he said, 'it's time we set off on foot to visit that old lady at Overton Hollow. What was her name? Protheroe. Mrs Agnes Protheroe.'

* ★ *

'Well, well,' said old Mrs Protheroe, 'so you're trying to find Rose Potter? It must be thirty years since I last saw her, climbing up on to the Warwick coach at the Volunteer on Thornton Heath. She was a cheerful soul, for all that she'd been a school mistress. That's how she put up with Mrs Sourpuss and her precious husband for so long. By being cheerful, I mean. Mind you, she was a born gossip. Not that I minded, because in these out-of-the-way places a bit of scandal's always well received.'

Agnes Protheroe, a stout, white-haired old lady who wore horn spectacles on the end of her nose, sat in a chair drawn up beside the chapel door of the old almshouses at Overton Hollow. Some disregarded knitting lay on her ample lap. She had welcomed Jackson and Bottomley, explaining that in these days she had precious few visitors.

'Mrs Sourpuss?'

'Well, Mr Jackson, that's what I called her. Mrs Hector Paget, her real name was. She was a handsome woman, I'll give her that, but her heart was as cold as a stone. *He* was entirely under her thumb, and seemed devoted to her in his way. He was civil enough, but he was one of those vague, cringing kind of men

63

that you'd never trust. They didn't stay for long after that little girl who stayed with them went off to school.

'They left Mayfield without a word to anyone, leaving Rose Potter as caretaker. This was in the November of 1864. Just before Christmas, Rose got a letter from them telling her to close the place up, as her services were no longer required. They enclosed a money order for four pounds, in lieu of notice.'

Old Mrs Protheroe laughed.

'It was typical of those two skinflints that they made it four pounds. Why not five? Anyway, they went, and good riddance. After that, no one came to live in Mayfield Court, and the place went from rack to ruin.'

'You've a very good memory of those days, missus,' said Herbert Bottomley. He looked kindly at the old lady. She was dropsical, and the awkward angle of her neck told of arthritis, but she seemed immensely cheerful. There was nothing of the sourpuss about Mrs Protheroe. 'Did you live in Mayfield village in those days?'

'I did, Mr Bottomley. I was the midwife, and over the years I brought over forty children into the world. I got on very well with Rose Potter, because — well, never mind about that. She was a class above me, of course, having been a schoolteacher in one

64

of the National Schools, but we were good friends.'

'You mentioned the little girl who stayed in the house for a night,' said Jackson. 'Her name was Helen, Helen Paget.'

'Yes, that's right. Miss Helen. No one ever saw her, to my knowledge, except the Pagets and Rose herself. She said she was a dear little girl of ten or eleven, very well mannered, and nicely spoken. A young lady, you know. She only stayed a short while, and then a carriage came to take her away to a school for young ladies. I often wonder how she got on in later life. She'll be grown up now, and married, with children of her own, I've no doubt.'

'Do you know where I can find Rose Potter?' asked Jackson. 'I want to have a talk to her about her time at Mayfield Court.'

Mrs Protheroe gave both men a sudden, shrewd glance.

'You think that child's dead, don't you?' she said. 'You think the Pagets made away with her. There were always rumours about that, and about ghosts and suchlike, and we've heard tell that a little skeleton's been unearthed at Mayfield. But Rose will tell you differently. A carriage came in the night, and took the little one away to school. Do you know the little town of Bishop's Sutton, a mile or two beyond Haseley Green? Well, you'll find Rose Potter there. She's a good age, now, like me, but she's still the post-mistress there. Find the post office, and you'll find Rose.'

★　★　★

On the afternoon of the next day, Jackson and Bottomley went in a hired trap to Haseley Green. This place was very much on their patch, a pleasant village just a few miles out of Warwick. A winding secondary road took them to the village of Bishop's Sutton. The ivy-covered remains of an old priory stood in a field behind the church, from the gates of which the village street made a gentle descent to a tributary of the River Best. The post office, housed in a whitewashed cottage, was also an oil shop; above a line of tapped drums stood a shelf displaying an array of lamps and lanterns for sale.

Rose Potter was a lady in her early seventies, grey-haired, and comfortably stout. She had shrewd but humorous eyes, and an unlined face, which made her look younger than her years. She seemed very pleased to meet the two detectives, and quickly handed over control of the post office counter to a young girl, her trainee assistant. She led them into a cosy little room behind the shop, and motioned to them to sit down in two chairs beside the unlit grate.

'Well, well,' she said, 'fancy you wanting to know about young Miss Helen! It's a lifetime ago since I first saw her, and that wasn't for long. Why do you want to know about Helen after all these years?'

'A few days ago, Miss Potter,' said Jackson, 'the skeleton of a little girl was unearthed in the rear garden of Mayfield Court. We were referred to you as someone who remembered the child Helen Paget, and what happened to her when she stayed in the house — '

'A skeleton! Well, you do surprise me,' said Miss Potter. Jackson was puzzled by her response. She showed natural curiosity, but did not seem to link the fact of the skeleton with the fate of little Helen.

'Let me tell you everything that happened,' Rose continued. 'I have a very good memory, and the events of that day have stayed with me ever since. It was the year 1864, and our little night visitor came to us on the 28 October.

'I was waiting to receive this little girl, and was standing in one of the upstairs rooms of Mayfield Court, with the curtains drawn back, peering out through the driving rain. It was half past ten at night, and as black as pitch, but I could see along the drive, to where a lantern, suspended on its bracket on the south wall of the lodge, threw its light on to the lodge gates.

'After a few minutes, a closed carriage stopped at the lodge, and I saw the driver, impatient and soaked to the skin, clamber down from the box, and bang on the iron scroll-work of the gates with the butt of his whip. Poor man, he'd had enough of the elements for one night!

'Well, John Lewis, the lodge keeper, came out, hauled the tall iron gates open, and then coaxed the two black horses over the cattle-grid and so into the grounds. As the carriage passed under the oil lamp I caught a glimpse of a small, round, pale face, half hidden by the hood of a travelling-cloak, peering out of the carriage window. Poor little soul! She looked about ten or so, pretty enough, but with a frozen, expressionless look, in the way of children who are either frightened or overawed. Can you understand what I mean? That was my first sight of Miss Helen, and I've never forgotten it.'

'You knew that the child was coming? She didn't just arrive unannounced?'

'Well, yes, Mr Jackson, of course I knew she was coming. The master had come to see me in my sitting room early on the previous day, to tell me all about it. 'Mrs Potter', he said — he was always correct in that way, calling me 'Mrs' because I was the house-keeper, even though I wasn't married — 'Mrs Potter, my late cousin's daughter, Miss Helen, will be arriving here some time tomorrow evening. See that there's someone on the gates, will you?' Quite pleased, he was, I thought.'

'Pleased?'

'Yes. Maybe he liked the idea of having a child about the place. After all, there'd never been children there, and he was a kindly enough man when left to himself.'

Herbert Bottomley threw her a shrewd glance.

'But for most of the time he wasn't 'left to himself'? I expect his good wife had a lot of influence over him.'

'Oh, yes, she did. Miss Helen wouldn't have got any joy from *her*, that's for sure. She was as cold as ice, and with a will of iron. She'd throw him the occasional word of comfort like throwing scraps to a dog, and he'd be happy for the rest of the day. Mr Hector Paget was too weak-willed to withstand her. As long as he had his laudanum, he'd be content to do whatever *she* suggested. Still, it wasn't any of my business.'

'He took laudanum?'

'Yes, Mr Jackson, he did. I've never had any truck with doctor's bottles and cure-alls from the chemist, but he needed such stuff to give him courage, and to make him forget what a pathetic creature he was. So he took laudanum. It's like opium, and he became a slave to it. Half the time, he walked around that house in a kind of waking dream.'

'And what happened when Miss Helen came into the house?'

'Well, I received her myself in the hall, and took her through to the kitchen. I told the man to leave the little girl's bit of luggage beneath the stairs, as I'd carry it upstairs myself, later. Cook had long gone by then, but there was a cheerful fire burning, and I gave her a nice warm supper. She didn't say much — no more than yes and no, but I could see that she appreciated being looked after.

'When she was finished, I picked up her valise, and went upstairs with her. I'd done what I could to furnish one of the first-floor rooms for her, but it was a gloomy, ill-furnished place. I told her to wash her face in a bowl of warm water that I brought up, and then I combed her hair, and made her all tidy. It was time for me to take her down to the drawing room, to meet the master and mistress.

'Well, there they were, waiting for her. He was stooping, and nervous, with a fixed smile on his face. He looked done in, if you'll pardon the expression — exhausted. *She* was as majestic as ever — oh! She was a frightening woman, very handsome, and very domineering. They shook hands with the child. I expect his was limp and warm; hers would have been as cold and as hard as steel. They both spoke briefly to her, and informed her that she was to be sent to school somewhere across the county. She was too overawed to make any reply, and I took her up to her dreary bedroom. I helped her to unpack, and asked her whether she would like a warming-pan for the bed. She shook her head, but for all that I expect she would have liked it. I could see that she was very tired, and I stayed with her until she went to sleep.

'As I was making my way downstairs, I heard *them* talking to each other in the drawing room. The door was partly open, and I stood in the passage, trying to make out what they were saying.'

Rose's round face suddenly broke into a smile. 'Yes, I was listening at the door, and no doubt it was very remiss of me, but there it is. And the fragments I heard were so peculiar that I sat down in the kitchen and wrote them down on a piece of paper.'

71

Rose Potter opened a drawer in a bureau, and after some rummaging, produced a folded piece of greaseproof paper. Holding it up close to her eyes, she read its contents aloud to the two detectives.

''I tell, you, Hector', (she said) 'the subject is closed. We agreed that there was no other way. All that is needed tonight is that you give your consent. You may leave the execution of the matter to me'. I couldn't catch all they said after that, but then he started to speak, and for once his tone was strong and firm.

''I'd give it until next August, Arabella', (he said), 'no earlier than that, and certainly no later. It would be a good idea if a local man did it. That way, he could let others know in the normal way of things.'

''So by next August — ''

''By next August, I can assure you', (he said), 'the thing will be complete. Remember that I managed the other affair without unnecessary scruple, just as I can leave you to manage this business without my assistance. This is what I think we should inscribe.

''There are three or four other names there, so underneath we can have something like this: *Also Gabriel Forshaw, beloved son of the above Henry, perished of a fever at Bonny, in Nigeria, 7 August, 1865, aged 24 years, and buried there.* What do you think?'

'And that was all, Mr Jackson,' said Rose. 'They were getting uncomfortably near the door, and I quickly retreated to the kitchen, where I wrote down what parts I could remember. Here, you can take this paper with you, if you like. And that very night, while I was still asleep, little Helen was taken away. A carriage had called for her, they said, and carried her off to that school I mentioned. I was astonished, Mr Jackson, when I was told. I went into the bedroom, and the little girl's bed was still warm. As for Mr and Mrs Paget, I suppose they're long dead. I left their service soon afterwards, and came out here to Bishop's Sutton.'

'You say that the child was removed from the house by coach while you were asleep, Miss Potter,' said Jackson, as he and Bottomley prepared to leave. 'Are you quite certain that she left Mayfield Court? I told you that we have found the skeleton of a child — '

'Oh, but that couldn't have been Miss Helen, Inspector,' said Rose. 'I met her, you know, many years later, and she told me all about the school, and how glad she'd been to get away from that gloomy house. She gave me a calling-card, with her address printed on it. It's somewhere in this drawer — yes, there it is. You'd better take it. She looked very well and prosperous, I thought. She was married by then, she told me, apparently to a young accountant in Birmingham, and had a little baby of her own.'

4

Catherine's Narrative: Death in the Afternoon

I am not a vain woman — at least, I don't think I am — but when I have just put on a new dress or coat I survey myself in the cheval glass that stands to one side of the window in my dressing room. The grey dress, I thought, fitted very well, even though it had not come from Peter Robinson or Liberty.

An older neighbour of ours, Mrs Buckmaster, had taken me to visit Sophie Solomon, a seamstress who occupied a little shop near Spitalfields. Sophie was as adept as any fashionable modiste at tailoring dresses and suits that could be worn anywhere with confidence. The little matching hat was neat enough, and the mauve feathers were small and skilfully clipped. Michael, I felt, would approve.

How wonderful it was to be back in dear old London, and away from that dreary, ghost-ridden ruin at Mayfield! It was five days since we had hurriedly decamped at dusk on the eighth, and neither I, nor Uncle

Max, would ever go back to that place again. Uncle and I both belonged to London: the great, smoky city seemed to sustain us, as though recognizing one of its own. Uncle Max seemed much better in himself, more even-tempered. As for me, I was beginning to put the events of our visit to Warwickshire aside. It had been an uncharacteristic interlude in our life, and was best now forgotten.

That afternoon — it was Monday, 13 August — Michael and I were going to a matinée at the Gaiety Theatre in the Strand. Mr George Edwardes had enlivened the place for the last two years with his musical comedies, and his plethora of young ladies in the chorus. Uncle Max had called it 'all froth and nonsense', but there had been a twinkle in his eye as he said it. He seemed more than satisfied that Michael and I had become friends.

Outside, in the railed garden in the middle of Saxony Square, people were walking about, enjoying the August sun. A few nannies were seated on one of the long benches, their perambulators forming a kind of defensive line in front of them as they chatted to each other. Would they be talking about their charges? Probably, but maybe they were discussing their young men, too.

Although I was willing myself to forget Mayfield and its dark secrets, I kept Sergeant Bottomley in my remembrance. After that day's matinée I would tell Michael the whole story of what Mr Bottomley had described as 'the bones of a child hidden away in the overgrown garden of a broken-down old manor house.' Secrets of that kind, he'd said, were best shared with someone outside the family.

Uncle Max began to call up to me from the lower landing. I went out into the passage and looked down at him. He stood with his hand on the banister, gazing earnestly up at me, his face conveying some ill-concealed worry, his brow creased with an anxious frown.

'Catherine,' he said, 'come down to the study for a moment. I want to speak to you before you go off to the theatre.'

Uncle Max's study was on the ground floor, at the rear of the house, with a view of the old walled garden. It was a pleasant room, its walls lined with bookshelves, and in the window bay was a massive mahogany desk, at which my uncle conducted his business. I had once asked him what kind of work he did, and he had told me that he specialized in conveyancing, and the proving of title deeds to property.

Since his return from Mayfield he had remained closeted in this room, emerging only for meals. At night, when I went up to bed, I could see the line of light under the study door, showing that he was still up late, working.

On the third night following our return he had emerged from the study at five o'clock, clutching a handful of letters destined for the evening post. He put them as usual on to the brass tray on the hall stand, whence Milsom would collect them. Then I saw him pause, and extract a single letter from the pile. He threw on his overcoat, fetched his hat, and went out through the front door. From the hall window I saw him hurrying in the direction of Brandenburg Street, where the post box was to be found. I wondered then who was so important that a letter to them merited a special journey. I was, of course, too much in awe of him to ask him when he returned.

'Sit down, my dear,' said Uncle Max, when we entered the study, 'I shan't detain you long, since Michael will be calling very soon. I — Do you think I have done well by you, Catherine? Have I been a good uncle to you? I know that I'm snappy and curmudgeonly at times, but there's no harm intended. Everything I have done, I have done with your best interests at heart — '

'Dear Uncle,' I cried, rising in alarm from my chair, and taking his hand in mine, 'why are you speaking to me like this? No girl could have had a better guardian. You know that I love you, and always have.'

'Well, well,' he replied, withdrawing my hand from his, and looking away shame-facedly for a moment. 'Well, well, let us say no more about it. You see this desk? When I am — when I am gone, you will find a copy of my will in there, together with the name and address of my solicitor, who holds the original copy — No, Catherine, do not try to stop me. What is there to fear? At my age I must think of the inevitable.'

Uncle Max seemed to be controlling himself by a supreme effort of will. There was something gravely wrong with him today — perhaps it was connected with that pile of rotting papers that had so preoccupied him at Mayfield Court.

'After my death,' he continued, 'you must go to my solicitor to hear the will proved. On that occasion, he will hand you a sealed envelope, addressed to you in my handwriting. You must read the document contained in that envelope, and act upon its contents as your conscience directs.'

I said nothing in reply to his words, because it seemed to me that any protestation at that point would be inappropriate. But I was deeply disturbed. Why today, of all days, had he chosen to speak in such solemn tones? They would remain in my mind all through the comic play that Michael and I were about to see.

'I know that you are very much attached to Michael,' Uncle continued. 'Do you think you could ever marry him? There, there, don't blush, for goodness' sake! He is a fine young man, very personable, and following a noble vocation. He is many years older than you are, but still a young man, and I hope very much that you will marry him. If you do, whatever . . . whatever may happen, you will both have my blessing. But there's the front doorbell ringing. Goodbye, Catherine. Enjoy yourself this afternoon. Is Michael taking you to tea after the theatre?'

'Yes, Uncle. We'll go to Palfrey's Café in Bedford Street, and then Michael will bring me home. We'll catch an omnibus to Marble Arch and walk from there. Will you be all right here by yourself?'

'All right? Of course I'll be all right. I'm — I'm expecting a visitor this afternoon, so I'll not lack for company.'

My uncle took my hand in his, and pressed it kindly. When he looked at me, I saw that tears were beginning to well up in his eyes.

I left the study, closing the door behind me. I was very disturbed by his attitude and demeanour, and his gloomy talk about death, wills and lawyers. It was almost as though he was bidding me farewell.

The door to the parlour across the hall was open, and I saw that Milsom, the house-keeper, had placed a small table near the fireplace, laid for afternoon tea for two. She had set out the best Spode china tea service. I wondered who my uncle's visitor could be. Even in the midst of his perturbation, he had characteristically not thought to tell me.

Milsom, a neat, competent woman in her mid-fifties, had been with us for six years. She emerged from the kitchen passage, and went to open the front door to admit Michael. I detained her for a moment.

'Milsom,' I said, 'who is my uncle expecting this afternoon? Is it another lawyer? It's not often that he has visitors at this time of day.'

'Well, miss, it's not a lawyer, unless there are lady lawyers these days! Mr Paget told me to set out tea for two, as he was expecting a lady at half-past three. He said that I was not to ask her name, but to show her straight into the parlour. But there's Mr Danvers ringing again. He's very impatient, I must say! He'll not want you both to be late for the theatre.'

81

As always, the management of the Gaiety Theatre did full justice to its reputation that afternoon. They were presenting a revival of their popular musical farce *In Town*, which had been hugely successful in the previous year. The doors opened at two o'clock, and Michael had bought two tickets for the pit, at 2/6d each. Uncle, of course, had been right: it was indeed 'all froth and nonsense', but it was hugely enjoyable, particularly as the original principals of the farce, Arthur Roberts and Miss Florence St John, were performing that day.

Goodbye, my dear .... Why had Uncle Max used those words? After all, I was only going to the theatre for part of the afternoon. It sounded as though he were bidding me farewell ...

Nonsense! I still hadn't thrown off the baleful influence of Mayfield Court and its hateful secrets. What had happened to Helen — if that was really her name? By what evil course had she ended up as a skeleton, concealed in the ruins of the washhouse? Hateful place! Child and house had decomposed together.

I shuddered, and glanced at Michael, who seemed totally absorbed in the comic antics on the stage. There came a sudden gale of laughter, and the performers obligingly froze for an instant until the audience's mirth had subsided.

All the light in this building is false, I mused, man-made light; it comes from gas mantles along the walls and from the powerful lime-lights fixed on to the front of the circle. At any moment they could be plunged into darkness. Outside, the brilliant August sun would still be shining, and there would be a breeze, perhaps. Here, while the performers threw all their energies into the two-act farce, the air reeked of tobacco smoke and stale gas. It was stifling . . . Oh, Uncle Max, came my inward cry, what did you mean when you said those words: *Goodbye, my dear?*

When the performance ended, we emerged, blinking, into the bright sunlight of the Strand. The wide thoroughfare was, as always, thick with horse-traffic, characterized by the drumming beat of iron tyres on the setts, the 'clip clop' of countless horses, the cracking of whips and the curses of cabbies in a hurry.

It was a relief to turn into Bedford Street, and seek out a secluded corner in Palfrey's Café, where Michael ordered tea and toasted muffins. The little shop smelt of freshly baked bread, and coffee, served from steaming silver urns standing on the marble counter.

'Well, did you or didn't you?' Michael's

voice held a tone of slightly resentful amusement. Bother! He'd asked me something, and I had been miles away. I was usually all ears when he had something to say to me.

'Did I what?'

'Enjoy the show. What's the matter with you today, Cath?'

Tea and muffins arrived, and I gave all my attention to pouring out.

'Michael,' I said, 'I'm worried about Uncle Max. I've a premonition that something awful is going to happen to him — No, it's nothing to do with Marguerite and séances. He spoke to me today as though he was bidding me farewell.'

Michael stirred his tea thoughtfully. Even in my agitation of mind I could not resist admiring him. How handsome he was! His fair hair curled at the nape of his neck, and when he half-closed his eyes in thought, his long lashes swept his cheeks as though he was still a little boy. Yes, Uncle, I thought, I may have blushed when you spoke of marriage, but if he were to ask me now, I would accept him like a shot . . .

'It's that business of the old house in Warwickshire,' said Michael at length. 'What was it called? Mayfield Court. Perhaps he knows something about that skeleton — something that he dare not tell you. He's always been a

84

hoarder of secrets.'

'Well,' I said, rather lamely, 'I shall be relieved when the secret of Mayfield is finally revealed to the light. Maybe then the ghost will be able to find rest.'

Michael finished his tea, and began to make inroads into his muffin.

'Lay the ghost? Well, that rustic policeman did that for you, didn't he? Helen, the little lost waif.'

'It was that 'rustic policeman', as you call him, who urged me to tell you all about the secrets of Mayfield Court. Detective Sergeant Bottomley, his name is.'

'And how did he know about me?'

'He — he played a trick on me, a trick which made me tell him all about you — well, not all, but enough! That's when he advised me to confide in you.'

'Hmm . . . Not so rustic after all, then. But I say, Cath, what's all this about? I don't like secrets. Finish your tea, and we'll walk down to Trafalgar Square. We can catch an omnibus there to the corner of Upper Berkeley Street, and cut through into Saxony Square.'

★ ★ ★

As we came into Saxony Square we saw a crowd of loiterers gathered on the pavement in front of our house. They were, I knew, a pointer to the nameless dread that had hovered in the back of my mind since early that morning. The tall, elegant eighteenth-century houses, with their wrought-iron balconies, basked quietly in the afternoon sun, but the crowd, and the fact that the front door of the house stood wide open, showed that my premonition of evil had been more than a mere fancy. A stalwart uniformed constable stood impassively on the doorstep, keeping guard. The sun reflected from the silver 'C' badges on his collar.

Michael shouldered a passage for us through the crowd, and we made towards the door. The constable stepped forward, and held up his hand as though to bar our entry to the house.

'Are you family?' he asked, and when Michael replied in the affirmative, he moved aside, and we entered the house.

As soon as we stepped into the hall, Milsom came running along the kitchen passage towards us. Her usually placid face was ravaged with tears, and she was wringing her hands in anguish.

'Oh, Miss Catherine!' she cried. 'Your uncle's dead — poisoned! That wicked woman — I wish I'd never let her into the house. She poisoned him! And it was such a lovely day!'

She poisoned him . . . I suddenly recalled poor Uncle's words in the ruined garden, after he had rescued a packet of letters from destruction: 'The harpy will be pleased — maybe she will take her claws out of me once I have given her that elusive deed!'

I clung tightly to Michael's arm. I was not surprised at the terrible news. My uncle had bade me farewell, as though he knew that he would not survive that day. Perhaps he had a premonition that the 'harpy' would be the death of him. For a fleeting moment I saw him in my mind's eye, shaking his fist at the heavens while he burnt letters and papers on the bonfire in the garden of Mayfield Court. I, too, had had a strong premonition of impending disaster.

'What woman?' I asked, and was surprised at how strong my voice sounded.

'The woman who came to tea, miss. She arrived not fifteen minutes after you and Mr Danvers had left for the theatre. She came in a private-hire carriage, and the driver came down from the box to open the door. Well, she was a recent widow, as far as I could make out, clothed entirely in black, and with a long mourning veil, which she didn't lift. She — she looked like an angel of death.'

'What kind of woman was she, Mrs Milsom?' asked Michael. 'Did she say anything?'

'She spoke only to the carriage driver, telling him to wait for her. She was a lady, and I'd say she was about sixty years of age. I took her into the parlour, and poor Mr Paget rose to greet her. Then they both sat down to tea. I'd already brought the teapot in, and placed it on the table. And then I left. I came back again in less than half an hour, to see if they needed anything more, and found him — he was still alive, but gasping and shaking like a leaf. There was no sign of the woman. He looked at me, and there was terror in his eyes. And then he died! He gave a kind of muffled shriek, and fell back in his chair, dead — '

The door of the parlour opened, and a tall man in the uniform of an inspector came out into the hall. He had a red face, a fleshy neck, and thick silvery hair, but his quiet, thoughtful voice belied his truculent appearance.

'Miss Paget?' he said. 'I'm very sorry to tell you that your uncle, Mr Max Paget, has been murdered. Your housekeeper found him dead, and sent for the local constable. Very commendable. I am Inspector Blade, of 'C' Division, at Little Vine Street Police Station.'

He turned to look at Michael.

'And you are, sir?'

'I am Michael Danvers, Miss Paget's friend. I am a doctor at St Thomas's Hospital.'

'St Thomas's? Then perhaps you'll know our divisional police surgeon, Dr Whitney? He's in the parlour now, examining the body of the late unfortunate Mr Paget. I suggest you join him, sir. Meanwhile, Miss Paget, it would be a good idea if you took your house-keeper to some private room elsewhere, and listened to her story. I've already questioned her, and will ask for a written statement later.'

The two men watched as I led the weeping Mrs Milsom up the staircase. I heard the inspector say to Michael in low tones: 'It's always a good idea to get the ladies out of the way at a time like this. A police hearse will arrive in a few minutes' time to take the body away to Horseferry Road mortuary, and I need the hall clear for that eventuality. Go in now, sir, and talk to Dr Whitney, if you like.'

He nodded towards the parlour, and left the house by the open front door.

★ ★ ★

I have my own sitting-room on the first floor, facing the long, well-tended rear garden of our house. I made Mrs Milsom sit down on a sofa, despite her protests that it 'wasn't right'. The housekeeper had gained control of herself, though she was still very obviously shocked and bewildered.

89

'Miss Catherine,' she said, 'I've already told that police inspector all I know. The woman arrived here not long after you'd left for the theatre. From the way she spoke to the carriage driver I judge that she was a lady — an educated person, at least. When I showed her into the parlour Mr Paget rose to greet her — '

'Did he show any signs of agitation?' I asked. 'I'm sorry to have interrupted you.'

'Not at all, miss. Mr Paget seemed quite at ease, in fact he took the lady's hand and bowed over it in that old-fashioned way he had. Oh dear! I can see him now, in my mind's eye. Whoever she was, miss, Mr Paget knew her. After all, he was expecting the visit, and for all I know he may have asked her to the house himself. Who was she? And why did she commit such a wicked murder? I hope Inspector Blade hunts her down, and that she ends up on the gallows!'

For the last few minutes I had felt myself growing strong enough to cope with the horror of my uncle's violent death. I would grieve for him, but some inner recess of my mind bore a message of liberation from his life-long domination over me. I was my own woman now, free to make my own choices.

'Now, Mrs Milsom,' I said, 'I want you to tell me whether you heard any scraps of the

90

conversation between my uncle and that woman. No, this is no time for niceties about eavesdropping. Did you hear anything?'

'After I'd shown her in, miss,' said Milsom, 'I left the room and closed the door. As I was doing so, I heard the woman say: 'The old fool gets loose, and God only knows what he'll blab about unless we get him permanently under restraint.' I'll confess to you, Miss Catherine, that I stood outside the door for a while, wondering what those words could mean. The master seemed agitated, and he raised his voice, so that I heard him say something about 'making away with him'. It was like a question, as though he was saying, 'Shall we make away with him?' or 'Are you going to make away with him?'

'I began to get frightened then, miss, and hurried away into the kitchen passage, but not before I heard the woman's voice again. I don't know what she said, but I did hear the single word 'Forshaw'. And that's all I can tell you, miss, because that's all I heard.'

* * *

Later that evening, before he left for his billet in St Thomas's, Michael told me what had occurred when he joined Dr Whitney in the parlour.

91

'Whitney's a good fellow,' he said, 'a lithe, restless kind of man with a short spade beard. He pointed towards — Look, perhaps I'd better spare you the details — '

'No!' I cried, surprised at my own vehemence. 'I am tired of men trying to deprive me of information. Tell me what happened! Tell me what you saw!'

Part of me was horrified at my unbecoming forcefulness. I saw Michael suddenly look at me with something approaching awe.

'Very well, Cath,' he said. 'Your uncle was still sitting at the tea table, but he was quite dead. His head was thrown back, and his features convulsed in what had been a last, agonizing spasm. I have seen many dead bodies, of course, but I had never seen a victim of murder before. Your uncle sat there dead, clothed in his dark suit, with a lined silk waistcoat, his watch still ticking in his pocket, and his hands clenched so tight that his nails have drawn blood from the palms.'

I shuddered, but made no motion of protest.

''I know what you're thinking, Danvers', said Whitney. 'Or as good as know. You're still seeing him as the living, breathing man whom you knew. But he isn't that, anymore. He's a corpse, and can't speak for himself, to tell us what happened to him. We have to do that for him in the only way we can. Inspector Blade will bring in a detective, I've no doubt. But doctors — you and me — have to bring in the scalpel. So what do you think?'

'I looked at the body, realizing how inexperienced I was. 'There's no sign of a physical assault', I said. 'As far as I can see, he's not been stabbed, or shot, or bludgeoned. So I suppose he must have been poisoned.'

''He has indeed', said Dr Whitney, rubbing his hands together in what seemed to be a gesture of satisfaction. 'Poisoned by a substance put into that teacup you see there, now standing demurely on its saucer. I think he must have gulped down a good half of the tea before the cup jerked from his hand, and fell to the floor. You can see the stain, just *there*. Once he was dead, his companion — the lady who was taking tea with him — put the cup back neatly on its saucer. Some killers, you know, have genteel ways.'

''Do you know what poison she used, Dr Whitney?' I asked. 'Or is it too early for you to say?'

''I won't know for certain until I've opened the body up, which I'll do this evening. But I'm sure in my mind that he was poisoned with aconite, or wolfsbane, as it's called. I'll take away that teacup, and a section of the stained carpet, for chemical analysis. Yes, *Aconitum napellus*, or wolfsbane. It disrupts the balance in the cells of the heart muscle, and a lethal dose produces fatal arrhythmias, including ventricular tachycardia. That housekeeper's description of Paget's last moments suggest aconite poisoning — excessively rapid heart rate, et cetera.'

'And that was it, Cath,' said Michael. 'The poison brought on an immediate and fatal heart attack.'

'Wolfsbane?'

'Yes, Cath. The alkaloid, you know. I don't suppose our genteel killer came here with a bunch of lethal buttercups in her hand! Somehow, and somewhere, she knew how to obtain the pure alkaloid. But that's Inspector Blade's concern.'

It was time for me to confide the whole mystery of Mayfield Court — at least, all that I knew of the matter — to Michael. I told him of our stay in the old house, of the 'ghost' that I had seen, and the story of Helen, the child wraith. I told him all the details of the skeleton, and of Sergeant Bottomley's investigation. Michael was particularly interested in Uncle's obsession with the bundles of letters and papers that he had spent most of his time examining.

'Did he find anything of interest?' he asked.

94

'Yes, one document, which he actually clutched to his chest when he discovered it. I've no idea what it was, or where it is now. Uncle Max may have sent it in the post to someone else.'

'Another mystery,' said Michael. 'Somehow, Cath, I don't think the truth of this strange business will ever be brought out into the light of day.'

★   ★   ★

That night, I stood once more beside the cheval glass in my dressing room. I had sought out my darkest dress, which would serve the purpose until I went to a mourning warehouse tomorrow. There was much to do, particularly with respect to my uncle's funeral. When would the authorities release his body for burial?

Outside, the gaslights had been lit in Saxony Square, and all was quiet. I was now the mistress of this house. Why had Uncle had a premonition of his own death? The answer could only be that he knew the character of the deadly woman who had visited him . . .

There was something that I intended to do as a matter of urgency. I would write to the man who hadn't laughed at my belief in ghosts, and tell him all that had happened. I would tell him, too, the little scraps of conversation that Milsom had overheard. He had told me to confide in Michael about the sinister discovery at Mayfield Court. Well, I would return the confidence and tell him of my uncle's murder. I would look out his calling-card, write to him first thing in the morning, and send the letter to his home address, a farmhouse in the Warwickshire countryside.

I was conscious of a throbbing headache, and went to bed early, refusing dinner. I was surprised and relieved when I fell into a sound sleep almost immediately.

NOTE. Reading through what I have written so far, I can scarcely credit how gullible I was at that time. I always had an uneasy suspicion that I was too naïve, even for a twenty-year-old; but I was more than that, wasn't I? You and I have been married now for ten years, and I have always been quietly grateful for your saving me, when the need arises, from the consequences of my own continuing gullibility!

(March 18, 1905)

5

A Letter from Saxony Square

'Dad, there's a postman coming across the yard. Whatever can *he* want?'

Herbert Bottomley paused in the act of eating his breakfast of fried gammon and eggs. The dim farmhouse kitchen, as always in the morning, resounded to the noise of his girls, vying with each other to help their mother get him ready for work and out of the house. The baby was crawling under the table. Judith, their eleven year old, was brushing his overcoat, and scolding him under her breath for his untidiness.

'Well, Poppy,' said Bottomley, 'maybe he's bringing us a letter.'

Poppy, a fair-haired girl of fourteen or so, looked doubtful.

'Maybe he wants to buy some fresh vegetables,' she offered, but at that moment she heard the flap of the letter-box raised, followed by the slap of something falling on to the flags of the front kitchen. With a shriek of delight Poppy dashed out of the room, and in a few moments had returned with a bulky

97

letter, which she handed to her father.

'What's it say, Dad?' she asked eagerly.

Bottomley had looked at the postmark: London W. Franked at Grosvenor Street Post Office, 10.00 a.m., 14 August. He thrust the envelope in his pocket.

'I'll not know what it says, Poppy, until I've read it. Now while I finish my breakfast you can rescue Baby from under the table. She's untying my boot laces again. Judith, that's enough with the brush — there'll be no coat left by the time you've finished.'

Mrs Bottomley, busy at the kitchen range, looked at her husband. He'd not been his usual cheerful self since he'd come back from finding a little skeleton at Mayfield. Any crime involving children sat heavily upon him.

'Herbert,' she said, 'that letter — is it police business?'

'It is, Esther. It bears a London postmark, which tells me who it was that sent it. I'll take it out to the barn and read it before I saddle the horse.'

Bottomley finished a cup of strong tea that had accompanied his breakfast, and embarked upon the ritual kissing of his daughters before donning coat and hat and leaving the house. Behind the farmhouse, and across a narrow lane, there stretched a smallholding of about an acre, well tilled, and planted with a range of vegetables.

At the far end of the large field was a barn. Bottomley went in, and sat down on a bench. From an overcoat pocket he produced a pair of wire spectacles, and tore open the letter.

He had realized at once that it had come from Miss Catherine Paget, but had not anticipated the devastating news that it contained.

> *11, Saxony Square*
> *London, W.*
> *14 August '94*

Dear Mr Bottomley

My dear uncle, Maximilian Paget, has been cruelly murdered. It happened yesterday, 13 August, while I was absent on a visit to the theatre with my friend Dr Michael Danvers.

Our housekeeper, Mrs Milsom, told me that Uncle Max was expecting a lady visitor to tea at half-past three. He told her that she was not to ask the visitor's name, but to show her into the parlour. Milsom told me that the woman came in a private-hire carriage, and that the driver came down from the box to open the door. The woman was clothed entirely in black, and wore a long mourning veil, as though she were a recent widow. Milsom said that she was a lady in her bearing and manner of speaking, and about sixty years of age. Milsom took her through to the sitting room, where Uncle was waiting to receive her. He seemed quite at ease, and rose to greet her. When Milsom returned to the room a short time later, she found him in the last extremities of poisoning, and the woman gone.

Milsom told me that she had heard a few words of the conversation between Uncle and the woman. I reproduce those words exactly as she heard them. She heard the woman say: 'The old fool gets loose, and God only knows what he'll blab about unless we get him permanently under restraint.' She said that Uncle seemed agitated, and she heard him say, 'Shall we make away with him?' or 'Are you going to make away with him?' Milsom became frightened, and went into the kitchen passage, but not before she heard the woman say the single word 'Forshaw'. I write these details for what they are worth. They mean nothing to me.

'But they do to me, my dear,' Bottomley muttered. He recalled the fragment that he had discovered in the burnt remnants of letters in the incinerator at Mayfield. *Gabriel Forshaw tells everybody that he will go to Africa.* He continued to read Catherine's letter.

Uncle was poisoned with aconitine, or wolfsbane, placed in his teacup. The policeman investigating his murder is called Inspector Blade, of 'C' Division, and he can be found at Little Vine Street Police Station.

Dear Mr Bottomley, you were so kind and understanding when we met at Mayfield Court, which is why I am writing to you about Uncle's death. I took your advice and confided in my friend Dr Michael Danvers. My uncle very much approved of him as a suitor, and I hope one day that he and I will be married.

Please feel free to show this letter to your inspector, if you wish to do so. I think you told me his name, but I have forgotten it.

Yours sincerely
Catherine Paget

To Saul Jackson, Barrack Street Police Office in his native town of Warwick was a kind of home-from-home. No matter how far afield his investigations took him, the familiar

101

surroundings of Barrack Street helped him to think more clearly. Or so he thought. The front of the premises was occupied by Sergeant Hathaway and his three uniformed constables, but the back room, with its scrubbed and sanded floorboards, was the undisputed territory of himself and Detective Sergeant Bottomley. A laconic notice, pinned on the door, read: *Detectives. Knock and Enter.*

Sergeant Bottomley sat in the window seat, waiting for his guvnor to finish reading Miss Paget's letter. So it was two murders, now. Little Helen Paget out here in Warwickshire, and Mr Maximilian Paget up in London. And both murders, it would seem, committed by a woman.

'I'm thinking of what Rose Potter told us, sir,' said Bottomley when Jackson had put the letter down on his desk, 'about overhearing that conversation between Hector Paget and his wife. It was all about a monument to a man called Gabriel Forshaw. It's just a name to us, but maybe we could flesh it out with a few facts.'

'And then there's Miss Helen, Sergeant,' said Jackson, 'your little ghost. Rose Potter says she's still alive. What do you think? Maybe she's telling lies. Or maybe she's telling the truth. Because if the lady she claims to have met is not Helen, then the skeleton almost certainly is. It's time we made a move. I'll contact this Inspector Blade in London, to let him know that we're investigating a linked crime here in Warwickshire.

'Meanwhile, I want you to go after this 'Miss Helen' that Rose says she met. It's vital that you establish the identity of your skeleton as soon as possible.'

'And what will you do, sir?'

'Me? I'll go to this place Upton Carteret, and see what I can find out there. Whoever Gabriel Forshaw was, he seems to have a monument of sorts at Upton Carteret. The only way for me to find out is to go there.'

* * *

It had been a hot, tiresome train journey from Warwick, involving a change at Copton Vale Central, where Jackson had caught a little single-carriage train that had skirted the old town of Coventry before plunging into a belt of seemingly impenetrable woodland. Saul Jackson was a Warwickshire man born, but this part of the county was completely unknown to him.

Finally the train had drawn up to a wooden platform, where a sign-board informed the inspector that he had reached Monks'

Stretton. The man in the ticket office at Copton Vale had told him to get off here — 'alight' was the word he used. You always *alighted* from a train, apparently. The sign-board also told him that the little exit gate would take him on to the public footpath to Upton Carteret.

The footpath bordered a seemingly endless array of ploughed fields, sheltered by tracts of woodland. The dark-blue sky was cloudless, and there was not a soul in sight. It was on hot August days such as this one that Saul Jackson began to feel his age. His clothes seemed to hang heavy about him, and his boots pinched more cruelly than usual. The trouble was that he was becoming stout, and stout men could never abide hot weather. Perhaps he would exercise more in future.

The path began a steep climb through a grove of young birch trees, and suddenly Jackson found himself on the crest of a hill, from which he could look down at the village of Upton Carteret. It was just after ten o'clock on Friday, 17 August.

Upton Carteret had a wide main street of beaten earth, with cottages and shops on either side. At the end of the street, nearer the foot of the hill, stood an alehouse, a single-storey white-washed building, with a small shady garden furnished with a few rustic tables. A sign painted below the gable-end told Jackson that this was the Carteret Arms.

Opposite the alehouse was an ancient church. Here, perhaps, he would find some kind of monument or inscription relating to Gabriel Forshaw, 'the man of the fragment'. Jackson descended the hill path, and made his way into the churchyard, where he sat down thankfully on a stone bench set beneath the grateful shade of a sturdy old oak.

How quiet it was! Even the birds, Jackson mused, had been defeated by the heat of the August day, though a few bluebottles managed to buzz and drone among the gravestones. Jackson recalled the words found on the charred fragment of paper that he and Bottomley had found in the ravaged garden: . . . *inscription on their monument in Upton Car* . . . . Presently, after he had rested, he would examine some of the gravestones, and then quench his growing thirst at the Carteret Arms.

Facing the bench where he sat, and half hidden by tall rank grass and weeds, was a row of three tombs, which seemed in his fancy to be huddling together for company. They were built of soft sandstone, which had proved no match for the clinging ivy that was twining its way across the deeply-incised inscriptions. Jackson drew in his breath. Surely Providence had led him to this secluded spot? There in front of him he saw the name that the veiled woman had uttered before she had murdered Maximilian Paget.

All three monuments, it seemed, provided last resting places for a family called Forshaw.

Forshaws . . . John Forshaw, gent, died 3rd March, 1798, aged 58, a benefactor of the poor, deeply regretted by Monica, his wife . . . Edward Forshaw, died 15 December, 1853. Also Laura, beloved wife of the above, died 7 March, 1861, and buried at Leatherhead . . . Also Henry Forshaw, brother of the above John, unfortunately killed, 14 September, 1862.

These were some of the names that Arabella Paget, the dominating wife of Hector Paget, had been talking about when Rose Potter had lingered in the passage to hear what they were saying. Forshaws . . .

It was too hot even to think, today. It was very peaceful in this secluded spot — no wonder his eyes were shutting! This was an old, closed churchyard: there'd be no more burials here, and probably hadn't been for years. His eyelids drooped, and for a few minutes he yielded himself to the pleasurable sleep of a man fatigued.

He jerked awake as a lusty bluebottle droned past his ear. He saw it alight on one of the three adjacent tombs, where it began an erratic progress across an incised epitaph, added near the bottom of the third tomb. Yes! There he was!

Also Gabriel Forshaw, beloved son of the above Henry, perished of a fever at Bonny, in Nigeria, 7 August, 1865, aged 24 years, and buried there.

He recalled another of the rescued fragments of burnt paper: . . . *Gabriel Forshaw tells everybody that he will go to Af . . .* Well, it was true. Whoever Gabriel was, he had suited his action to his words, and had gone out to Africa, never to return. Could he safely conclude that poor Gabriel had nothing to do with the business in hand? Perhaps. But that black-garbed murderess had uttered the name 'Forshaw'. It was too early to dismiss anything from his mind as irrelevant.

'Bonny?' said Jackson aloud. 'It wasn't so bonny for that young fellow of twenty-four, who died there thirty years ago.' Gabriel . . . He'd have been fifty-four, now, perhaps with a wife and grown children of his own, had not the fever claimed him in far-off Africa.

Suddenly, Jackson realized that he was not alone in the churchyard. He became aware of an old clergyman sitting on another stone bench placed in the shadow of the church.

The figure seemed to emerge from the dim shade of a clump of over-hanging beeches like a photographic image slowly appearing on a glass slide.

Why had he not seen the old man? Probably because he was sitting so very still, almost motionless. He looked cheerful enough, but very frail and wraithlike. His hands rested on a stout walking-stick. He wore a broad-brimmed straw hat, and was rather carelessly dressed in a rusty old black frock coat which contrasted with the starched whiteness of a Roman collar. Perhaps he was the rector?

The old cleric was regarding him with an amused smile. The figure was so like a wraith that Jackson almost jumped in alarm when he began to speak.

'I heard you make a rather droll remark about Bonny just now, sir,' said the old clergyman. 'It was a terrible place for fevers, you know — still is, I expect. And a very convenient place to choose if you wanted to explain away the sudden disappearance of a healthy young man like Gabriel Forshaw. You know, as you get older — and I'm well over eighty — you begin to get impatient with the conventions.'

'The conventions, sir?'

'Yes. Agreeing with people so as not to make a fuss. Did I know you at Exeter?

Sometimes, I . . . They said it was fever, you know, and we all acquiesced. It was thirty years ago, you see, and we were younger then. Convention was all-important. But it was murder, right enough . . . I don't suppose it matters much, now. All the Forshaws are dead and gone, lying peacefully in those three great tombs till the Last Trump. But you won't find Gabriel there; and you won't find him in Bonny, either . . . Are you a resident here? My name is Walter Hindle, and I suppose you could say that I'm a visitor to Upton Carteret.'

'I, too, am a visitor here, sir,' said Jackson. 'My name's Saul Jackson, and I'm a detective inspector in the county constabulary.'

'A detective? So, I'm not the only one to be undeceived by a contrived legend. But it was a very long time ago. I shouldn't bother yourself about it. How hot it is today, Mr Jackson! Very hot indeed.'

The old gentleman's head nodded, and he fell asleep. Jackson, his eyes half closed, listened to the droning of bees, and felt the heat of the morning sun on his back. What a strange old man . . . He seemed to have emerged from the background of ancient beeches like a ghost. What did he say his name was? He'd sit there for a little while longer. It was a day for sleeping . . .

So this was Bonny, dark, dank, beneath the scorching African sun! Whose funeral was this? They were burying Gabriel Forshaw in a jungle graveyard. But hadn't someone said that it was not true? They were singing hymns and beating drums. 'He is not there', said a stern voice, 'you must look elsewhere.'

Jackson woke with a start, and looked around him. The old man had gone. He moved uneasily on the stone bench. The sun was passing now over the church, and the graveyard was being invaded by shadow. Had he dreamt the whole thing? Had there really been an old clergyman sitting over there on the other stone bench? Was he a ghost — a revenant, they called them — coming soundlessly to visit his last resting-place? Or had he been a dream-figure, suggested by the names of all those Forshaws carved on the three tombs?

Whether man of flesh and blood or a dream-figure, the old cleric had certainly been talkative — and his talk was of that dangerous variety that could lead to trouble. He had blandly accused someone — or some people — of murder, and then had advised Jackson, a police officer, to do nothing about it.

Well, it was time to pay a visit to the alehouse. As Jackson reached the churchyard gate he stopped abruptly. A garrulous old clergyman . . . What had the housekeeper

110

Milson overheard that murderous woman say? 'The old fool gets loose, and God only knows what he'll blab about unless we get him permanently under restraint.'

Jackson crossed the road and entered the garden of the Carteret Arms, where he sat down gratefully at one of the tables. At the same moment the landlord came out into the garden. He was a genial man with a shining bald head, and he was wiping his hands on a towel.

'Yes, sir,' he said, 'what's it to be?'

'I don't suppose you could give me a glass of Sherman's mild ale? Perhaps you'd fancy something for yourself?'

'That's very kind of you, sir,' said the landlord, 'I'll join you in a glass of mild, if I may.' In moments he had procured two glasses of beer from the inn, and had joined Jackson at the table.

'I don't think we've seen you here before, sir,' he said. 'From the looks of you I'd venture to say that you're a seed merchant, or maybe a corn factor. My name's Joseph Hardacre.'

'Saul Jackson's the name, Mr Hardacre, and I'm from Warwick.' He was content for the moment to be taken for a seed merchant. 'I was looking at some of the tombs in the churchyard. There seemed to be a lot of Forshaws there — three big sandstone tombs

111

full of them. I suppose the Forshaws are the local squires?'

'Squires? The Forshaws? Oh, no, Mr Jackson, nothing like that.' Joseph Hardacre swallowed a generous mouthful of beer, and wiped his lips on his sleeve. 'The Forshaws lived here, right enough: they'd been here for nigh on two hundred years. But they were never landowners. They made their money in shipbuilding — I don't mean modern ships, it was in the great days of sail. They had yards south of London, so they say, and they built warships for the navy. This would be in the seventeen hundreds, seventeen-ten, something like that.'

'So there are no Forshaws here now?'

'Oh, no, Mr Jackson, they're long gone. The last one died in the 1800s, but not here. Gabriel, his name was. They say he went out to Africa, and never came back. The Forshaws used to have a grand house on the road to Monks' Stretton, a little way beyond the village, but it was burnt down in — when was it? 1868, that's right. Waterloo House, it was called. Oh, it was a grand fire! If you're going back to Monks' Stretton the way you came, you'll see the ruins, all covered in ivy, set back from the road in a tangle of bramble and bindweed.'

'And they were never the squires here?'

112

'No. They were moneyed folk, and highly thought of, but not gentlefolk. The squire here is Sir Leopold Carteret of Upton Carteret. He lives at Providence Hall, which lies in its own little park a hundred yards or so beyond the church. The Carterets of Upton Carteret have been squires here since the days of Henry the Fifth.'

'You're a mine of information about this village, Mr Hardacre,' said Jackson.

'Well, sir, I've lived here, man and boy, for nigh on fifty years, and an innkeeper has to be interested in people and their doings.'

'I saw an old clergyman in the churchyard earlier this morning,' Jackson continued. 'What did he say his name was? The Reverend Walter Hindle. I expect you know him?'

'Hindle? No, sir, there's no clergyman of that name in these parts. Perhaps it was the rector you saw? Mr Bold, his name is. Youngish, and a bit prim and proper.'

Jackson was content to let the matter drop. He had watched the landlord when he had denied any knowledge of a clergyman called Hindle, and was inclined to believe that he was telling the truth. But he would not let the Reverend Mr Hindle slip from his mind. What had he said of the young man who had died at Bonny? 'It was murder, right enough'.

Jackson got to his feet. He rummaged in his pocket, drew out a few coins, and put them on the table.

'This Providence Hall, Mr Hardacre,' he said, 'I expect the grounds are open to the public? I fancy a stroll before I make my way back to Monks' Stretton.'

'Yes, Mr Jackson, the park's open right enough. Sir Leopold is very good in that way. A quiet man, quietly spoken, but nobody's fool. Well, I must be doing things. Nice to have met you, sir. I hope you have a safe journey back to Warwick.'

★ ★ ★

Jackson retraced his steps through the old churchyard, glancing at the stone bench where the Reverend Walter Hindle had sat earlier that morning. Had he really hoped to see the old clergyman again? Of course, he was no longer there.

A narrow lane confined by blackthorn hedges ran behind the church, and at the end of this lane an iron wicket gate gave entrance to the pleasant park surrounding Providence Hall. It was evidently a deer park, because a miniature grove of saplings growing there had been protected by little rings of paling fixed carefully around each tree. The whole estate spoke of quiet opulence. For a moment Jackson recalled the dreary, half-ruined house and grounds of Mayfield Court, blighted, as far as he could ascertain, by a lack of money. That was clearly not a problem faced by the owners of Providence Hall.

The great house lay basking in the hot August sun. Half-hidden by trees to the west, it was a long, low-roofed Elizabethan mansion, all black and white timbers, mullion windows and lichen-covered roof slates, merging dramatically towards the east with a three-storeyed Georgian extension in Cotswold stone. The whole venerable pile was surrounded by formal gardens well planted and maintained; an elaborate hedge of box flanked an ornamental iron gateway through which visitors gained access to the front entrance.

What was it, thought Jackson, that was compelling him to seek admittance to this great country house? He knew nothing of Sir Leopold Carteret, or of his family, always assuming that he had one. What was he to say if he was ushered into the presence of this gentleman, who would, no doubt, stand politely, waiting for him to state his business? He would ask some vague questions about the aged clergyman whom he had met in the churchyard, and be content with that.

'Sir Leopold, there's a stranger coming up the drive from Church Lane. I've not seen the likes of *him* in these parts before.'

'What kind of a man is he, Lucas?' asked Sir Leopold Carteret. A slightly built, sandy-haired man in his fifties, he was sitting on a brocade sofa in the oak-panelled parlour of Providence Hall. On the wall behind him hung a dim painting of a man who, at first sight, could have been taken for Sir Leopold himself, but the man was wearing the court dress of the late fifteenth century. Lucas was a strong, beetle-browed man of thirty, with a jutting jaw and a voice that placed his origin somewhere in the south of London.

'He's middle-aged, sir,' said Lucas, 'falling into flesh. He's wearing a thick brown serge suit — not very suitable for weather like this. He's got one of those brown blockers on his head, and I can see his gold watch-chain and seals glinting in the sun. He's limping a bit. Tight shoes, I expect.'

Sir Leopold turned a page of *The Times*.

'Probably a seed merchant or a provender factor. I expect he's come to see Owens in the estate office.'

'He's coming to the front door, sir,' said Lucas. 'So he can't be a seed merchant.

116

There, he's pulled the front door bell — '

'You'd better make yourself scarce, Lucas,' said Sir Leopold, throwing his paper down with a sigh. 'Even when her ladyship is away I can't get five minutes' peace in the morning. First you, hovering about, and now this visitor — Yes, Hopkins, who is it?'

A middle-aged, silver-haired butler had entered the parlour.

'Sir,' said the butler, 'a Detective Inspector Jackson from Warwick has called to see you. He regrets that he was not able to send in his calling-card.'

'Very well. Lucas, go through the other door into the library. Hopkins, bring the inspector in here.'

The butler waited until the man called Lucas had quietly closed the library door, and then ushered Saul Jackson into the parlour of the ancient house.

'Inspector Jackson?' said Sir Leopold, once more abandoning his attempts to read the newspaper. 'Well, how very interesting. How can I help you? Sit down, won't you? Whatever can have brought you here, to Providence Hall?'

Jackson began to feel more than a little foolish. Here was a landed gentleman, regarding him with pale-blue eyes, and waiting for him to answer his question. What was he to say? A little white lie was called for if he was not to lose all credibility.

'Sir Leopold,' he said, 'I'm making some preliminary enquiries concerning an aged clergyman, who may be staying in this parish at the moment. I thought perhaps you could help me. His name is the Reverend Walter Hindle, and he's a man over eighty. He dresses in rather careless fashion, and is known to wear on occasions a wide-brimmed straw hat.'

That, at least, was better than admitting that the clergyman in question could possibly be nothing more than a figment of his own imagination, conjured up during his morning doze in the churchyard.

'A wide-brimmed straw hat?' said Sir Leopold. 'How very interesting, Mr Jackson. And over eighty, you say?' The baronet seemed to be totally absorbed by the topic of the elusive clergyman. 'But how can I help you? What do you want me to do?'

The landlord of the Carteret Arms had been right. Sir Leopold was very soft-spoken, with a kind of caressing tone that was oddly flattering. He spoke as though everything Jackson said to him was of paramount interest, demanding an immediate answer. Jackson studied at him. He saw a willowy sort of man, slightly built, with a clean-shaven face animated by a kind of permanent smile. His sandy hair was beginning to turn grey at the temples.

'I wondered, sir, whether you'd seen such a man as I've described, or whether you are, in fact, acquainted with him. The Reverend Walter Hindle.'

Sir Leopold's brow became furrowed, as though he was making a monumental effort to recall some memory of the old clergyman. Then he shook his head in something like vexation, and smiled rather shamefacedly at Jackson.

'No, Inspector, I must confess that I've never heard of this Walter Hindle. He's certainly not here, in Providence Hall, and I don't recall ever having seen such a man in the parish. What I would suggest, is that you call upon Mr Bold, the rector. Perhaps he knows something about this Walter Hindle . . . And he wears a wide-brimmed straw hat? How very interesting. Call at the rectory, in Upper Ward. Mr Bold may be able to help you.'

'I'll do that, sir,' said Jackson. 'Thank you for receiving me without an appointment. I'm sorry to have troubled you.'

'It's no trouble, I assure you, Inspector,' said Sir Leopold, rising from his chair and accompanying Jackson to the door. 'I'm so disappointed that I was not able to help you.' The squire's voice held a quality of contrition that was positively moving. 'What makes you think that this old gentleman has any connection with Upton Carteret?'

'He was seen here, sir, only this morning. I'm not allowed to reveal my sources, but he was positively identified by someone who saw him in the churchyard.'

'In the churchyard? How very interesting. Let me accompany you to the front door. There's no need to summon the butler. You should certainly ask the rector, but, you know, I don't think he will have heard of the Reverend Walter Hindle either. Do call again if you're ever in the district. I have so much enjoyed meeting you.'

★ ★ ★

Mr Bold, a serious, carefully spoken man in his late thirties, with black hair thinning at the crown, had never heard of the Reverend Walter Hindle.

'I have never heard of the Reverend Walter Hindle,' he said. 'I can tell you confidently, Inspector, that there is no clergyman of that name living in these parts, and certainly not in this deanery. There's me, and there's Mr Lodge at St Peter's, Abbot's Sutton — he's

120

an elderly man, but not like the person that you have described. There are no Dissenters in this part of the shire, though there's a Roman priest who keeps a chapel near Mill Ford. He's a young man in his twenties.' Mr Bold smiled, half to himself, and added, 'None of us wears a straw hat with clerical dress.'

He reached up to a crowded shelf and took down a weighty volume with a fat gilded spine.

'Crockford's Clerical Directory, Jackson,' he said, 'a work which lists the names and details of all the clergy in the Church of England. Let us see . . . '

It took the rector only a few minutes to ascertain that no clergyman called Walter Hindle held office in the Church. He closed the book, and regarded Jackson critically for a moment. Then the ghost of a smile once more played around his lips.

'You told me that you dozed off more than once, Mr Jackson,' he said. 'Is it possible that you could have dreamt this clergyman? A man in Holy Orders wearing a straw hat, of all things! Most unclerical, I should have thought. Going to sleep in a churchyard on a hot day could give rise to what I'd call ecclesiastical dreams! Have you thought of that?'

It was, thought Jackson, time to go. He was making himself look a complete fool over this silly business. The more he listened to other people's explanations of his experience, the more he was beginning to think that they were right. There were mysteries here at Upton Carteret waiting to be solved, but a straw-hatted clergyman was not one of them.

Leaving the rectory he made his way back to the quiet churchyard. It was shadier now, and he could hear the fussy chirping of sparrows among the tombs. The three sandstone monuments of the Forshaws seemed to draw him like a magnet. John Forshaw, aged 58, deeply regretted; Also Simon, son of the above . . . Elizabeth Forshaw, died 4th April, 1798. And Gabriel, the young man who had perished at Bonny, in Africa, but who, in his waking dream, had been murdered. 'It was murder, right enough.'

Jackson strode along an overgrown path that would bring him out further along the road to Monks' Stretton. It was then that he saw, lying to one side of the path, a wide straw hat, that someone had attempted to conceal among the flanking weeds.

6

Helen Paget

Herbert Bottomley stood at the garden gate
of a detached 1850s' villa in Aston Road,
Erdington, a genteel suburb to the north of
Birmingham. This was the address printed on
the calling-card that Rose Potter had given
them, the home of Helen Paget. In a few
moments, if he was lucky, he would come
face to face with the woman who, as a forlorn
little girl, had arrived at Mayfield Court on a
rainy night in the October of 1864.

It was evident from the state of the house
and its gardens that Helen's husband, who,
the rate books had told Bottomley, was a
certain Adrian Robinson, Esquire, Chartered
Accountant, and was very comfortably off.
Bottomley's knock on the door was answered
by a trim maid in cap and apron, who asked
him his business, and then conducted him
into a sitting-room at the back of the house.

A dark-haired lady in her early forties,
handsome, and elegantly dressed, rose from a
sofa to greet him. She seemed nervous, but
then, Bottomley mused, most people were,

when brought into close proximity with a police officer.

'Detective Sergeant Bottomley,' she said, after he had presented his warrant card, 'what can I do for you? My husband is in town at his offices. Perhaps it is Mr Robinson whom you wish to see?'

Helen Robinson, also known as Helen Paget, spoke with the cultured tones of an educated woman.

'No, ma'am,' said Bottomley, 'it's you I've come to see. I was able to obtain your address from a lady called Rose Potter. You remember her, perhaps?'

It was impossible for Helen to mask her start of surprise. At the same time, her nervousness was superseded by an air of alert wariness. What did this rough man in the yellow overcoat, clutching his battered brown bowler with both hands, want of her?

'Rose Potter? Yes, I remember her well. Do sit down, Mr Bottomley. Rose was the housekeeper at a place called Mayfield Court, here in Warwickshire. She was a kind person, as I recall from my stay there. I met her again about ten years ago, and we talked about old times. But I fail to see — '

'Well, ma'am,' said Bottomley, 'I'm involved in a criminal investigation that's connected with the house you've just mentioned, and

I'm checking up on some historical facts to do with Mayfield Court and its tenants. What I'd like you to do, if you'll be so kind, ma'am, is to tell me something about your stay there in 1864. I know it is a very long time ago — '

'I remember it only too well, Sergeant. I was only eleven years old, and both my parents had died within days of each other in the August of 1864. My name then was Helen Walsh, but a lawyer, or guardian, or somebody of that kind — children have often no idea who these people are who take control of their lives when they're orphaned — where was I? I've lost the thread of what I was saying.'

'You were telling me that your name then was Helen Walsh, ma'am.'

'Yes, that's right. Well, this lawyer told me that I was to take the name of my only surviving relatives, which was Paget. And so I became Helen Paget from that day until I married Mr Robinson.'

Helen glanced at a framed photograph standing on the mantelpiece. It showed her with a sternly bewhiskered gentleman and two attractive young children, a boy and a girl.

'We married in 1876, when I was twenty-three. We have two children, Albert and Alexandra, who are both at boarding-school.'

Bottomley could see that Helen seemed

more at ease as she talked about her family, but the wariness, he noticed, had not left her.

'And is it true, ma'am, that you were only at Mayfield Court for a day, and that you were taken away in the night in a coach to go to school?'

'It is quite true. And let me tell you at once, Mr Bottomley, that it was the best thing that ever happened to me! Rose Potter was a kindly soul, but my aunt, if she *was* my aunt — I never knew for certain — was a domineering, frightening woman. There was a husband, too, an ineffectual sort of man. Mayfield was a dilapidated place, cold and forbidding. My new life began when I was taken in the darkness across the county to Meadowfield School.'

'And you were happy there, ma'am?'

'I was. Very happy. I never saw that aunt and uncle again, but the fees were paid faithfully until I left the school at sixteen, in 1871, and went to Homerton College in Cambridge, to train as a teacher. I taught at a local school there for a year, and then I met Mr Robinson.'

This lady, thought Bottomley, is very obliging to tell me all this about her life. Almost *too* obliging . . . But it was rapidly becoming clear that the legend of the coach carrying off little Helen in the night was true.

Solomon Williams, the old gypsy man on Piper's Hill must have been mistaken.

'And this school, ma'am,' said Bottomley, rummaging in a capacious pocket for his notebook and a stub of pencil, 'would you tell me where it is?'

'Why, certainly, Mr Bottomley. Meadowfield School for Girls is at a place called Upton Cross, here in Warwickshire. Are you going to visit them?'

'I am, Mrs Robinson. Just to tie up a few loose ends. Thank you very much for seeing me today. I'll be off, now, ma'am.'

Mrs Robinson rose from the sofa, and pulled a bell beside the fireplace.

'My maid will see you out, Sergeant. I must say that I am intrigued about the crime that you are investigating, and my role in the affair. What exactly are you engaged upon? Or must I not ask?'

'Oh, it's no secret, ma'am,' said Bottomley, pocketing his note book. 'We — the police, I mean — have just uncovered the skeleton of an eleven-year-old girl hidden in the grounds of Mayfield Court — '

'Oh, God!'

Helen Robinson, *née* Walsh, also known as Helen Paget, uttered a shriek of anguish and fainted away just as the startled maid entered the sitting room.

'Meadowfield School, Mr Bottomley, is well known to discerning families. Old girls will send their daughters here, and those daughters, ultimately, send us their offspring. We have a long waiting-list. We were established in 1802.'

Helen Paget's old school occupied a very fine mock-Tudor house, set in extensive grounds. Miss Jellicoe, the principal, strolled with Bottomley along a shale path that cut across the front lawn. A number of senior girls were playing a rather listless game of tennis on a hard court.

'I'm nearer seventy than is decent,' said Miss Jellicoe with an engaging smile, 'and I suppose I should retire. But somehow, that prospect appals me.'

This school-marm, thought Bottomley, isn't a bit like some of the vinegary old parties he'd met in the course of his life. He recalled Miss Fitt, (aptly so named), who had hated boys, and had a habit of hauling them around the classroom by the short hairs of their sideburns when she was in angry mood.

'And so you'll remember Helen Paget, ma'am? I saw her yesterday, and she told me how much she'd enjoyed being here.'

'She was a good pupil,' said Miss Jellicoe.

'She was unceremoniously dumped on us, you know, arriving very early one October morning in a closed carriage. She fitted in immediately, was good at her studies, and at games, and went on to become a teacher herself for a short time. Then she fell, smitten by Cupid's arrows.'

Miss Jellicoe laughed.

'And did you ever see her guardians — her aunt and uncle?'

'Never. All we ever knew was that she had come to us from a place called Mayfield Court on the other side of the county. Her fees were paid faithfully, and stopped when she left.'

'Was she very shy when she came to you?'

'Shy? No, not particularly. She was quiet and polite. This is a Froebel school, Mr Bottomley — do you know what that means?'

'No, ma'am.'

'Well, Froebel was a German educationist, who invented kindergartens — schools for little children. He also introduced the rewards system, where children are given little gifts to mark their progress. Helen Paget responded very well to this. She was in every way a model pupil. Shy? No, I don't think so. Do you have daughters of your own?'

'I have eight daughters, ma'am,' said Bottomley, with what sounded like a stifled sigh. 'Eight daughters, all living. Two are married, two are in service, and the rest are at home with the wife and me.'

'Good heavens! So you have a ready-made girls' school of your own. How do you cope?'

'Well, ma'am, I follow the same system as that German chap you mentioned. What I can't achieve by looking stern I achieve through bribery.'

Miss Jellicoe laughed again, and motioned towards the house.

'Come, Sergeant,' she said, 'it's a hot day. Let us go indoors and partake of some refreshment. I have tea, or I can send for beer if you'd prefer that. It's time for you and me to compare notes on the education of children!'

★ ★ ★

On the following Tuesday, Jackson and Bottomley, each fresh from his own investigation talked together for over an hour, sitting in the back room at Barrack Street.

'So that's that,' said Jackson. 'Helen Paget was indeed whisked off to school on that night in October 1864, and the old gypsy man was wrong. But I wasn't dreaming when I spoke to that old clergyman. I found his straw hat half-hidden in the graveyard, suggesting that he had been discovered and hustled away for some reason. He said that this Gabriel Forshaw had been murdered.'

'It looks as though he's the 'silly old fool' the murderous lady talked about,' said Bottomley. 'I wonder how *he* fits in?'

'And another thing,' said Jackson. 'I don't trust that blandly helpful baronet, Sir Leopold Carteret. Too obliging by far, he was. He saw me politely off at the door of his house, and sent me to the rector, who clearly thought that I'd dozed off and imagined the Reverend Walter Hindle.'

Jackson glanced at the tall railway clock fixed high on the wall of the office.

'It's nearing twelve,' he said. 'I think you and I should stroll up to the cottage and partake of some refreshment. Then we can go over a few things again in peace and comfort.'

★ ★ ★

A steep walk uphill from Barrack Street Police Office took Jackson and Bottomley very quickly into the green countryside. The cobbled road changed into an unmade winding track, along which several hundred years' worth of sparse buildings had sinuously arranged themselves into a hamlet. The summer sun flooded the quiet enclave of

131

Meadow Cross Lane, as the winding track from Warwick was called, bathing the walls of the cottages in golden light.

It was cool inside Jackson's cottage, because the back door on to the orchard was open, secured with an iron weight in the form of a goblin. Jackson motioned to Bottomley to take a seat and, after he had divested himself of hat and coat, he went into the kitchen, where a jug of mild ale stood in an earthenware bowl of cold water. He filled two pewter tankards, and returned to the living room.

'There you are, Sergeant,' he said, and sat down gratefully in his old wicker chair by the empty grate. 'Mrs Jackson's talking to the tenants she got for Brown's Croft after we married. She'll be coming back across the orchard soon.'

Herbert Bottomley had chosen an upright chair near the front door, which meant that he was uncomfortably near an old grand-father clock that stood in the corner. He had retained his yellow overcoat, but had placed his battered bowler carefully on the floor. He took the tankard from Jackson, and drained half its contents in a single avid gulp.

'So what it amounts to, sir,' he said, 'is this. Rose Potter says that Helen was carried off in a carriage from Mayfield Court on such a night, at such a time, etcetera. I interviewed Helen in Birmingham, the other day, and she confirmed that that had been the case. Helen Robinson she is, now, and she told me how much she'd hated that house and its owners, or lessees, or whatever they were, and how much she'd enjoyed being at school.'

'That's what she told you,' said Jackson, 'but your gypsy, Solomon Williams, says that Helen never left that house in a coach — in fact, she never left it at all. If your gypsy is right, then your Helen Robinson is telling fibs. Down there in the office, I believed what 'Helen' told you. But now, I'm not so sure. As you know, Sergeant, in our profession it's not a good idea to believe everything that we're told.'

'But sir,' said Bottomley, after refreshing himself by draining his tankard, 'after I visited Helen, I paid a call on her old school. The headmistress, a lady called Miss Jellicoe, confirmed that Helen had arrived on that very date at Meadowfield School for Girls, early in the morning in a carriage, and that she had stayed there happily until the age of sixteen. Her fees were regularly paid, and she proved to be a very happy and successful pupil. All of which, sir, gives the lie to our old gypsy.'

'Which leaves us with our little skeleton,

Sergeant. She can't be ignored, or left out of the equation. Dr Venner told us that it was the skeleton of a girl child of eleven, whose body had been concealed in that garden for thirty years. How far do we stretch coincidence?'

Sergeant Bottomley looked into his empty tankard, and Jackson got up to replenish it. When he returned from the kitchen, Bottomley was ready with a question.

'Sir,' he said, 'that place where you saw the old clergyman in the churchyard — Upton Carteret. Meadowfield School was at a place called Upton Cross.'

Jackson rummaged through a number of papers on a small table beside the fireplace, and produced a rather tattered county map. With some difficulty he opened it out and spread it across his knees.

'Let me see . . . There's Copton Vale, so we follow the railway line as far as Monks' Stretton. And there's Upton Carteret, where I saw old Mr Hindle, and there's Providence Hall, standing in its grounds. That's where I had that rather embarrassing interview with Sir Leopold Carteret, an interview that seemed to lead nowhere . . .

'Ah! Yes, there it is, just half a mile beyond Sir Leopold's demesne — Upton Cross, and there's a little plantation of trees drawn on this map, with the word 'school' written above it. That's a curious point, Sergeant, Helen Paget's school being so near to Providence Hall. There's something about that proximity that I don't much like.'

'There's a picture of sorts emerging, sir.'

'There is, and it all holds well together, Sergeant. But there's still the stumbling-block about little Helen. Is she the woman that you met, the woman who fainted at the mention of a skeleton, or has she been dead for thirty years, hidden until recently in the ruined washhouse at Mayfield Court? It seems to me — '

Jackson stopped speaking as his wife Sarah came into the cottage from the orchard. By force of habit she still knocked on the back door, as she had done when she was just a welcome visitor, coming through the trees from her own house, Brown's Croft. She had been a widow then, a woman who had lost both her first husband and her three little boys in the cholera outbreak at Sedley Vale, in the spring of 1880. She was carrying a bowl of russet apples, which she placed on the table.

Herbert Bottomley had risen from his chair near the grandfather clock, and had given Mrs Brown a clumsy bow. Sarah was a friendly, quiet woman without airs and graces, but she was the guvnor's wife, and had to be treated accordingly.

'Oh, do sit down, Mr Bottomley,' said Sarah. She took her place opposite Saul Jackson at the hearth, smoothing her white linen apron, and folding her hands in her lap. Bottomley glanced at the inspector, as though seeking permission to speak. Evidently Jackson knew what he was going to say, because he gave his sergeant an almost imperceptible nod.

'I was wondering, missus,' said Bottomley, 'if you'd let me tell you a story, and when I've finished, maybe you'd like to tell us what you think about it.'

Herbert Bottomley proceeded to give Sarah an account of their investigation of the mystery unearthed at Mayfield Court. From time to time Jackson added a few comments, but he was content to give Bottomley his head. The sergeant was possessed of a remarkably retentive memory, and very rarely got any fact wrong when discussing a case.

When he had finished, Sarah Jackson seemed lost in thought for some minutes. The grandfather clock ticked away in the corner. Out in the orchard, a lively blackbird was informing all and sundry that this was his territory, and that they had better watch out.

'Well,' said Sarah at length, 'it seems to me that there's a very wicked person at work, someone who's single-minded enough to sweep away anyone who stands in his path. Or her path, because it could be a woman — perhaps that heartless woman who lived at — what did you call the place? — Mayfield Court.'

'You're right, missus,' said Bottomley, 'and in my mind it is a woman who's left a trail of deaths behind her for thirty years. I think I know who she is, but now's not the time for me to speak. The insoluble mystery, as I see it, is what happened to Helen. One of our informants, an old gypsy man, is convinced that she was murdered, and that it was her little skeleton that was revealed to the light of day not so long ago at Mayfield Court. But I actually met Helen, now a married woman with children, so if Helen's alive, whose is the skeleton?'

'Well, Mr Bottomley,' said Sarah, 'I don't see any difficulty there. You can't just have a skeleton, you know, hidden in a garden without someone having put it there. From what you told me in your story — and a very wicked story it was — they were the bones of a little girl of eleven. Helen was eleven, and lived for one night in that house, never to be seen again. Why complicate matters? Of course that skeleton was poor little Helen's. She was murdered, most like, by that horrible couple who lived in the house, the aunt and uncle, or whoever they were.'

'But what about the Helen I interviewed, missus? That's the stumbling-block, you see.'

'Well, she must have been an imposter,' said Sarah. 'She told you how much she disliked her domineering aunt, and how kindly the servant-woman was — Rose Potter. And she said that the husband was a weak-willed kind of man. She knew a lot about that old house and its occupants — but she was only there for part of one night! Whoever that woman in Birmingham was, Mr Bottomley, she'd had all those details drilled into her, to repeat when required to do so, like a piece of poetry.'

'But Sarah,' said Jackson, 'if the woman in Birmingham was an imposter, where did she come from? I don't quite see — '

'Saul, the aunt told the servant that Helen was going to school that very night across the county. So she must have arranged for another child — the daughter of some poor, improvident woman, perhaps — to take her place. This other child was drilled as to what to say, told to accept a change of name, and sent to the school. You'll have to find out all that. As for the real Helen — well, it doesn't bear thinking about.'

'Sarah,' said Sarah's husband, 'what you've just said is pure supposition — '

'Well, of course it is, but it's an explanation, isn't it, Saul? It leaves you with an identity for your skeleton, and sends you off after the imposter. If I ever met that woman in Birmingham, I'd soon get the truth out of her.'

'But — '

'Why do you think she fainted away when you mentioned the skeleton, Mr Bottomley?' said Sarah, turning to the sergeant. 'She suddenly realized that she had been groomed to take the place of a child who had been murdered! That's why she fainted. Grown women don't faint at the mere mention of a skeleton. Dear me, is that the time? I must put the cabbage on the kitchen fire.'

Sarah Jackson rose from her chair and left the living room. Jackson and Bottomley sat absorbed in the ramifications of what she had just suggested. Two Helens, one of them an imposter . . .

'It might be an idea, sir,' said Bottomley, 'if you were to interview the Helen that I saw in Birmingham. You could take a local uniformed constable along with you, to put the wind up her, asking pardon for the coarse expression. I don't expect she knows much, but she'll know enough to put us back on the right trail of our mad, bad killer.'

7

Margaret Gates's Story

Helen Robinson stood at the door of her smart house in Aston Road, and watched her husband as he climbed into the cab that would take him to the station of the London and North Western Railway. They had enjoyed a night out with friends who played whist, but it was now Wednesday morning, and the office beckoned.

How smart he looked! And how settled! She and Adrian had both turned forty not too long since, and the word 'settled' was one that appealed to them both. The children, too, were content at their respective boarding-schools.

Her husband, as well as being a very successful businessman, was a pillar of the community, who had been appointed Chairman of the Board of Guardians at the Union Workhouse in May. There was a suggestion that he might become chairman, too, of the parish council.

She herself was an active member of the Gentlewomen's Sewing Guild, and an able organizer of clothing collections in the borough, but whatever she did as an individual was ultimately designed to reflect the glory of her husband. They both loved their spacious villa in Aston Road, and hoped to remain there for life.

The cab clattered away from the kerb, and Helen closed the door. She went down the hallway and into the morning room, where her maid was clearing away the breakfast things.

'Emily,' said Mrs Adrian Robinson, also known as Helen Paget, 'Emily, I'm worried about that big, shambling man who came here last Thursday.'

Emily put down the tray on the table, and regarded her mistress with open affection. She loved this handsome, kindly lady, who had brought her from an orphanage when she was twelve, and had trained her as a domestic servant. Emily was seventeen, the same age as Miss Alexandra, and the mistress treated her at times as though she were a second daughter of the house. Miss Alexandra was very clever and accomplished, but she didn't have much sense.

'He were the policeman, weren't he? Wanting to hear all about when you were a little girl. When I came in to see him out, you'd fainted away on the rug. I told him to be off, and that he'd no right to frighten a lady, policeman or no policeman. Why are you worried about him, mum?'

'It was something he told me about a skeleton that was discovered in the garden of a house near to a place where I once stayed the night when I was eleven. It gave me a turn, you see, because . . . Well, I can't really tell you the secret, Emily, but it's left me worried ever since. If that policeman comes back with more questions, what shall I do?'

Emily thought to herself: whatever the secret is, she'll tell me when she's good and ready. But we want no trouble here in Aston Road. This is a genteel area, and if I give satisfaction, I hope I'll stay with the Robinsons for life. Unlike some other servant-girls in this street, I don't want to work in a telegraph office, sitting on a stool, and pushing wires into sockets.

'Well, mum,' said Emily, 'if I was you, I'd tell them the truth. Whatever part you played in the secret, it couldn't have been much, if you were only eleven. You tell them the truth, mum, and then you'll have nothing to worry about. I'd better clear in here. Mrs Winchester will be here by ten.'

Tell the truth? Yes, Emily was right. But as far as she could tell, it was a furtive, lying business altogether. All her success in life had

142

been based upon a deception, and now — oh, God! — they had found a child's skeleton buried in the garden of that hateful, gloomy house. What did that portend? Adrian knew nothing of her secret.

She had no interest whatever in her past. She was wrapped up in her husband and her children, and this beautiful modern house, which had a bathroom, and water plumbed to the kitchen taps instead of to a hand-pump over the sink. And she loved her wise little maid, who had long ago become her *confidante*. None of this must be challenged or changed.

* * *

Towards eleven o'clock, a heavily built man in a brown suit with matching blocker walked up the path of the Robinsons' house, and knocked on the door. Emily, who was looking out of the landing window, saw the man, and hurried down the stairs to answer the door. Maybe he was from the gas company, or perhaps he was a new shopkeeper drumming up trade. She'd certainly never seen him before.

When she opened the door, she saw that a uniformed constable was standing at the garden gate, and her stomach turned over in alarm. The man held up some kind of card for her to read, and said that he was Detective Inspector Jackson of the Warwickshire Constabulary. He had come to see Mrs Helen Robinson, and would brook no denial. Emily made no reply, but led Jackson to the back sitting room, where Mrs Robinson was sitting on a sofa, reading the paper. She announced the visitor, and left the room, closing the door behind her.

Jackson had come prepared to attack and if necessary intimidate. This lady looked to be a nice, attractive person, but the time for prevarication had passed.

'You are Mrs Helen Robinson, *née* Walsh, also known as Helen Paget?' he said, and saw the colour drain from the woman's face. 'I believe you to be an imposter, and that, as a child of eleven, you collaborated with others to take the place of the true Helen Paget, who was then murdered. Recently, the skeleton of that poor child was discovered, and those pathetic remains lie exposed for the world to see, crying aloud for vengeance — '

Helen Robinson rose from the sofa with a cry of anguish, putting up a hand as though to ward off Jackson's denunciation. At the same time the door was flung open, and Emily came into the room. She rushed to her mistress's side and gently persuaded her to sit down again. Helen Robinson pulled the girl down beside her on the sofa, and held her hand. The mistress had burst into tears, but the maid, dry-eyed, stared at Jackson with unconcealed defiance.

'A fine man you are,' said the maid, 'coming into a lady's house and frightening her while her husband's away at work. What have you been saying to her? I tell you, I'll not leave her alone with you in this room. Why have you stood a policeman at the gate? Do you think this is a den of thieves?'

Jackson wilted under the young girl's diatribe. It was always like this. Bottomley could wheedle any information he wanted from girls and women, but he, Jackson, always managed to create scenes like this. He must calm this girl down, otherwise he would fail in the purpose of his visit, which was simply to hear Helen Robinson's childhood story.

Still clutching her maid's hand, Mrs Robinson made a tremendous effort to master her fear before speaking to Jackson.

'What do you want of me?' she asked quietly. 'Are you saying that I am a murderess? You accuse me of collusion. I tell you, I knew nothing of this other child. I never saw such a child. And I was only eleven years old when I went to that hateful place.' She repeated her original question: 'What do you want of me?'

Jackson sat down in an armchair facing the sofa, and the action seemed to lessen his intimidating air. He smiled at the two women, and some of the tension began to be leached from the air.

'I want you to tell me the truth about your origins, Mrs Robinson,' he said, 'and I want you to tell me all you remember about your visit to Mayfield Court over thirty years ago. I have not accused you of murder — no, certainly not that. But I know that you are guilty of collusion in a deception, and that you must have been willing to pass yourself off as the child Helen Paget, who was then murdered. Tell me all.'

'My husband knows nothing of all this,' whispered Helen Robinson. 'Must he be told? And will you arrest me?'

'You were only a child at the time of this murder,' Jackson replied. 'If you tell me all, without deceit or subterfuge, I will keep your story confidential, and will take no further action. Your husband need never know. As for you, young lady,' he continued, looking sternly at young Emily, 'I'd advise you to keep a civil tongue in your head. Meanwhile, if your mistress is agreeable, you can stay to hear what she has to say.'

Jackson saw how the mistress clasped her

maid's hand once more to indicate that she was to stay. There was obviously a strong bond between the two. Helen Robinson released Emily's hand, clasped her own hands in her lap, and after a few moments' silence, she began to tell Jackson her story.

'My name, in the days of which you speak, was Margaret Gates. I lived with my mother, Beulah, in a cottage on the fringes of the village of Newham Ford, a few miles to the south of Bicester. Mother was a seam-stress, employed by a lady of quality, a Mrs Arabella Paget, who lived in a house in the main street of the village. I had known her since I was a very little girl, Mr Jackson, as I often accompanied my mother on visits to return the sheets and pillowcases that she had hemmed for Mrs Paget.'

'Was there a Mr Paget?' asked Jackson.

'There was. I was afraid of him, because he was vaguely menacing — or so he seemed to me. He went completely in awe of Mrs Paget, who was a handsome, well-educated woman. Mrs Paget had two young children by her first husband, a boy and a girl. I believe they were away at school somewhere, or living with a relative. She had known Mr Paget as a friend, and married him very soon after her first husband's death.

'Mother was very poor, her husband — my

father — having died of drink when I was two years old. He was an agricultural labourer, she told me, kindly enough in his way, but a slave to gin. Mother eked out a living by her sewing, and by bouts of domestic service in the neighbourhood.

'I went to the village school, and very soon showed evidence of great natural ability for learning. I could read and write by the time I was six, and the schoolmaster declared that there was nothing much more that he could teach me by my ninth year. He was a good, devoted man, who gave me many books to read, and encouraged me to write essays and stories. He gave me a dictionary, I remember, and I would spend hours looking up words, and pondering over their meanings. Of course, I was destined, like my mother, for humble service, and neither of us thought otherwise. People of our class were not born to aspire to things beyond our station.

'And then, in the summer of the year 1864, when I was just eleven years old, Mrs Paget called upon us in our cottage — a thing that she had never done before — and told my mother that she and her husband were moving to a house called Mayfield Court, in Warwickshire. 'I shall have no further need of your services, Mrs Gates', she said, 'but I am going to make you a proposition which you would be very foolish to refuse.'

'Mrs Paget turned towards me, where I was sitting on a stool beside the fireplace. She gave me such a long, appraising look that I became embarrassed, and turned away in confusion. 'Margaret', she said, 'I hear from the schoolmaster here that you have become an exceptional scholar. How would you like to go to a first-rate private school for girls, with all your fees and expenses paid?'

'I heard my mother gasp in surprise, and from the look of joy on her face I knew what my answer to Mrs Paget should be. 'I should like it more than anything else in the world, ma'am', I said, and you'll understand, Mr Jackson, that I spoke with utter sincerity. 'Well', said Mrs Paget, 'here is what you must do. It involves telling a little fib, and sticking to the story that I shall tell you. You, Margaret, will call yourself Helen Paget, and when the time comes, I myself will school you in what you have to say and do. In return, you will go to one of the best girls' schools in England. You will be able to see your mother during the holiday periods, but you must keep her identity a close secret. Will you do this?'

'What else could I say, Mr Jackson, but 'yes'? I did not like Mrs Paget — she seemed to me to be a cold, heartless woman — but I had no intention of thwarting her in her desires. She was offering me a way of escape from a life of rural drudgery.

'Then she turned to my mother. 'Mrs Gates', she said, 'I will tell you also what I want you to do when the time is ripe. And as a reward for your co-operation, I will give you three hundred pounds in sovereigns.' And there and then, she went out to her carriage, and bade her coachman to bring in a valise, which contained the fortune in sovereigns that she had promised my mother.'

Mrs Robinson paused for a moment. All her previous agitation had disappeared. Telling her story evidently had a cathartic effect. Emily, the maid, sat round-eyed beside her. Jackson, too, seemed lost in thought.

'What happened next, Mrs Robinson?' he asked.

'What I have told you, Mr Jackson, occurred in the late August of 1864. On the twentieth of October, Mrs Paget called upon us again. We were to travel in a hired coach on the twenty-sixth of the month to the village of Mayfield, and stay in a cottage set in a coppice on the far side of the road from Mayfield Court. It would be rough and ready, she said, but we would only be there for a couple of days. Then I was to be 'spirited away' — those were the words she used — to my new school, and my new life. I was overjoyed, and forgot myself as far as to try to hug my benefactress. But she put me firmly aside. As I have told you, she was a cold, distant woman.

'After this, she began to teach us what we had to say. She had written it all down, and made us repeat what she had written until we were word-perfect. Then she burnt the paper in the flame of the candle which was lit on the mantelpiece. What she said, was — '

'Let me guess what she told you to say,' said Jackson. He was tremendously excited. Not only did all this mean that the skeletal remains at Mayfield were indeed those of the true Helen Paget, but that the woman whom Mrs Robinson was describing was surely her murderess. He began to speak, and it was soon his turn to be the object of Emily's round-eyed wonder.

'She told you to call yourself Helen Paget, and if anyone questioned you in the future, to say that your parents, whose name was Walsh, had both died. You were being looked after by relatives, who were anxious that you should receive first-rate schooling, and wished you to adopt their name of Paget. You were to tell anyone who enquired that you had travelled by coach to Mayfield Court, and that you had stayed there for one night, before being sent

151

to school. In fact, you never set foot in Mayfield Court, did you?'

'I did not. Mother and I arrived at the secluded cottage on the twenty-sixth, and found that it had been provisioned ready for our arrival. Mrs Paget had told me to say to anyone who asked me questions in the future that I didn't like Mayfield Court, and that I didn't like *her*! She laughed when she said this, and it wasn't a pleasant sound. She told me the name 'Rose Potter', and told me that she was the housekeeper at Mayfield. I was to say that I liked her, because she was kindly and compassionate. But I never saw Mayfield Court, and I never saw the woman called Rose Potter.'

'But you met her later, didn't you? About ten years ago.'

'Yes, I did. It was pure coincidence, and I won't tire you with explaining how the meeting came about. She introduced herself to me, and of course, although I had never seen her in my life, I pretended to recognize her. For her part, she seemed quite happy to accept me for who I was. I gave her my card, and we parted quite amicably. She was a pleasant, good-natured woman.'

'And then, I suppose,' said Jackson, 'the night of the twenty-eighth came, and you were told to get ready to leave. A coach came late that night to convey you to Meadowfield School. You said farewell to your mama and got into the coach. Did it stand on a main road?'

'No, it was waiting in a narrow lane near the cottage where we were staying. As we moved away, the branches of the trees scraped the roof.'

So Bottomley's old gypsy, Solomon Williams, had been right. The coach had been there, but not on the Warwick Road. How clever that woman had been to keep the two Helens apart! Rose Potter would have known nothing about the whole matter, and was innocent of any complicity. Meanwhile —

Jackson rose from his chair, and looked down at mistress and maid. There was nothing that he could do to make this woman atone for her complicity in a great and wicked deceit. She had been a child — a little girl — who had seen the road to freedom beckoning, and had seized the means of stepping out on to that road. But something had to be said, if only for the dead child Helen's sake.

'Thank you for telling me your story, Mrs Robinson,' he said. 'You were only a child in those far-off days, and cannot be held culpable. Besides, I don't suppose you knew that there was a real Helen Paget, also aged eleven, and that on the night when you set off for your new life, that other Helen was sleeping in a first-floor bedroom at Mayfield Court.

'As your carriage rattled away to take you to a new life, the real Helen was either poisoned or smothered, and her dead body was thrust into a crevice in a ruined wall in the garden. Helen Paget, aged eleven, murdered by your benefactor, and concealed, still in her nightdress, for the rats to gnaw until she became the little skeleton that Mr Bottomley discovered only days ago. I will prefer no charges against you, but I leave that part of your story for you to ponder on in future years.'

Minutes later, the now-subdued Emily was showing Jackson out. They could both hear the hysterical sobbing of Mrs Helen Robinson in the sitting room.

'You're close to your mistress, aren't you?' he said gently to the maid.

'Yes, sir.'

'Well, when she's recovered, tell her to confess the whole story to her husband. He'll know that something's wrong as soon as he comes home. Let there be an end to ancient secrets. For his sake, as well as hers, she must tell him all.'

'Bella, my dear!' cried Sir Leopold Carteret, looking up from his newspaper. 'So you're back. It's been ten days. How — How was Town at this time of year?'

Sir Leopold Carteret regarded his wife with unconditional affection. What would he have ever done without her? What a splendid woman she was, with enough personality to spare for both of them. He'd always been a faded sort of man, but Bella was the kind of person who created a stir wherever she went.

It was impossible to believe that she was sixty-five. Her expertly coiffeured hair was still dark, and her complexion flawless. Lady Carteret moved in the highest echelons of county society, and sat on many committees. She had always been ruthless about anything, or anyone, standing in the way of her ambitions, which made her a valuable addition to standing committees, and to the more progressive Boards of Guardians. He and she were bound together by ties of affection, and by their knowledge of things long forgotten, and known only to them.

Of her life before their marriage he knew only what she had chosen to tell him, and he was content with that. From unguarded remarks that she had made during their twenty years together he gathered that she had been married before, but he never alluded to the matter. It was none of his concern.

'Town, Leo,' said Lady Carteret, standing in her outdoor clothes at the parlour window, 'was hot, humid, and decidedly not the place to be in August. There was absolutely no one there. Still, my business there was soon concluded, which gave me time for a few pleasant visits. I lunched with Lady Kennedy last Saturday, and she regaled me with some of the latest gossip from Court. And yesterday I was able to go to the Army and Navy Stores, and then to Harrod's.'

Lady Carteret looked out of the window and gave a little hiss of annoyance.

'Hopkins,' she said, 'will you see that those parcels are taken upstairs immediately? And tell Andrews to move the carriage off the front drive *at once*. I see no point in having a coach house if we leave our conveyances exposed like that to vulgar view. And I'd like some tea — and biscuits, or cake, or something. See to it, will you?'

The butler gathered up the parcels and left the parlour. Lady Carteret removed her outer coat and flung it across the back of a sofa. She sat down beside her husband, and gently removed his newspaper from his lap. She put it down beside her on the carpet.

'And now, Leo, what, if anything, has been happening here since I went away? Do tell me. That is, if you can drag yourself away from your newspaper for five minutes.'

'If you don't like me reading *The Times*, dear, I can always change to *The Morning Post*. Was Dr Morrison happy about the arrangements?'

Bella Carteret laughed, and looked at her husband with a kind of amused regard. It was a way of his to counter a question by asking one himself.

'What choice does he have? Doctor Morrison has everything in hand, and Lucas will . . . will see to the matter tomorrow. So what's happened here since I went up to London?'

'A policeman called here the other day. A Detective Inspector Jackson from Warwick. He wanted to know — '

'You didn't tell him anything, did you?' Bella Carteret's face had suddenly drained of colour, and her voice was uncharacteristically sharp. Her husband put a reassuring hand over hers.

'*Tell* him anything, my dear? How could I tell him anything, when there's nothing to tell? He said he was looking for — for an old clergyman, who may or may not have been living around these parts. He'd met him in the churchyard, apparently. He mentioned a name, but I've forgotten what it was. I suggested that he have a word with John Bold. Maybe he did, but I don't know.'

'What kind of a man was he, this Jackson?'

'He was a stout, round-faced fellow in a heavy brown serge suit, a brown blocker to match, and stout boots. He looked completely out of his class in this parlour. I thought he was a foolish kind of man. Stolid, you know, and not very bright. But I may be wrong. He wasn't here long, and he left the village that afternoon.'

'Yes, Leo,' said his wife, thoughtfully, 'you may be wrong. We'll have to wait and see. But everything went well in Town, so I think you and I can relax.'

Sir Leopold leaned forward and put his lips close to his wife's ear.

'The old fool had wandered off yet again,' he whispered. 'Gave Lucas the slip. But we soon got him back.'

'Yes, well, very soon indeed we'll see a solution to the problem of our wanderer. But if it's to be a regular habit, we shall have to take positive steps to see that his wandering days are over. If not Doctor Morrison, then Doctor Zhdanov. You know what I mean.'

'Good God, Bella, he's your own brother!

Surely you wouldn't — '

Lady Carteret smiled, and sat back in her chair.

'Hush, dear,' she said. 'Here's tea coming in. You can read your paper now without further interruption. Don't worry: now that I've seen Doctor Morrison, the long journey away from *us* has just about concluded.'

8

Mr Brahms Remembers

Inspector Jackson turned out of St Paul's Churchyard and into Ave Maria Lane, walked up the white steps of a staid old house, and rang the bell. After a whole minute had passed, the door was opened by an old man in rusty black, who told Jackson that he was expected, and ushered him into the musty premises of Louis Brahms and Partners, Attorneys at Law. The old man led him into a dim room at the front of the house, and motioned towards another old man sitting behind a desk.

'Detective Inspector Jackson is here, Mr Brahms,' he said, in a little reedy voice, and then left the room, quietly closing the door behind him. Mr Brahms was old, but contrived to look comfortably middle aged. His hair, Jackson saw, was skilfully dyed, and his tailor knew how to flatter his aged body. When he spoke, his voice was disconcertingly loud and assertive.

'So you are Inspector Jackson, of the Warwickshire Constabulary,' he said, glancing at a letter that he held. 'I must confess that I've never met a provincial police officer before. You don't look like a policeman, if I may say so. I should have thought that you were a claims adjuster — something of that sort. Sit down. How did you hear about me?'

'Well, sir, during the course of an investigation I learnt of the existence of the Forshaw family. A Mr Hardacre, the landlord of an inn at Upton Carteret in Warwickshire, told me that the Forshaws had made their fortune from building ships for the Royal Navy in the great days of sail. Telegraphic enquiries to the Admiralty confirmed this. No one there knew anything of the family, who had ceased to be offered naval tenders when steam ships had come in, but they *did* know that all documents concerning their contracts with the Forshaws were dealt with by your very old-established and distinguished legal practice, Mr Brahms — '

' "Very old established' — yes, that's true enough. We've plied our trade here in the shadow of St Paul's Cathedral for the past hundred and fifty years. Don't know about 'distinguished', though. What exactly is it that you want to know about the Forshaws, Inspector? They have long gone, you know. Do you want a history of the whole family?'

Mr Brahms turned in his chair and began

161

to remove an intimidating leather-bound tome from a shelf behind him. When Jackson demurred, he pushed it back again with an expression of evident relief.

'No, sir,' said Jackson, 'it suffices for me to know that they were naval ship-builders, and that they had amassed a great fortune. I want to know about a young man called Gabriel Forshaw, who died on 7 August, 1864, aged twenty-four years.'

Mr Brahms removed the gold-framed spectacles that he had been wearing, and sat back in his chair. He had a heavily jowled face, and pale, watery-blue eyes. Jackson judged that he was well over eighty. He rested his cheek on his hand, and stared into space for a while before replying.

'I knew them all, you know, all the Forshaws who were alive in the fifties and sixties. They were thriving, and so was I — I was in the prime of life, then. I can see them all now, in my mind's eye, as though they were still alive . . . '

He motioned towards an array of papers that he had spread out on his desk.

'And there they are now, Mr Jackson, a labyrinth of names and dates written on reams and reams of paper. They're all history. All dead.'

The old solicitor picked up one of the

sheets of paper, stared at it for a while, and then put it down again on the desk. He saw that Jackson was looking at a tear-off calendar standing behind an array of inkwells. It was a day behind, and with a little flurry of impatience he ripped off the offending page. It now read Friday, 24 August.

'We'll start, Inspector,' he said, 'with Edward Forshaw. He was the head of the firm, which had extensive yards at Sheerness. He was born in 1799, and married a lady called Laura Blythe, one of the Blythes of Forest Acre, in Suffolk, though her branch of that family had long been established in Leatherhead. She was a charming woman, much admired for her taste in clothing. They were very wealthy, you know, but by the late forties, the navy needed ships of a different mettle. That's when the firm — John Forshaw & Son — began to retrench.'

'They failed to keep up with the demands of the time?'

'No, Inspector, not quite that. Edward decided that the Forshaws were rich enough to live like gentry, and he made that conscious decision to wind the company down. All the hands were paid off and given a gratuity. And that was the end of John Forshaw & Son, shipbuilders, established 1735, and closed down 1850. Why do you want to know all this?'

'Well, sir,' said Jackson, 'I'd like to say first how delighted I am that you're taking all this time to assist me. As for *why* I'm asking you these questions, I think one or other of the Forshaws may have been on the periphery of an old murder that I'm investigating. I can say no more than that at this juncture — '

'No, of course you can't, that is quite understood. A murder, hey? Well, well . . . '

At that moment the clock in St Paul's chimed eleven o'clock. The door opened, and the other old man — Mr Brahms's clerk? — came into the room carrying a tray on which sat two cups of coffee and a plate of Bath Oliver biscuits.

'Thank you, Steggles. Now, Jackson, let us refresh ourselves, and then I'll tell you some more about the Forshaw family of Upton Carteret and Sheerness. You'll never remember one half of what I tell you, because the family relationships of the Forshaws are a convoluted business. In 1853 Edward Forshaw, who was then living in retirement at his ancestral home, Waterloo House, in Upton Carteret, was found to have advanced consumption of the lungs. It was a particularly virulent strain of tuberculosis, and he died at his house on 15 October. He was fifty-three.'

'I suppose Mr Edward Forshaw had made a will?'

'Oh, yes, indeed. There were a lot of legal complexities to iron out, and his will was eventually proved in March, 1854. He left a vast fortune, some three quarters of a million pounds. There were a few bequests to relatives, and to a marine charity, amounting to five thousand in all. The residue went to his wife Laura absolutely. She was a very rich widow, Mr Jackson. Very wealthy indeed.'

'What did she do after her husband died?'

'She left a housekeeper to maintain Waterloo House, and went to live in her native town of Leatherhead, in Surrey. She outlived her husband by eight years, and died at Leatherhead, aged fifty-eight, in 1861. They had no children, so that branch of the Forshaw family came to an end.'

'But there were other branches?'

'Branch. Edward had a younger brother, Henry, and when Laura died, the family fortune passed to Henry Forshaw. The legacy was passing from party to party, from son to son, from relict to relict, and there was a danger of lateral claimants trying to get their hands on at least part of the fortune. It happens, you know, and can lead to ruinous litigation. Yes. What was I telling you?'

'About the fortune passing to a man called Henry Forshaw.'

'Yes, that's right. He was a cheerful,

sanguine sort of fellow, and I liked him very much. He had set himself up as a marine broker in a small way, but when he inherited, he gave that up, and set about enjoying the life of an independent gentleman. You can do that, you know, with that sort of money. It was I who warned him about family hangers-on, and advised him to let me draw up a Deed of Release — you know what that is, don't you?'

'No, sir.'

'Well, it's a document that must be produced whenever someone new inherits an estate. It is a legal confirmation that the estate belongs wholly to the inheritor, and cannot be disputed. There are two types of deed, open and closed — But never mind the legal complexities!'

The old man chuckled, but then suddenly assumed a solemn look, as though he had committed an impropriety.

'And then, in January, 1862, at the age of fifty-two, Henry Forshaw was killed in a railway accident. It was a terrible blow to his family — did I mention that he had a family? He had married a lady called Cecily Bancroft who, I believe, had been a schoolmistress. They had one child, a son, Gabriel, who was born in 1841. I'm not remembering all this, Jackson, without an *aide-memoire*: it's all written here, in these papers on my desk.'

'It's very interesting, Mr Brahms,' said Jackson. 'You're giving life to what could have been a mere list of names. And now you have placed Gabriel Forshaw in his context, if that's the right word. I believe he went out to Africa, and perished there?'

'He did. He was a very personable young man, who had been educated at Rugby School. He excelled at sports of all kinds and, at the time when he inherited his father's fortune — he was twenty-one — he had signed an engagement with the Oxford and Buckinghamshire Light Infantry to serve with them for five years. He was a determined young man, and saw no reason to alter his decision to take up soldiering. So his fortune was put in trust here, with us, until he returned.'

'And did he sign the Deed of Release? I assume that's what he would have done.'

'Indeed, yes. He signed it here, so that all was fair and square, and took it away with him. He was young, you see, and thought that it would be as well if he looked after the deed himself. As he was going out to Africa, I didn't try to dissuade him.'

'And so he went to Africa?'

'Yes, he did. As a matter of fact, I went down to Upton Carteret to see him off. I'd always liked him, you know; he was a manly, thoroughly decent lad. The Forshaws lived at Waterloo House, their old family home, just a few hundred yards outside Upton Carteret. It was burnt down, you know, later in the sixties.'

'And did you see him off, sir?'

'What? No. When I got there, I was told that he had left in the night, in order to say goodbye to an old friend of his before he caught the train to London from Copton Vale. I must say, I was rather vexed, but then, young folk have their own ideas about these things.'

'Can you recall, sir, who told you that he had left?'

'It was a woman — a lady, I should say. She was alone in Waterloo House when I arrived, and I assumed she was a distant member of the family who had also come to see young Gabriel off on his African adventure. No, I don't recall her name: indeed, I don't think she told me. It's a very long time ago, Inspector, and memory fades.'

Was that lady the murderous chatelaine of Mayfield Court? And had the young man supposedly left the house in a closed carriage? Easily arranged: the woman's compliant husband could have left the house muffled up in a cloak. Such details would chime well with her *modus operandi*. And then, with Gabriel out of the way, they would have been free to turn their murderous attentions to little Helen. That, at least, was a working hypothesis. What was Mr Brahms saying?

'At any rate, the regiment sent a battalion out to Bonny, in Nigeria, and poor young Gabriel caught a fever there, and died. We received a letter from a clergyman resident there, and much later in the year a confirmation from Gabriel's commanding officer. Poor boy. He was only twenty-four.'

Jackson recalled the words of the Reverend Walter Hindle, when he was contemplating the young man's epitaph on the Forshaw tomb: 'You won't find Gabriel there; and you won't find him in Bonny, either.' Was he to be found hidden in the burnt ruins of Waterloo House? Perhaps.

Jackson was beginning to see that the whole mystery of the Forshaws was centred on the movement of an unimaginable sum of money from one heir to another, and the pursuit of it by a vicious, perhaps half-mad killer. But surely with Gabriel's death, either in Bonny or elsewhere, the Forshaws had become extinct?

'You're wondering where the money went, aren't you?' asked old Mr Brahms. 'With Gabriel's death in 1865 the Forshaws came to an end. I was the trustee: what was I to do? I had no idea what Gabriel had done with the Deed of Release, so I took counsel with one of the judges in Chancery, who told me that the fortune should revert to Henry Forshaw's widow, Cecily, and so I arranged for that to happen. I suppose it was some kind of consolation for Cecily, for losing first her husband, and then her son.'

'And that's the end of the story, sir?' asked Jackson.

'Yes, I suppose it is, you know. All the Forshaws were dead, and the money had passed out of my trusteeship. Cecily married for the second time later that year. A few eyebrows were raised, of course, but that was only natural, I suppose. Her second husband was a very decent man called John Walsh; he was a widower with a little girl of nine. Her name, as I recall, was Helen.'

'Did you ever see the child, Mr Brahms?'

'Yes, I saw her once, when I was obliged to call upon the Walshes at their house in Edgbaston. She was a solemn little thing, I seem to remember. Yes, Helen, her name was. Helen Walsh. But I don't know anything about that side of the family, Mr Jackson. I did hear that both John Walsh and his second wife Cecily were dead, but I don't know for certain. It was all so very long ago, you see.'

Saul Jackson turned out of St Paul's Churchyard and into Cannon Street, which was thronging with carts, cabs, and lumbering lorries. On his rare visits to London, he was both impressed and disturbed by the roar and ring of the city traffic. Londoners never seemed to notice it.

Old Mr Brahms had presented him with a plethora of names and dates, most of which he had recorded in the fat notebook, bulging with letters and papers, and secured with an elastic band, that he always carried.

Names, yes; but behind the names there lay hidden a vast fortune, which was still in existence. Where was it? Who owned it now? It had passed out of the Forshaw family with the death of Gabriel, supposedly in Africa, and had been settled on a woman called Cecily Bancroft. The widowed Cecily had married a man called John Walsh, who had brought her a little stepdaughter, Helen . . .

As Jackson approached the entrance to Bread Street a four-wheeler, drawn by two horses, rounded the kerb with a screech of iron tyres. He jumped back in alarm, but in that moment he had seen an elderly man looking out of the cab window. Surely it was the Reverend Walter Hindle? Jackson began a half-hearted run along Bread Street, but the vehicle was soon lost in the press of traffic making its determined way to Cheapside.

Finding himself near a little public house, Jackson went in, ordered a pint of mild ale, and sat with it at a little marble table near the window. He was grateful to get out of the oppressive dust and heat of the London streets. Had he really seen the Reverend Walter Hindle? Perhaps. But he must not let himself be led astray from the task in hand. What should he do now? He would go to Somerset House, and start a search for John Walsh, and Cecily Walsh, formerly Cecily Forshaw, *née* Bancroft. After that, he would call upon Inspector Blade at Little Vine Street Police Station, and ask him what progress had been made in the investigation of the murder of Mr Maximilian Paget.

★ ★ ★

The heavy four-wheeler turned out of Cheapside into St Martin's Le Grand, passed the entrance to Noble Street, and drove into a quiet court lying behind Pewterers' Hall. The driver climbed down from the box and opened the door. A strong, beetle-browed man emerged on to the pavement. He turned to help a second passenger to alight, an amiable, frail old gentleman in clerical dress.

'How much will that be, cabbie?' asked the strong man.

'One and sevenpence, guvnor.'

'Here's a florin. Help me get this gentleman up the steps of number three.'

Together they assisted the old man to mount the four deep steps leading up to the black-painted door of number three, one of a terrace of tall, redbrick houses with railed areas accessible from iron gates let into the railings. The strong man rang the bell, and the cabbie turned his heavy vehicle on the cobbles, and made his way slowly out of the court. A stern woman in the starched uniform of a nurse beckoned the visitors to enter the house.

★ ★ ★

'Well, Mr Lucas,' said Dr Morrison, 'I'm very pleased that Sir Leopold and Lady Carteret have chosen me to look after this gentleman. How are you, sir? You're looking quite well! Excellent!'

Doctor Morrison was a man who had fallen into flesh, and was comfortable with his condition. He smiled a lot, and his voice was cheery. The eyes behind the gold pince-nez were shrewd and calculating. He was thinking to himself: this is the Reverend Walter Hindle, a retired Congregational minister and missionary. He is hovering on the borders of senility, and men of his temper can be dangerous if not controlled. Sir Leopold had always been generous to a fault, and he, Morrison, owed him a debt of gratitude.

The Reverend Walter Hindle acknowledged the doctor's greeting with an old-fashioned half-bow. He returned smile with smile.

'I am quite well, thank you, sir. I expect you were introduced to me just now, but I forget very quickly. Did you say that we are in Exeter? Lucas, I don't quite understand — '

'Exeter?' cried the jolly doctor. 'No, Mr Hindle, this is good old London! I'm sure you'll be very happy here with us at St Gabriel's House. It's a home-from-home for gentlemen like yourself, with all your needs consulted, and all your ailments treated with care and sympathy. Nurse, will you show Mr Hindle to his quarters? Perhaps he'd like some tea? A church? Certainly. We're only a stone's throw away from St Botolph's in Aldersgate Street. Or would you prefer a Protestant chapel? We'll have a little talk about that later.'

When the nurse had left the room into which they had been ushered, Dr Morrison's smile disappeared as if by magic. He motioned to a chair, and Lucas sat down.

'I gather that Mr Hindle has become a nuisance?'

'He has, Doctor. And more than a nuisance: a danger. All the parties in this business have scruples about making away with a clergyman — '

Doctor Morrison waved away with a pudgy hand the idea of 'making away' with anyone.

'Come, now Lucas, let's not have any talk of that nature. You're too — too physical, you know. We're not in the Middle Ages. These days, we need more subtle approaches to this kind of problem. I suppose he knew the Forshaws?'

'He knows far too much about everything, sir. That's the trouble. If there are any sleeping dogs around, Mr Hindle will be sure to waken them up. A bite from the kind of dog I'm thinking of could be fatal.'

'Well . . . He's safe enough here. Don't worry about St Botolph's. He'll never get further than the little walled garden at the back of the house. We . . . we have medications, you know, that inhibit memory. So tell Sir Leopold Carteret not to worry.'

Lucas rose to go. He looked vaguely dissatisfied. He had once been a warder at Hanwell Lunatic Asylum, and in his book Walter Hindle was a dangerous lunatic. The trouble with aristocrats was that they were too scrupulous. Admittedly, Mr Hindle was Lady Carteret's brother. But one silly old man wouldn't be missed.

'Doctor Morrison,' he said, as he rose to take his leave, 'is Dr Zhdanov still doing his sterling work at Chatham Court?'

Doctor Morrison's brow creased in a frown of annoyance. He rose from the desk where he had been sitting, and faced the beetle-browed man who stood opposite him. Morrison, to do him credit, feared nothing and no one.

'Don't ever mention that name in my presence, do you hear? I'll not stand by and see Hindle marched down that particular road. You're a good man, Lucas, but you're becoming too familiar. Get back to Sir Leopold, and tell him his worries are over. Hindle will see his remaining days out here with us. And when he dies, it will be from old age and senility. Nothing more than that. No! No more. Be off with you!'

★ ★ ★

The 5.35 afternoon train for Warwick drew out of the Great Western Railway's terminus at Paddington exactly on time. Saul Jackson leaned back in his seat in a half-empty third

176

class carriage and gave himself up to thought.

With the aid of an interested and helpful clerk, he had unearthed the death certificates of Cecily Bancroft and her second husband, John Walsh. He had been described as 'independent gentleman', and she as 'housewife'. Their deaths had occurred at their residence in Mallard Lane, Edgbaston, Cecily's on the 18 August, 1863, and John Walsh's on the 19 August. The certificates, duly signed by two physicians, attributed their deaths to acute food poisoning, 'consequent upon the consumption of tainted lobster.' More poison ... They had been married for only a year.

Two months after the deaths of her father and stepmother, John Walsh's young daughter, Helen, had been claimed by her aunt, Arabella Paget, and taken to live for one day at Mayfield Court. And there she had stayed, killed in childhood and concealed in the garden of that baleful, half-ruined grange.

* * *

The woman stood in the darkened passage outside the candle-lit room, fearful to step over the threshold that would lead her to insanity. Was she awake or asleep? There were times, during the night, when she could no longer be certain. She had never liked that room, with its dark, oppressive Tudor panelling, and the high, intimidating Elizabethan bed. What vermin nested in those faded plumes atop the bedposts? What cobwebbed passages lay behind the panelled walls?

Asleep or waking, whenever these terrors assailed her, she forgot who she was, knowing only that she was an outcast, an abomination.

She had left the more cheerful part of the house behind her, venturing, candlestick in hand, further away from the present age and back into the dim and dangerous past. Was she awake? The floorboards creaked beneath her steps, and the slight internal breeze that blew constantly through this part of the house caressed her face. Why was she behaving like a silly girl? Press on, and enter the candle lit room.

There: she had hurried through the bedchamber without incident, and had passed through a door at its further end that led into the ancient library of the house, a long, dim room with a fireplace at either end. Neither she nor her husband — what was his name? — ever ventured there. Its walls were lined with shelves, bearing thousands of old books, some bound in vellum, others in costly leather. They looked as though they were not meant to be read, and never *had* been read.

The clock in the turret above her struck two.

Fool! She was awake, and putting her health in peril by this nocturnal wandering. She looked across the room at the long window, its panes containing their family's ancient armorial bearings in dim stained glass. Below the window was a long table, where something was hidden by a green baize cloth. She did not recall seeing that table before. She would look at it before retracing her steps to the sanctuary of her own bedroom in the other part of the house.

She flung the green cloth aside, and saw, gleaming white in the moonlight, the perfect skeleton of a young child. Shuddering, she groped her way out of the hellish library and into the sombre bedroom with the high four-poster. The room was not empty. Beside the bed stood the figure of a young girl of ten or eleven, gazing earnestly at the pillow. Yes, it was her burden, the externalization of a guilt that would one day sear her mind and leave her a lunatic.

How still she stood! She was wearing the dark olive-green dress with the lace at collar and cuffs, that she had worn that night . . . Her hair fell down across her cheek, partly hiding her face. The woman began to tiptoe towards the door, hoping that the child would not see her. Her limbs trembled so much that

179

she could scarcely walk. She glanced back almost involuntarily, and saw the child turn to look at her.

Little Helen's face was dark and cyanosed, her eyes protruding from their sockets. So had she looked when the woman had pulled the pillow away from her face to ascertain that she was dead. She was dead now, looking at the woman from her dead eyes, set in her dead face. Helen Paget, her accuser to Heaven.

The woman uttered a shriek of fear, and jerked herself awake. She was in her bed, in her own familiar room, and the clock at her bedside told her that it was just after six o'clock. The welcome light of dawn shone at the window. A dream, then. Another cursed dream. It was over thirty years, and the dead child would not let her alone.

And she was not the only ghost who came to haunt her, and to point her on the road to damnation. They were all there with her in the house, Cecily, and John, and the weak-willed Hector, and Gabriel, too. She would come across them unexpectedly in different parts of the house, both by night and by day. *All of them.*

She could not petition God for mercy, because He would not hear.

The wicked shall be turned into Hell.

9

Catherine's Narrative:
a Will and a Letter

I buried my Uncle Maximilian on the 17 August — the Friday following his death. Doctor Whitney, the police surgeon, had told Michael the details of the *post mortem*, which had shown unequivocally that Uncle had died of poisoning by wolfsbane. An inquest was to be held on the twentieth, the earliest date that the coroner could make available, but in view of the hot summer weather, it had been deemed advisable that the body should be released to me before that date.

Inspector Blade had come to see me briefly on the morning following Uncle Max's death, and had told me that the inquest would be opened and then immediately adjourned until the police investigation was completed. I was able to give my whole attention to the arrangements for Uncle's funeral.

I had been advised to use Dowbiggin and Holland, the distinguished funeral furnishers, and they proved to be an excellent choice.

They attended to every detail, and I must admit that I sighed with relief when the whole melancholy business was taken out of my hands.

Do I sound hard and unfeeling? I deeply mourned my poor dear uncle and, as you will see later in my narrative, I had no intention of leaving his foul murder unavenged; but at twenty I was still little more than a girl, and my loss had somehow opened a door that had been hitherto closed — a door into an independent future, with Michael at my side.

I had asked for a grave to be dug in Putney Vale Cemetery, and there I stood, with Michael and Marguerite, all three of us in full mourning, listening to the officiating minister consigning Uncle Maximilian to the earth. He spoke well, and they were beautiful words, but they gave no hint of the horror of poor Uncle's passing:

I heard a voice from heaven, saying unto me, Write, From henceforth blessed are the dead which die in the Lord: Even so, saith the Spirit, for they rest from their labours.

* * *

There was much that I had to do before some kind of normality could be established. I had no intention of leaving Saxony Square, and said as much to Milsom, much to her relief. She agreed with me that it would be prudent to retain our present cook, and that a second housemaid should be employed. The gardener, whom we shared with our next-door neighbour, the relict of a City underwriter, had always proved satisfactory, so no change was needed there.

On Saturday, Marguerite arrived with a young man of unprepossessing appearance, declaring that he was one of the most powerful mediums that she had ever encountered. I knew that she was going to suggest a séance, but somehow the idea no longer appealed to me. Uncle Max, according to the officiating clergyman, was resting from his labours. I gave them both tea, and sent them away.

On Sunday, I went to church as usual, forsaking the sober rituals of St John's for the heady ceremonies of St Mary's Bourne Street. I knew then that I was in danger of losing contact with my own personality. I was starting to drift into unknown and untried paths, relishing the novelty of my new independence at the expense of that latent self-knowledge that told me I was not a hard, unfeeling young woman at all, but someone desperately in need of reassurance.

When Michael called in the evening,

solicitous, kind, and unassuming, I found the new façade that I had erected around myself was crumbling, and for the first time since Uncle's death, I dissolved into tears.

I was myself again — the Catherine Paget of old — when, on Monday morning, the 20 August, I called upon my uncle's solicitor. Mr Finbar was a man in his fifties, the son of the gentleman who had managed my uncle's affairs for him since the 1860s. He occupied a small set of chambers in a sort of cul-de-sac of an alley halfway between Crutched Friars and Cooper's Row.

Uncle's will, as I knew from the copy that he had left for me in his desk, and revised and dated 10 January 1893, was a very simple affair. After a bequest to Milsom of £200, everything came to me absolutely. This included the house in Saxony Square, a portfolio of shares in a number of railway companies, currently worth £6,500, and cash deposits in two London banks amounting to £12,000.

'You see, Miss Paget,' said Mr Finbar, leaning back in his chair and regarding me with a kind of detached interest, 'your uncle, the late Mr Maximilian Paget, always fretted that he had not enough money to live as he would have wished. He was constantly planning and devising ways to unlock some hidden fortune or other that lay tantalizingly out of sight on the fringes of his acquaintance.'

'And what, pray, do you mean by that?' I asked. ' "The fringes of his acquaintance"?'

'He was very tenuously connected with a number of families who had once been very wealthy, and it would seem that nobody knew where this wealth had gone. My father knew far more about all this than I, but one of these families were the Forshaws, the naval shipbuilders at Sheerness. Your uncle spent many fruitless years delving into family trees and other similar matters in order to find where the money was, and to lay some claim to part of it — why, I don't know, because he never confided in me. He told me what to do regarding his day-to-day affairs, and I did it.'

Mr Finbar had clearly taken offence at my manner of speaking to him. That word 'pray' had rankled. I tried to look sufficiently contrite, and he gradually relaxed.

'When all's said and done, Miss Paget,' he said, 'your legacy is a very tidy one. Very tidy. Your house alone is worth three thousand, you know, and those shares and deposits amount to eighteen and a half thousand pounds. And that property in Warwickshire should fetch four hundred or so. Wisely invested, the whole sum will bring you in a very respectable annual income.'

I was more than inclined to agree with him. Uncle's constant talk of making economies had vaguely alarmed me, but now I saw that there had been no valid reason for his fears. Had he become a miser? No, because in anything respecting my well-being and happiness, he had always been generous. It was merely that he had become obsessed with the game of fortune-hunting.

Mr Finbar rose from the table, and unlocked a drawer in a desk standing against the wall behind him. He came back to the table holding a letter, which he handed to me. My heart leapt with excitement when I saw that it was addressed to me in my uncle's handwriting, and sealed heavily with three red wax wafers. This was the letter that Uncle Max had told me would be given to me after his death.

'I will tell you at once, Miss Paget,' said Mr Finbar, 'that I have no idea what that envelope contains. I have had it for only a short time, and I was given strict instructions not to give it to you until after your uncle's death. That moment has now arrived. I'm going through to confer with my clerks, and will leave you here in peace to read your uncle's letter.'

He suited his action to his words, and left

186

the room, closing the door behind him. I broke the seals, opened the envelope, and spread the enclosed letter out on the table. It was written on our family's headed notepaper, but was undated.

Dearest Catherine

For some time now, I have had a premonition that my days on earth are numbered. I have wandered where I should not have gone, and stirred old and dangerous memories in the minds of those whom I most fear. It is time that I told you about Mayfield Court.

It was never a true dwelling place; it was rather a staging-point, a meeting place for the exchange of information in the quest for a lost fortune. People went there, and stayed there, in order to set various plans in motion. It had once belonged, I suppose, to some ancient family long extinct. I will return to the matter of Mayfield Court presently.

There was once a rich family called Forshaw, which owned the great shipyards of John Forshaw & Sons, established at Sheerness since 1735. The owner of the company, a man called Edward Forshaw, closed down the firm in 1850, because he decided the time had come to live the life of a gentleman. In 1853 Edward Forshaw, who was then living in retirement with his wife at Waterloo House, in the Warwickshire village of Upton Carteret, contracted tuberculosis, and died, aged 53, at his house on 15 October of the same year. He left a fortune of £750,000.

His widow, Laura, died eight years later, in 1861 and, as there were no children, the fortune passed to Edward's younger brother, Henry Forshaw. And then, in 1862, Henry was killed in a railway accident.

It was then, dear Catherine, that my brother Hector and I began to feel the lure of the Forshaw wealth. Every heir seemed to be seized by death within a few years of inheriting it, and Hector and I were struggling to establish ourselves often literally by the sweat of our brows. In what way, you will ask, were we — the Pagets — related to the Forshaws?

Henry Forshaw — he who perished in an accident in 1862 — had married a lady called Cecily Bancroft, and they had produced a son, Gabriel, born in 1841. When Henry was killed, his son Gabriel inherited the family fortune.

Now, Cecily Bancroft had a much younger sister, Arabella, and it was this woman who married my brother Hector. She was a native of Newham Ford, near Bicester. I will tell you now, Catherine, that she was a very wicked, ruthless woman, and that I have been aware of her, and afraid of her, since those far-off days in the sixties. Wicked? Evil, I think, would be a more accurate description.

Arabella had lived with her first husband at Newham Ford, but when my brother Hector married her, she was already living at Mayfield Court. I have never been able to find out whether she bought it or rented it, but there they lived, and there — God forgive me! — I connived at and condoned their wickedness. For my brother, morally weak and addicted to laudanum, did whatever his wife told him to do, so that in the end he was a moral imbecile — finding innocuous phrases to cover a multitude of atrocities.

The first of these involved the young heir, Gabriel Forshaw. He was a very decent young man, educated at Rugby, and eager to serve in the Army. His fortune was put in trust, because he was to serve a military engagement in Africa for a number of years. When he returned, his fortune would be released to him. It was said that Gabriel Forshaw did indeed go out to

Africa, to a place called Bonny, and died there of a tropical fever. That was in the August of 1865.

Towards Christmas-time of that year — I cannot be certain of the date — my brother Hector called upon me at Saxony Square. He told me that he and Arabella had left Mayfield Court for good, but when I asked him where they were living, he became vague and confused. I knew without having to ask him that he was too afraid of his wife to divulge what was evidently a secret matter. He seemed very pale and fevered, a shadow of what he had been, but when I asked him what ailed him, he became very agitated, and looked not at me, but over my shoulder, as though he could see something frightful there.

'What ails me?' he cried. 'It is nothing to do with the body, it is a disease of the soul! You cannot imagine what diabolical things she has made me do . . . I shall not see you again, Maximilian, and so I must tell you that she and I connived to make away with Gabriel Forshaw, and gave out that he had sailed for Africa. It was I who did the deed — can there be any forgiveness in the next life? Her brother, a missionary clergyman, was deceived into saying that he had indeed died in Africa — but I, of all men the most wretched — knew better than that.'

I was horrified, as you can imagine, but I held my peace.

'Not long since,' Hector continued, 'Arabella, too, added murder — with my connivance — to her catalogue of wicked deeds. She — Ah! It was a child! What's to become of us? And recently, I have seen her eyeing me with a horrible speculation, as though I am to be next. Why? What is she contemplating now?'

He grew more and more agitated. I urged him to stay the night, but he refused. For a while he grew calmer, and was able to tell me that he had hidden a cache of documents at Mayfield Court, in which I would find a Deed of Release, drawn up by Henry Forshaw's solicitor in 1861, which Gabriel Forshaw had endorsed before his supposed embarkation for Africa. The whole of his inherited fortune was held in trust at Hoare's Bank in London, and could only legally be released, and the trust broken, by production of this document. It had been duly produced and endorsed when the estate passed to Cecily, but Hector told me that he had managed to get it into his possession, and had hidden it at Mayfield Court. He saw it as a kind of insurance policy to prevent his wife from acting any further without his knowledge.

It was that document you saw me searching for when we were at Mayfield Court. I found it, and will in due course give it to Arabella. She can enjoy her ill-gotten gains in peace, with no interference from me. She will probably destroy it, though there will most assuredly be copies of it elsewhere.

My brother left the house, and from that time forward I never set eyes on him again. It was only in July of this year that I heard that he had died, and had left me Mayfield Court in his will. You remember that country lawyer who called on me? He was the bearer of the news. That man knew more than was good for him, so I shall not mention his name. He told me that the Forshaw fortune, now grown to one million pounds, was almost in Arabella's grasp. You see, she had killed all those who stood in the way of her inheriting: Gabriel was dead, and Arabella's sister Cecily had died suddenly, as had her second husband, John Walsh. Were those deaths from natural causes? Who knows? Who *dares* to know?

In 1864, only the child Helen stood between Arabella and unimaginable wealth. I know what she did, and that Hector connived at it. I remain terrified of Arabella, and it is for that reason that I will not tell you where she is now. I will ensure that she receives the Deed of Release, and have written to tell her that I want no part of the inheritance. I hope and pray that she believes me.

And so, dearest Catherine, I stand revealed to you as an accessory after the fact of murder. I remained silent when I should have spoken out; but had I brought Arabella to justice, I would most likely have gone to the gallows with her. And I could never have betrayed my poor brother.

I am resigned to my fate, and deserve whatever is coming to me. Farewell, dear Catherine. Try not to think too harshly of your old uncle. I hope with all my heart that you will marry Michael Danvers, and start out on a new life of happiness and fulfilment.

Your loving uncle,
Maximilian Paget.

10

The House in Barbary Court

'I'm one of seventeen inspectors here, Mr Jackson, and we've got thirty-seven sergeants and — let me see, how many just now? — three hundred and eighty-six constables, and it's still all we can do to stem the tide of crime here in St James's Division.'

Inspector Jackson looked at the smart, uniformed officer who stood, one arm resting on the mantelpiece, before the unlit grate in his office at Little Vine Street police station. He was a tall, commanding figure, with a red face and thick, silvery hair, but his voice was quiet and thoughtful. He could have been a bully, had he so wished, but it was clear that that kind of stance was not in his nature.

'I can see how busy you must be, Mr Blade. And this police station is a regular warren! But then, it's a divisional headquarters . . . So can you see your way clear to helping us? This Mayfield Court affair is obviously linked with the murder in Saxony Square.'

'Oh, yes, I'll certainly help you in this

matter — Sergeant Bottomley, why don't you sit down? You're making me uncomfortable hovering there by the door like a daddy longlegs. Sit down!'

Herbert Bottomley did as he was bid. He didn't like these big London places. It was all very well for the guvnor, but he preferred the quiet obscurity of little county police offices.

'Tell me again about this clergyman,' said Inspector Blade, 'the one you think you saw in a cab turning into Bread Street.'

'The more I think about it, Mr Blade, the more convinced I am that it really was the Reverend Walter Hindle. He is quite a striking old man, and I'm good at faces. He turned up in the churchyard at Upton Carteret, where all and sundry tried to persuade me that I was dreaming. Well, I wasn't. I found the straw hat that he'd been wearing hidden in a hedge. I want to interview this gentleman. He as good as told me that a young man called Gabriel Forshaw had been murdered.'

Inspector Blade thought for a moment, and then said, 'Was it a hackney carriage the old gentleman was in, or a four-wheeler — a 'growler', as people call them?'

'It was a four-wheeler. He was accompanied by another man, strong, thick-set, in his forties.'

Inspector Blade left the office abruptly, and

the two detectives could hear him talking to someone in the corridor.

'Sergeant Parker, suppose you wanted to go somewhere leading off Bread Street, and particularly wanted to hire a four-wheeler? Where would you go to find one?'

'There's a cab rank in St Martin's Le Grand — '

'You're not listening to me, Sergeant. I want a growler. Where would you go?'

'Well, there's a little bit of pavement half-way along Poultry where you'll get a growler, sir. It's one of old Abe Thompson's franchises.'

Inspector Blade returned.

'We'll follow up this business now, Mr Jackson, if that's all right with you. We can take an omnibus as far as Cheapside, and walk from there.'

Sergeant Bottomley, who had maintained a respectful silence for the last half hour, suddenly spoke. Inspector Blade jumped in alarm.

'Inspector Blade, sir,' he said, 'how is the young lady in Saxony Square bearing up to all this? Losing her uncle, I mean. Begging pardon, sir, for speaking out of turn.'

'Miss Catherine Paget? She's away from Town at the moment, Sergeant. She's gone to stay for a week in a hotel in Bournemouth. She's taken a friend of hers, a Miss Danvers, to keep her company. I rather think that she's returning home today. But come, let's not waste time talking. It's time we went to this franchise rank in Poultry.'

★   ★   ★

'Yes, I remember him, guvnor. An old parson. And the man with him was one of those well-dressed thugs you see chucking drunks downstairs at the music hall. That's why I remember them pertickler. Maybe the old gent was going to convert him.'

They had found four old-fashioned growlers standing in a strip of cobbled thoroughfare halfway along Poultry. The second cabbie they questioned, a hard-bitten, almost toothless man wearing an old overcoat tied round the waist with string, had recognized the fare that Jackson had described.

'And can you recall where you took them to?' asked Inspector Blade. 'This old clergyman and his minder?'

'Minder, hey? So that's the way of it . . . ' The cabbie treated the three officers to a smile, revealing his few remaining crooked and yellow teeth. 'I may remember, guv, if I give my mind to it. Now where was it I took them?'

Inspector Blade took a shilling piece from

his pocket, and gave it to the cabbie.

'Maybe that'll jog your memory,' he said.

'It does, sir, it does! I was returning empty from dropping a fare, and the well-dressed thug hailed me halfway down Cannon Street. He told me to take them to Barbary Court, behind Pewterers' Hall. Number 3, Barbary Court. I charged him one and seven, and he gave me a two shilling piece.'

'And what happened then?'

'What happened? Well, nothing happened, did it? I helped him to get the old clergyman up the steps to the house, and then took myself back to the rank.'

'And if I was to give you a florin, would you take the three of us there, now?'

'I would, sir. Climb in, gentlemen.'

'When you get there, cabbie,' said Inspector Blade, 'stop somewhere behind Pewterers' Hall. Wait for us there. We'll go to this Barbary Court on foot.'

★　★　★

'I don't like the look of this, Mr Jackson. I think I know who lives in that house.' The three officers stood on the side of the road opposite number 3, which seemed to be a well-kept house with a smart painted door at the top of a flight of four deep steps.

'It's a private nursing home run by a Dr Morrison. People go there to recover from attacks of nerves, others go there because they're becoming absent-minded, and can't be trusted to be alone.'

'And why don't you like it?' asked Jackson.

'Because people — particularly awkward people — have been known to disappear from that establishment. Morrison's a smooth-talking customer, Mr Jackson, and he always has an explanation. This one's gone abroad, that one's been reclaimed by a relative — here's a letter to prove it. I don't like him, and I don't like his nursing home. I expect your old clergyman — what did you say his name was? — the Reverend Walter Hindle — I expect he's in there, now. I've got a general warrant here, though I won't show it unless I have to. Let's go and find out.'

* * *

'You want to see the Reverend Mr Hindle? Certainly. I do hope he has not committed some foolish indiscretion. He's not always in full possession of his faculties, you see.'

Inspector Blade eyed Dr Morrison with barely concealed distaste. What a humbug the man was! Stout to the point of grossness, with steely eyes behind his pince-nez, his cheery demeanour and ready smile could not deceive a man skilled in the reading of criminal character.

'Mr Hindle has done nothing untoward, to my knowledge, Doctor,' said Blade. 'But we need to speak to him on a private matter. Where is he?'

'He's here, Inspector. I'll summon the nurse, who will take you to him.'

Morrison rang a small hand-bell, and in a moment a stern woman in nurse's uniform came into his office.

'Nurse,' said Dr Morrison, 'would you please take these gentlemen to see Mr Hindle in his room?'

'Mr Hindle?' said the nurse. 'Oh, he went out for a walk, Doctor, about half an hour ago. I expect he'll go as far as St Botolph's, and sit in the churchyard for a while.'

'You must understand, Inspector,' said Dr Morrison, 'that our patients are not prisoners! They're free to go out whenever they wish. All we ask is that they inform us first.'

Inspector Blade glanced briefly at Jackson, and saw from his expression that he, too, did not believe a word of the bland physician's statements.

'Well, Doctor,' said Blade, 'I'm sorry to have missed the reverend gentleman. Perhaps we can call again at a more convenient time.

Meanwhile, it would be an idea if you would show me your fire certificate for these premises. One can't be too careful where old, frail people are concerned.'

They saw the surly suspicion break through the cheery mask.

'Fire certificate? I don't think — '

'Well, no matter. We'll just make a quick inspection of the premises, and let you know if we find anything that contravenes the fire regulations. No, it's no bother, I assure you. Inspector Jackson, will you accompany me?' Lowering his voice, he whispered to Herbert Bottomley, 'Sergeant, there's a large garden to the rear of these premises. I saw it from that window, and there's a kind of summer house and a number of sheds. Have a look there, will you?'

Doctor Morrison had regained his cheerful *persona*, but the two inspectors could sense that the man was now consumed by fear. They asked him to accompany them on their round of inspection, and he was obliged to comply. The house was well furnished, and the patients' rooms held nothing remotely sinister. The Reverend Walter Hindle's room was tidy and comfortable, and various religious magazines were strewn around on tables and chairs.

There were only six resident patients, five

of whom were assembled in a pleasant dining room, where morning coffee was being served. They were all very old and frail, but they were clearly well looked after. At the back of the house a modern iron fire escape led down from the first floor to the garden.

'Excellent, Doctor,' said Blade. 'A very well-run establishment, with a responsible approach to the dangers of fire. Ask your staff to find that fire certificate, and post it to me at Little Vine Street. I'll arrange for it to receive an updated endorsement.'

They had reached a little terrace at the back of the house, bordering on a well-tended garden. Sergeant Bottomley came towards them, walking rather jauntily across the grass. Ignoring his superior officers, he addressed himself to Dr Morrison.

'Well, fancy that, Doctor!' he said. 'Mr Hindle hadn't gone out for a walk after all. I found him sitting in that little potting shed beside the summer house. I could see him through the window. He looked very comfortable, surrounded by hoes and spades, sitting on a backless chair all among the spiders. And guess what? Somebody had padlocked the door! A mistake, I'm sure. Perhaps you could find the key?'

Doctor Morrison had gone very pale, and began to stammer some kind of denial, but

Inspector Blade had decided to play Bottomley's game. He held up his hand to stem the doctor's attempts to explain the unexplainable.

'These things happen, Dr Morrison,' he said. 'You can't have eyes everywhere. I expect you've plenty to do, so we'll not detain you. Meanwhile, we'll go and have a talk with Mr Hindle. I don't suppose you'll mind if we break your padlock.'

★ ★ ★

'Well, well,' said the Reverend Walter Hindle, 'this is very nice! I remember you, of course, Mr Jackson. We had a talk about murders in a churchyard — I think it may have been at Exeter, though I'm not quite sure of that. Have you seen the cathedral there? It's very fine of its type.'

Saul Jackson looked at the old clergyman, smiling contentedly as he sat on the broken chair. Somebody had brought him here, and locked him away from prying eyes until the police had left the house. It would be fruitless to ask him who had imprisoned him, because he had almost certainly forgotten. He was a Congregational minister, which was why he had not appeared in Crockford's Clerical Directory. That worthy tome did not

203

recognize the existence of clergy who were not of the Church of England.

'And these are your friends? Mr Blade, I can see from your uniform that you are a police officer. And Mr Bottomley — I didn't quite catch — '

'Mr Bottomley's a detective sergeant,' Jackson explained. The old clergyman looked doubtful.

'You don't look like a detective,' he said, 'but if Mr Jackson says you are, then I suppose he must know. And, of course, it would be part of your vocation *not* to look like a detective, so . . . Yes. There you are.'

'That graveyard, sir,' said Jackson, 'was in a place called Upton Carteret, in Warwickshire. And when we met, you told me that a young man who had once lived there, a man called Gabriel Forshaw, had not died in Africa, but had, in fact, been murdered.'

The Reverend Walter Hindle smiled, and nodded his agreement.

'Yes,' he said, 'I was assistant at a small chapel in Exeter, many, many years ago, before I went out as a missionary to Bonny. Yes, indeed. I was there, in Bonny, you know, when Gabriel supposedly arrived to join the regiment. We were told he was coming, but I knew that couldn't have been so. He was supposed to have been stricken down with fever the moment he arrived, and to have died the same night. A sealed coffin was produced, and a death certificate issued. I wrote to my sister and told her what was being said. And later, the commanding officer there posted Gabriel's death as official. It was probably some poor native's body that had been passed off as Gabriel's. But I knew that it could not have been he. At one time I thought of retiring to Exeter, but I don't suppose I ever shall.'

'You said that Gabriel Forshaw had been murdered,' Jackson persisted. 'How do you know that? Who told you? And if you know how he was murdered, Mr Hindle, do you then know where his body is to be found?'

Tears sprang to the old man's eyes. He was silent for over a minute, while he recollected what it was that he wanted to say.

'Even in those days, when I was only in my fifties, my mind was failing. Not my intellect, you know, but — but my mind. Upton Carteret, yes, that's right. I was staying there, as I often did, and one night — I cannot recall the date, but it was a little while before Gabriel was supposed to have embarked for Africa. I was restless, having been unwell for some months, and I went out for a night walk through the lanes. As I approached the gates of Waterloo House, where Gabriel lived,

I saw him running down the drive towards the road. It was dark, but there was just enough moonlight to make out what was happening. And — they are very kind here, you know. Very attentive.'

So near, thought Jackson, and yet so very far away. He glanced at Sergeant Bottomley, who placed his hand over that of the old clergyman.

'It's all very interesting, sir,' he said, 'this story that you're telling us, about Gabriel Forshaw, and how you saw him one night running along the drive of his house towards the road. Why was he running, sir? Was someone chasing him?'

'Yes, Mr Bottomley, someone was chasing him, a dark, vengeful figure, bearing down upon him. He raised something in his hand and struck poor Gabriel down. Then I heard voices — the vengeful man had been joined by another — and saw that Gabriel's body was being dragged back into the shadows towards Waterloo House. That's how I knew he had been murdered.'

'And where were you staying in Upton Carteret when you saw this happen?'

'Well, Mr Jackson, I was staying with Mr Forbes, who ran the Congregational chapel there in those days. I was conducting a little preaching mission there before I embarked for Africa. Did I tell you about that? I went out there, just in time to see the coffin of the man passed off as Gabriel Forshaw. But I knew it couldn't have been he. Oh dear! I did nothing. I wanted to forget it all, you see.'

'And where do you think I shall find the body of young Gabriel Forshaw?' asked Jackson.

'I expect it's somewhere in the burnt-out ruins of Waterloo House. But don't bother yourself about it, Mr Jackson. It's all past history, now. Leave well alone.'

'Sir,' Jackson said, 'when I first met you, you were sitting in the churchyard at Upton Carteret. What were you doing there? Were you staying with the Congregational minister?'

'Oh, dear me, no! There's not been a chapel of that kind in Upton Carteret for many years. No, I was staying with my sister and her husband as a more or less permanent guest. They're very kind, you know. Very indulgent of a foolish old fellow like me.'

'And can you give me the names of your sister and her husband?'

'Why, certainly. This has been very pleasant, Mr Jackson, meeting you again. But I don't think I like sitting in this shed very much. I wonder could we go back to the house, now? It will be lunchtime soon, and they keep a good table, you know.'

'Yes,' said Jackson, 'we'll go now. And the names of your sister and her husband?'

'My sister is called Lady Carteret, and she's the wife of Sir Leopold Carteret, Baronet, of Providence Hall. Did you say you'd been to Africa? No, well, it's very hot, and very dusty. Not a bit like Exeter, even in the summer.'

★ ★ ★

In the back room of an alehouse in the shadow of St Mary-le-Bow, the three police officers conferred. Evidently the landlord was well known to Inspector Blade. He had ushered them into the empty room, and returned in a moment with three glasses of draught bitter. Blade had given him 1/3d, and told him to keep the change.

'I'll not leave your old clergyman alone to the tender mercies of that hypocrite,' said Blade, sipping his beer. 'I don't know whether he's a lunatic or telling the cold, sober truth, but he's been put away there because he can't control his tongue. Did you make any sense of his story, Mr Jackson?'

'Oh, yes, Mr Blade,' said Jackson. 'I know exactly what he was talking about. That young man, Gabriel Forshaw, was murdered, so that someone else could inherit his fortune. Sergeant Bottomley and I believe that the murderer was a woman, the same woman who, nearly thirty years later, did away with Mr Maximilian Paget at his house in Saxony Square, on your patch. *Our* murders in Warwickshire — and there were many of them — are directly connected with *your* murder.'

'Well, Officers,' said Blade, 'I'll help you all I can by keeping a close eye on any developments here in London. Have you consulted your superintendent about calling in Scotland Yard? Or am I being a bit premature, as they say?'

'If we have to, Mr Blade, then of course we will. But I think at the moment we know what has to be done. One important fact we learned today is that the Reverend Mr Hindle is the brother of Lady Carteret, of Providence Hall. That is very interesting, because when I called on Sir Leopold Carteret he blandly assured me that he'd never heard of anybody called the Reverend Walter Hindle — the man who is, in fact, his own brother-in-law.'

'What will you do?'

'I intend to unsettle Sir Leopold Carteret, Baronet, and his good lady, by conducting a very open and public search of the ruins of Waterloo House, which is very near indeed to his country seat. Maybe we'll find the remains of Gabriel Forshaw; maybe we won't. But what we *will* do is unsettle Sir Leopold Carteret and his wife — give them the jitters, if that isn't too vulgar an expression — and then Sergeant Bottomley and I will launch our offensive against him. Where else could Mr Hindle have been staying when I met him that day in the churchyard, but at his brother-in-law's house? Sergeant Bottomley and I have been following that hidden fortune all over Warwickshire, and here in London. I'm more and more convinced that its final resting-place is Providence Hall, in the village of Upton Carteret.'

'And where is your homicidal woman?' asked Inspector Blade. 'The woman whom poor Mr Paget invited to his house, only to be poisoned by her? Where is she? And, more to the point, *who* is she? You and I have both got warrants out against her, but we don't know who she is.'

Sergeant Bottomley, who had fortified his beer from the battered flask of gin that he carried in the tail pocket of his overcoat, suddenly spoke.

'As for that, sir,' he said, 'we may not know who she is for certain, but the guvnor and I have a pretty shrewd idea who she *could* be. And we do know *what* she is: a woman who must be in her late sixties, a lady in speech and bearing, according to Mrs Milsom, the housekeeper in Saxony Square. Asking your pardon, sir, for speaking out of turn.'

'There's one woman in this case who so far has only been a name,' said Jackson, 'and that woman is Lady Carteret, poor Mr Hindle's sister. I've met her husband, but I've never set eyes on her. I wonder, with Sergeant Bottomley: is she a lady in her late sixties, well-spoken and lady-like? And does she know that her own brother has been shut up in a shady nursing home? You'll see the way our thoughts are tending.'

Inspector Blade rose to his feet.

'I wish you well, Mr Jackson,' he said. 'Meanwhile, I'll arrange for a constable to keep an eye on Dr Morrison's nursing home. Nothing must be allowed to happen to that muddled old gentleman.'

★　★　★

'Sir,' said Sergeant Bottomley, after Inspector Blade had taken his leave of them, 'I don't like the idea of a single constable standing guard over that place. He'll be no match for those people. I was wondering — '

'Yes, so was I, Sergeant. I'm catching the afternoon train to Warwick. You'd better stay

211

here and conduct your own investigation as you think fit, and if you can, rescue that poor old man from the clutches of Dr Morrison and his cronies. If you don't, then I very much fear that the Reverend Walter Hindle will not be long for this world.'

11

Catherine's Narrative:
An Interlude of Impertinence

'Catherine, will you put down that magazine and listen to what I am saying?'

I was half successful in stifling a sigh of vexation as I abandoned the copy of *The Lady* that I had been reading. I had been grateful when Marguerite had offered to accompany me to Mrs Forster's boarding-house in Bournemouth. Marguerite was much older than I, and in some ways more worldly wise, except in the matter of spiritualism, which she approached with a naïve enthusiasm.

The week's holiday at the seaside had been an excellent idea, but Marguerite never really left me to rest and recuperate. If I went for a stroll in the gardens, or along the promenade, she was there beside me, talking about Uncle's murder, and the resultant police investigation.

We had returned home on the twenty-seventh, and Marguerite offered to stay with me for a few days, in order to make herself 'useful', as she put it. And now there was to be another interruption — something to stop me relaxing in my own sitting room in Saxony Square with my favourite magazine.

Somewhere in the depths of my mind I detected a very faint warning: Marguerite was beginning to establish an ascendancy over me. As yet the idea was tentative, but it rankled. We had been friends and equals, but the relationship was undergoing a subtle change.

'What is it, Marguerite?' I asked.

'I think that now is a convenient moment, Catherine,' she said, 'to tell you what Michael and I think about your situation. Your uncle never liked me, but I have always had your happiness at heart. And, of course, so has my brother. But there, I needn't tell you that, need I?'

'So what is it that you and Michael think?' I asked.

'We are both convinced that you should take no further interest in this business of your uncle's murder. You told Michael such a lot of things — things about a great fund of money that some terrible woman is trying to secure for herself at any cost. You told him about murders committed in the past — dreadful things, that someone like you shouldn't concern yourself with.'

'But Marguerite,' I replied, 'you can hardly expect me to forget all about my uncle's murder! While that remains unsolved, I *must* retain an interest.'

'Well, yes,' she said, 'and I quite understand you receiving visits from Inspector Blade. But you told Michael that you'd written a letter to some rural detective whom you met when you went to stay in that tumbledown old house in Warwickshire. Why get yourself involved with him, and the cases he is investigating? Give it all up, Catherine. Let the police do their work, and report when all's over. Start looking to your future, and leave the past alone.'

It is difficult, even now, to express in writing how impertinent I felt these words to be. There was nothing tentative about Marguerite's suggestion: it carried an intimation of scolding, as though I was a little girl in the nursery, and she my disapproving nanny.

'It's very kind of you and Michael to take such a close interest in my affairs,' I replied, 'and I can assure you that I have no intention of becoming an amateur sleuth. You've given me sound advice, and I'll think about what you've said. And there's an end to the matter.'

Marguerite shot me a glance, a curious, speculative look, but said nothing more. She wandered from the room on some errand of her own, and I returned to my perusal of *The Lady*.

So Marguerite had metamorphosed from friend to mentor. And she and Michael had discussed my life and my present situation behind my back. Marguerite was a chatter-box, but Michael? He was, I felt sure, about to ask me to marry him. Well, it ill became a man to discuss his lady-love with a third party, however close in blood. That, too, rankled. When next I saw him, I would tell him so.

There was a picture of Archduchess Stephanie wearing one of the new high-collared shirt-blouses with what appeared to be a man's spotted tie — it interested me hugely, as did the rather boyish boater that she was wearing. But soon my attention wandered again to my late uncle, and his guilty secret — accessory to more than one murder, and living all his later life in terror of the murderess.

If only I could have seen that woman! But fate had decreed that I should be out at the theatre on the very day that she called at our house on her murderous errand! How I regretted having asked Michael to take me to the theatre that afternoon! If only —

I let the magazine slide unheeded from my lap on to the floor. It was not I, but Michael, who had suggested that theatre visit. But what of that? What difference did it make? A chill breeze rustled the trees in the garden of Saxony Square, seeking its way through the half-open sash window. I got up from my chair and drew the window down.

I lingered for a moment, watching the few solitary people walking along the shale paths behind the protecting railings. There were a few loiterers, too: men and women with nothing to do on a working weekday but lounge about in public open spaces. There was a man standing almost motionless beneath the centre oak, seemingly looking up at the windows of our terrace, a man with a yellow overcoat and a battered bowler hat . . . It was with a sudden rush of delight that I recognized him: it was Detective Sergeant Bottomley, my friend and guide to the mysteries of Mayfield Court.

★ ☆ ★

'I'm very pleased to see you again, Miss Paget,' said Sergeant Bottomley. 'I've been watching your house more or less all this morning.'

He and I were sitting in Uncle's study, with the door closed, so that we could not be overheard. I had wanted Marguerite out of the house, and had sent her off in a cab to the circulating library in Oxford Street. It was only when her cab disappeared from sight that I had opened the window again, and beckoned to Mr Bottomley to come over to the house. It was Milsom's day off, so I had gone downstairs and opened the door to him myself.

'I received your letter, miss,' he continued, 'and was shocked, but not surprised, at the sad news that it contained. In a moment, we'll share our knowledge of what all this business is about, but first, I'd like to know who the youngish lady was who left your house in a cab about fifteen minutes ago. Nicely dressed, and well turned out, but looking none too pleased with herself — or with somebody else, perhaps.'

'That was my friend Marguerite Danvers,' I replied. 'She's gone to the library in Oxford Street.'

'Gone, has she? Or was she sent?' I saw the twinkle in the sergeant's eye, and smiled an acknowledgement of his perceptiveness.

'And is she the sister of your Michael — begging pardon, miss, for being so familiar?'

'She is. As I think I told you, Michael is a doctor, working at St Thomas's Hospital here in London. The three of us have been friends for quite some time. We like to go on excursions together to theatres, concerts and the like. Uncle Max didn't like Marguerite, because she was so very keen on spiritualism, but he wholly approved of Michael. But now I have something to show you that will reveal the terrible truth about the fate of Helen Paget, and a good deal more, besides.'

I rose from my chair and brought my uncle's last letter to me for Mr Bottomley to see. I watched him as he produced a slightly bent pair of wire-framed spectacles from his overcoat pocket, and read the letter, silently mouthing some of the words as he did so. Occasionally he ran a finger along a line where Uncle's writing had become a little uncontrolled. He put the letter down, and held his head in his hands for quite a minute. I realized that he was committing most of the letter to memory.

'Nothing of what your uncle had written there surprises me,' he said at length. 'The guvnor and I had already deduced much of it from other evidence that we've examined. There's a mass of fact and speculation waiting for us to make full sense of, miss, and I'm going to tell you all that Mr Jackson and I have discovered about the Forshaws, and what happened to them, and about little Helen.'

Sergeant Bottomley proceeded to tell me about the examination of the little skeleton at Mayfield Court, the mortal remains of a child which we both knew were those of Helen Paget. I still mourned for that child, and in my mind confused her often with the forlorn little 'ghost' whom I had seen at Mayfield, and whose hand Mr Bottomley had held. He told me of Inspector Jackson's experiences at Upton Carteret, and finally of his discovery of the aged clergyman, held a virtual prisoner in a London nursing home.

'We're on the threshold of solving this case, miss,' he concluded. 'We believe that the wicked woman — the harpy, as your uncle called her — is a titled lady living in Warwickshire. Very soon, we should be able to bring her to justice, and so lay the ghosts of Mayfield.'

'A titled lady? Do you mean the woman who came here, bent on murdering poor Uncle Max? Oh!' I suddenly recollected seeing one of Uncle's letters waiting on the hall plate to be taken to the post box. Lady Carteret . . .

'It's a Lady Carteret, isn't it?' I cried. 'My uncle wrote a letter to her not too long ago — it was to a house called Providence Hall, somewhere in the country.'

'That's right, miss. And when your uncle

wrote that letter, he unwittingly summoned his murderess to come with her poisons and her subtle wiles to Saxony Square.'

It was my turn to tell Sergeant Bottomley of my visit to the solicitor. All that I had to tell him merely confirmed in his mind the conclusions that he and Mr Jackson had already reached.

When he rose to leave, he stood looking at me gravely for so long that I began to feel alarmed.

'I'll leave you, now, Miss Paget,' he said, 'and before I go I want to give you a solemn warning. Don't speak to anyone about what you and I have discussed today. Somebody once said that knowledge is strength, but knowledge can also be danger. Above all, don't tell Dr Michael Danvers or his sister. One is more or less your fiancé and the other the friend you'd normally share secrets with, but if you tell them what you know, you may be exposing them to danger. So in this instance, miss, keep your own counsel — and therefore mine, as well.'

He left me, then, and I sat in Uncle's chair, possessed of a growing unease for which I could not account. That day, his legacy of suspicion and murder sat heavily upon me.

Marguerite returned to the house an hour after Mr Bottomley had left. She seemed her usual cheerful self, with no trace of the unwelcome intrusion into my affairs that had so vexed me earlier. She brought with her a number of library books, secured with a leather strap: Richard Jefferies' *Toilers of the Field*, J.K. Jerome's *Told After Supper*, and Olive Shreiner's *Dreams*.

At four o'clock Milsom brought us tea and buttered scones, and Marguerite read me the first pages of *Dreams*. Anything by Miss Shreiner is worth reading, and as Marguerite read to me — she read well — I felt my earlier annoyance receding. She left just before five, and I felt very glad that she did so with my fondest, though unspoken, regards.

That evening, Michael called. He seemed flushed and rather nervous, as though the day's duties at St Thomas's had left him exhausted. I thought that he would want to stay to dinner, but he said no; could we instead go for a stroll in the gardens? It was a lovely evening, with a steady though declining sun, and I readily agreed. I thought he had meant for us to cross the road into the gardens at the centre of the square, but it turned out that it was the garden behind my house that he had in mind.

Our garden is very long, and well tended, with a neat lawn surrounded by borders of fragrant flowers. There was a miniature coppice at the end of the garden, in which, at some time in the past, Uncle had had a pergola erected. When we reached it, Michael stopped, and took a small black box from one of his pockets. I knew then what he was going to do. The blood raced to my head, and drummed in my ears. He looked at me with an almost pained expression, as though what he was about to do was in some way reprehensible. Even in that moment of overwrought emotion, I wondered why.

Michael made a little faltering speech — I will not record what he said here — and then asked me if I would marry him. I said yes, and he produced a beautiful betrothal ring from the little box. The declining sun glanced off the circle of diamonds, and I watched the dancing darts of light as he slipped the ring upon my wedding finger.

I felt so happy. This act of commitment seemed to banish, at least for that moment, the dark and evil shadows that hung about the house, the remnants, as it were, of Uncle Max's own gloomy forebodings. I learnt that Marguerite had deliberately made herself scarce before five o'clock, to leave the scene free for her brother to make his proposal!

We walked hand in hand back to the house, and I wondered why Michael should be trembling so. Had he for one moment thought that I would refuse him? Milsom had spotted us from an upstairs window, and came bustling out on to the back terrace to congratulate us. I had never seen her smile so broadly before.

It was Milsom who persuaded Michael to celebrate our betrothal by staying to dinner after all. At first he demurred, saying that he was still in his working clothes, but he was overruled. We dined alone, the two of us, sitting opposite each other at the long polished table in the dining room. Uncle's great chair still stood at the head of this table, and there were times while we were talking when I fancied he was still sitting there, a shadowy figure, come to attend his niece's betrothal feast.

It was after Milsom had served coffee that I looked across at Michael, and said, 'Now that we are engaged, will you stop discussing me with your sister as though I were a recalcitrant child in need of chastisement?'

He had the grace to blush, and began to stammer an *ad hoc* explanation of his conduct, but when I started to laugh, he immediately regained his humour, and the matter passed off lightly. Nevertheless, I think my barbed words hit the mark.

There was brandy on the sideboard, and I proposed that we had a glass each, to complement our coffee. I watched him as he crossed to the sideboard, where the decanters had been set out. One day, if all went well, this would be his house, too.

The Married Women's Property Act, passed only last year, would give me full and entire control over my own property, and any further legacies that might fall my way. But I had always intended that ownership of my house in Saxony Square would be made over to Michael if we were to marry. I was old-fashioned enough not to want a husband who was daily made conscious of his dependency upon his wife for a roof over his head.

We sat in companionable silence at the table long after both coffee and brandy had been consumed. The sun was fast fading, and shadows were gathering in the room.

I have mentioned before — have I not? — that I have always had a certain psychic awareness, an ability at times to sense things beyond our normal level of perception. Well, that evening, as we two sat there in the gloaming, I was suddenly conscious of a strong, agonized voice addressing me, pleading with me, admonishing . . .

I saw nothing, of course, and I heard nothing in the usual way of mortals; but I knew that a voice from beyond was straining to make contact with me. And then suddenly, the 'voice' stopped. I mastered my response to this psychic intrusion so effectively that Michael did not even notice any change in my demeanour.

We went on to discuss days and dates, what church to go to, what guests to invite. And then, pleading a night-shift at St Thomas's, Michael made his departure. I was very happy that night, and went to bed in a sort of waking dream. But when my eyes finally closed, I found myself standing in the first-floor room at Mayfield Court, where a solemn little girl ghost mouthed the name 'Helen', and immediately put a finger to her lips.

NOTE. As I read through this account of the Mayfield Court affair, I wonder whether it is honest, or indeed right, to contemplate turning it into a novel. Since my first work, *A Dream of Heroes*, came out in 1898, I have culled my fiction from the depths of my own mind, whereas this would be a story based upon passages in my own life. Still, I am fortunate in having in you, my dear, a husband who seems able to resolve these literary dilemmas for me, using a doctor's insights into what is viable and what is improper, and so I shall go ahead and turn this narrative into a full-blown fiction. I am minded to call it *The Garden of Bones*, or, if that is too morbid, then *The Ghosts of Mayfield Court*. What do you think? Or can you come up with something else?

(March 18, 1905)

'It's not often that we see you here, Mr Temperley,' said Dr Morrison. His words were more a reproach than a mere statement of fact. 'How is your mother?'

Morrison thought: I know quite well how your mother is. She's dangerous to all life, and particularly those of her own clan. And you're no better, for all your good looks and your fine head of yellow hair.

'My mother's well,' replied the man called Temperley, 'well and flourishing, and will be even more so when you've handed the old man over to me.'

'Where will you — ?'

'I've no time for explanations! I'm due elsewhere in a very short while. In any case, Dr Morrison, what you don't know, you can't fret over. When people come to ask where he is, you can tell them that he'd managed to slip away again. Be as vague as you like. It will be of no consequence. I'm wasting time. I want the old man now.'

Temperley went over to the window of Dr Morrison's study and cautiously parted the curtains.

'There's a police constable watching the house from the other side of the road which is why I came in to see you from the back entry. I have a closed carriage at the end of the mews. Inspector Blade's posted that man there, and he'll just stand and look at the front door until he's relieved.'

Doctor Morrison said no more. In less than half an hour, the bemused and drugged Walter Hindle was brought out of the house in a wheeled chair, and taken across the garden to the rear gate, which gave on to a walled entry. Temperley and another man wheeled him to the waiting carriage. A few moments more, and they had gone.

Morrison, standing at the window of an upstairs room, quietly cursed the day when he had become involved with Temperley and his murderous mother. His practice had been built up on the principles of discretion and confidentiality. A client brought him an ailing patient, and that patient was looked after and treated until he or she died. It was tacitly understood that his 'guests', as he liked to call them, would never leave the premises except in a hearse. They were free to write letters, but those letters were always passed, unopened, to the client.

But the Temperleys were drenched in the blood of innocent victims, and he should never have agreed to look after the Reverend Walter Hindle. From time to time he would wander off, and a search-party had to be sent out to find him. Inevitably, he forgot that he had ever been there, and thought he had just been brought for the first time. True, he had, from time to time, been collected and taken off for holidays — there was some remnant of conscience, apparently, because the old man had been close to some family member. When he was returned, they had to go through the rigmarole of pretending that he had just arrived for the first time. It was a tiring business altogether. Now that the vicious son had arrived to take charge of him, Morrison held out little hope of his survival.

Well, he had nothing personal with which to reproach himself. He didn't know where young Temperley was taking the old man, so it was no longer any affair of his.

The door opened, and the stern nurse came into the room.

'Doctor Morrison,' she said, 'here is a letter from Mr Joel Gernsheim, the banker. He would like to place an aged relative of his in our care.'

The doctor's face broke into a smile.

'Mr Gernsheim? Well, let us see to the matter at once. Perhaps we could increase our fees a little? A banker, you know, has access to a lot of money!'

The doctor laughed heartily at his little joke, and together he and his co-conspirator descended the stairs and made their way to the office.

★ ★ ★

The carriage stopped at a dismal house in a secluded court on the Guildhall side of Moorgate, as it prepares to cross London Wall. It was a blank, dark brick house, with square windows hidden by shutters. Its only neighbours were a livery stable and a public house. A tarnished brass plate beside the door read:

> Dr Igor Zhdanov, Consultant Physician.
> By Appointment Only.

In answer to their knock, the door was opened by the doctor himself, an austere, bearded man, dressed impeccably in a black suit. Most of his wide, Slavic face was covered by a massive black beard.

The Reverend Walter Hindle was helped into the house, and taken in charge by a silent orderly, who was wearing an ankle-length white coat. The two men, patient and keeper, disappeared into a back room. The man who had helped Temperley opened the front door, and left the house without a word.

'So you have come to me at last,' said Zhdanov. 'What is it you want?'

'I want to hear of the sad fate of an aged clergyman, his mind wandering, who escaped from Dr Morrison's nursing home in Barbary Court, despite all the measures that had been taken to secure him. And then — '

'This man, this Hindle, is your own uncle. Are you quite sure that you wish to avail yourself of my services? For once I put my hand to the plough, I do not turn back.'

'He has become too dangerous to contain. If he blabs any more to strangers, we shall all end up on the gallows — Mother, my sister, and myself. A detective sergeant from Warwickshire is at this very moment asking dangerous questions at Saxony Square. The police are getting too close for comfort. An event has to take place.'

In spite of himself, Temperley blushed, and found himself unable to meet Zhdanov's grave, cold eyes.

'You will . . . you will see that he is unconscious?'

'When do you want the event to happen?'

asked Zhdanov, ignoring the question.

'It's the twenty-ninth today. Let it be this coming Friday, which sees the month out.'

'You know that I do not arrange these things on credit, and that I do not, for very obvious reasons, accept cheques. You must give me, now, five hundred pounds.'

Temperley had brought a heavy valise with him. He opened it, and produced ten paper rolls, each containing fifty sovereigns. Dr Zhdanov nodded his satisfaction.

'The event will take place on Friday,' he said. 'Look in the evening papers, and you will see what happened. Please give my kindest regards to your mother.'

Temperley said nothing. He glanced with something like anguish towards the door through which the Reverend Walter Hindle had passed, and then hurriedly left the house of the consultant physician.

12

Three Dead Men

The sun, a great orange disc, was beginning to slide down behind the horizon, bathing the dim woods and fields of Warwickshire in its dying glow. Before long, thought Jackson, the men would need to light the tarred wicks in the iron torches which earlier had been placed among the ivy-clad ruins of Waterloo House. The men had been digging for hours, but so far nothing sinister had been found.

What had once been a great mansion was now a collection of irregular tumuli, all trace of brick or stone hidden for decades by conquering ivy and bramble.

Across the road from the village of Upton Carteret, and beyond the old churchyard, now in dark shadow, where Jackson had first met the Reverend Walter Hindle, the gracious old mansion, Providence Hall, could still be seen. Well, thought Jackson, the smooth and shifty Sir Leopold Carteret, and his murderous lady, will have been told what's going forward here.

He and Sergeant Bottomley were virtually

certain that the baronet's wife was the Fury who had attacked and annihilated the Forshaw family, and murdered Maximilian Paget, but it was still too premature to move against her. But this excavation of the ruins would get her rattled; and when folk were rattled, they could do foolish and imprudent things.

Earlier, he had visited his old acquaintance the landlord of the Carteret Arms, who had rummaged about in a drawer under the bar and produced an old faded daguerreotype of Waterloo House taken in the 1850s. It showed a substantial four-square dwelling, neither beautiful nor ugly, with a coffered entrance and an array of rectangular windows. You could see the pathway, too, neat and well tended in those days, but now almost invisible under the depredations of Nature. Three men, a gentleman and two farmhands, stood on the path, looking with grave dignity at the camera. House, path, and men — all had gone long ago.

The landlord had told him that the house had burned down in 1869, or thereabouts. It was thought that a lamp had been knocked over, and there was no reason to seek other, more sinister, explanations. Men with buckets and hoses had done their best, but were no match for the engulfing flames. No one had lived there except the housekeeper: the last owner, Mr Gabriel Forshaw, had gone out to Africa and perished there. Nothing remained.

The sun went down, and darkness rushed across the sky. The men went round the ruins, lighting the tar-wicks. Across the fields, Jackson could see the sudden eruption of candlelight in the rooms of Providence Hall.

★ ★ ★

She was safe — safe, here, with her husband and her household. She had been lady of the manor for what seemed a lifetime. What could this fellow do to harm her? She had said to Leopold earlier: 'That was the bumpkin fellow who called here when I was away, was it not? What harm can he do? What can he possibly know about our affairs?' And her husband, calm and smiling as always, had replied: 'That's the man who tracked down the killer of Sir Nicholas Waldegrave and his son last year at Langley Court.[1] A very astute fellow. I only found that out after he'd called here. But don't worry: we have rank and social position on our side. Just deny everything. If we do that convincingly enough, my dear, they'll begin to think that they've made

---

[1] *The Calton Papers*

a ghastly mistake. I'll invite the chief constable to dinner. Don't worry.'

What were they doing? They'd lit bonfires or something of the kind, so they intended to dig there all night. Gabriel Forshaw ... A silly, callow youth, who yearned for travel in savage lands. What use would he have made of that fortune? Why should he, brought up in luxury and educated at Rugby, live to dissipate the Forshaw inheritance on harebrained schemes of philanthropy?

He'd called upon them once, at Mayfield Court, very early in the sixties, and told them that he intended to establish a boarding-school for the children of serving officers. He could live quite well, he said, on his army pay, and he hoped that he would be remembered for the school that he intended to found.

Hector had been very clever. Poor, dear Hector! Weak, addicted to opiates, his moral integrity crumbling with every day that passed, she had loved him for his loyalty to her, and had fought tooth and nail to wrest him from his addiction. But it had all been in vain. He had died, hardly knowing her, and calling on God for mercy.

But Hector had been very clever. 'You can't very well have boys and girls together in the one school,' he'd said. 'Officers do have daughters, you know! What about them?' And

Gabriel had replied that he would endow a second school for girls. When he had left, Hector had looked at her, and said: 'Well, that's it, then.' And so the silly fool's fate was sealed. Her sister Cecily had died suddenly, and it had been a simple affair to send her second husband, John Walsh, speedily after her.

The way was then clear to remove the would-be philanthropist Gabriel from this world, followed by his newly orphaned little heiress, Helen. Gabriel had been Hector's affair, because he could not face the prospect of silencing a child, but she had had no qualms in the matter.

Lady Carteret moved away from the window, and retreated into the as yet unlighted upper chambers of Providence Hall. At once, she passed into that dark other world where she knew herself for what she was: an outcast and an abomination. She was afraid of these old Tudor rooms, with their dark, oppressive panelling. What noises were those? The scuttling of rats behind the wainscot. How her head ached!

What room was this? Ancient, and smelling of rot, with faded, moth-eaten tapestries hanging on the walls. There was a man sitting at a small table, seemingly reading a book. Her heart pounding with fear, she drew closer, and realized that it was Hector. She looked down, and saw that he was reading the Bible. It was the Book of Psalms, and Hector's finger was pointing to a particular verse: *The wicked shall be turned into Hell.* He turned to look at her, but his face was the face of a skeleton.

Another room. But this was a low-ceilinged, comfortable place, with a cheerful fire burning in the grate. Where was she? Yes! It was her old home in the cottage at Newham Ford, and there, sitting beside the fire was Colin Temperley — Colin, her first husband, cheerful and kindly, the father of her son and daughter. He raised the clay pipe that he was smoking in greeting, and motioned to her to join him at the fire.

But that could not be. He was long dead, killed when a horse had bolted, and thrown him, leaving her a widow with two young children. The horse had stood beside his dead body, nonchalantly cropping the grass. She had fetched Colin's gun, and shot the beast herself.

From far off, a voice was calling her. What horror was she to face now?

'Bella, Bella! Where are you, my dear, dinner's about to come in.'

The dark dreams receded, and she found herself standing at the top of the stairs, looking down upon Sir Leopold Carteret, his hand extended to take her in to dinner. She gasped in sheer relief, and left the ghosts of the past in order to join her noble husband in the dining room.

Nothing must happen to him. She had told him that if the truth ever came to light, he was to deny all knowledge of past deeds. Of her children, a son as ruthless as herself, and a half-imbecile daughter, he knew nothing. They had been brought up in London, where her great wealth had secured them the best of care and education. They had their parts to play in her schemes, but they would never be a threat to her husband, who knew nothing of their existence. Nothing could ever be traced to him. He must remain what he was, squire of Upton Carteret, baronet, and wealthy aristocrat. If she went to the gallows — or the madhouse — then Leopold was to be her legacy.

★　★　★

'Master!'

The labourer's voice came urgently to Jackson from somewhere deep in the day's excavations. He looked down into one of the dark pits that the digging had created, and saw the man, his face shining in the torch-light as he looked up at him. He scrambled down the precarious slope into the floor of the pit.

'Master, this stone tank that my spade's uncovered lay in the foundation of this part of the house. I think it may have been an ice pit. But now it's a coffin, as you can see. Take a look.'

It had been a good idea to recruit these twelve farm labourers, thought Jackson. Some of them had been laid off, and were glad of the money that he offered them. All were used to the cruel hard work associated with arable farming. They had started to dig just after nine that morning; it was now after seven in the evening.

The labourer had revealed the remains of a body, partly preserved, so that Jackson could see the wizened, mummified face and the shock of hair. He noticed a long slab of granite, which the labourer had dragged off the stone tank: this body, unlike that of little Helen, had not suffered the depredations of hungry rats.

The digger stood resting on his spade, looking down at the remains.

'He's still got his clothes on, master,' he said, 'so they must have been in a hurry to get him safely buried. They're old-fashioned clothes, like my old father wore. What will you do with him?'

'We'll raise him just after dawn, and take

him to the police mortuary in Copton Vale. But there's a gentleman waiting in the police van who'll come down now, and have a preliminary look at him. What's your name? I forgot to ask.'

'Samuel Vokes, master. My old father used to tell me about this house, and the Forshaws who lived here. Fine folk they were, too, though not gentry. So you reckon this here body was one of them?'

Jackson smiled, and shook his head. This was no time for sharing confidences.

'That remains to be seen, Mr Vokes,' he said. 'I'll leave you to stand guard, while I go to fetch the gentleman who'll cast an expert's eyes over those remains.'

Doctor Venner was wearing a long overcoat and a kind of cap fastened with straps beneath his chin. Evidently he had come prepared for a certain amount of dirt, and the unexpected chills of a summer's night.

He slid down into the pit, and produced a dark lantern from the valise that he carried. Placing it open on an exposed piece of brick footing, he bent down close to the remains, and slid both hands behind the head. They saw him prise open the jaws, and peer inside the mouth. Then he slid, rather like a serpent, the length of the body, and felt the legs, still clothed in trousers. They heard him utter a little grunt of satisfaction, and Jackson proffered a hand to help the police surgeon out of the pit.

'What do you think, sir?' asked Jackson, drawing Venner aside out of earshot. 'Can I assume that we have uncovered the murdered remains of Gabriel Forshaw?'

'How old was this Gabriel when he died?'

'Twenty-four, sir.'

'Then no, Jackson. This dead man is not your Gabriel Forshaw. He was a man approaching fifty, with only a few teeth remaining. I can't say more than that until I've opened him up, which I'll do tomorrow, if you can get him to Copton Vale before midday.'

Doctor Venner picked up his dark lantern, blew out the candle, and returned it to his valise.

'I'll not stay any longer, Jackson,' he said. 'It's time I took myself home. If you find any other bodies, send them along tomorrow, too. Oh, and by the way: that man in the pit had his head cloved in with a spade. Good evening.'

★ ★ ★

'You're looking radiant tonight, my dear! You are the brightest, lightest thing in this room. Indeed, I'd go as far as to say that you're the

242

light of this entire house.'

Lady Carteret looked across the dining table at her husband. There were three people in the world whom she loved: Sir Leopold, and her two children by her first husband. Of the three, it was her husband she loved the best.

That compliment that he had just turned — he meant, and, of course, she *had* retained her good looks into late middle age. Yes, he meant it. He was a slight man, by no stretch of the imagination a heroic figure; but he was an aristocrat to his fingertips, enormously respected in the county. He knew all her secret plottings, and pretended that none of them existed. Whenever she was with him, she felt safe. He had an almost uncanny power of denial, as though he really believed his various untruths. Whatever came to pass, he must not be harmed.

The meal, superbly presented by their Belgian chef, and served with all the skills of well-trained footmen, began to bring a welcome calm to her nerves, and she relaxed. What did that policeman hope to find? And if he *did* find anything, how could he link it to her? It had all happened a lifetime ago.

The wines seemed to have been particularly well selected that night. She felt disinclined to withdraw and leave her husband to his port and cigar. She looked across the table at him, and he immediately interpreted her unspoken wish. He said a few words to the head footman, and coffee was served at the table, together with a sweet dessert wine.

It has all been worth the danger and the anguish. She had rescued this dear man from what would have been a scandalous crash involving social and financial ruin, and he had repaid that with utter love and loyalty. He had given her the social *cachet* that she had hitherto lacked. Her title, and her position in the county, were a kind of impregnable armour. Yes, she was safe with Leopold, and with their factor, Mr Lucas, a man who had the knack of making things happen. Lady Carteret relaxed in her chair, and sipped the sweet dessert wine.

★ ★ ★

Just after nine o'clock Samuel Vokes, who had moved deeper into the ruins to work with two of the other men, uncovered a bricked-up recess in what had probably been the wine cellar of the house. Part of the wall had crumbled away, and all three men saw the twisted and desiccated body that had been concealed there.

Saul Jackson watched as Vokes and his

helpers pulled down the crumbling wall with their pickaxes. This body, too, was fully clothed, and the material had survived the passing decades well. It was frustrating not to have Venner there to make a quick but skilled examination. The body, arranged in a sitting position with knees almost beneath the chin, certainly looked like that of a young man. A lantern was brought, and the inspector surveyed the remains.

The dead man had been wearing a jacket of some kind of serge material, and it was possible to see a flapped pocket on the side facing Jackson. Leaning forward, he gingerly slipped his hand inside. He had assumed that the man's killers had rifled through his clothes, and did not expect to find anything, but his fingers closed on something soft, which he withdrew.

It was a damp-stained diary, its pages stuck together in a solid block; but the mildewed cover opened easily enough, and Jackson saw written on the flyleaf in lead pencil, the brief inscription: *Gabriel Forshaw. January 1865.*

'Does this mean you're finished here, master? If so, we'll all be off to our homes.'

'Yes, we've finished here, Mr Vokes,' said Jackson. 'And I'm going to tell you something now that you're free to tell your neighbours. This body — bricked up here in this cellar wall — is that of a man called Gabriel Forshaw. It was said that he'd gone out to Africa in the sixties, and died there of fever. There's an inscription to that effect on one of the Forshaw monuments in the churchyard. But it wasn't true, Mr Vokes. Gabriel Forshaw was murdered, here, in the grounds of his own house, by two men. Done to death. And when that was over, one of the men killed the other with a spade. Dead men tell no tales.'

'Murdered? I've heard that old tale of the man who went out to Africa . . . So he was murdered? Well, it doesn't do to have a pot of money, does it? Somebody's bound to try and get it off you, one way or another. I'll bid you good night, Mr Jackson. Murdered, you say? The wife will be very interested to hear that. Her grandma was in service here when this was a real house, not this sad ruin. Yes, she'll be very interested . . . '

* ⋆ ⋆

She had long ago withdrawn to a separate bedroom, because her 'nightly fits and starts', as Leopold called her nightmares and sleepwalking, had made sleeping with her husband impractical for both of them. When she retired to bed that night, she had looked out of a window, and had seen the fitful

246

flames of the torches in the ruins of Waterloo House across the fields. Would they find it? And would it matter, after all these years — a lifetime — since Hector and another man, a discharged labourer desperate for work and prepared to do anything for money, had made away with Gabriel Forshaw?

She woke in the depth of night, and found herself once more in the library, a room that she hated and feared: a long, claustrophobic chamber, its walls burdened with thousands of old, rotting books which no one had ever read. The two fireplaces, one at each end, threw a pale light into the room from their glowing embers.

Hector was there, as real as he had been in life. He was standing near the fireplace further from the door by which she had entered, so that he seemed far distant.

'Oh, no,' he said, 'it would never have done, to have a witness to that. Dead men tell no tales.'

She stumbled out of the library into an old gallery, leading to the former servants' quarters of the Tudor part of the house, quarters that had long been abandoned and bricked up after that part of the mansion was remodelled in the seventies. Her brother, Walter, was standing at the end of the gallery, his arms folded, his eyes regarding her with the kind of resigned pity that he had always shown towards her. Was he dead? Or was this a phantasm of the living? He began to speak, but she could not make out the words.

And then she saw, standing beside him, sheltering under his protecting arm, the figure of a young girl. She was still wearing the dark olive-green dress with the lace at collar and cuffs, that she had worn that night. She stood motionless, looking at her, but saying not a word. Helen Paget, aged ten . . .

Would Walter protect her from the fury of that wandering spirit? He had long ago been removed from her influence, adopted by a well-to-do merchant, John Hindle, whose name he had taken, and brought up as a Congregationalist. But she had always been fond of him, her own brother — dangerously kind, until she had realized that her affection for Walter, as his mind degenerated, would probably lead to her own death on the gallows. Would he protect her, now? Was he still alive?

At last, Walter's words began to make sense. A book had appeared in his hand, and he was reading from it. The little girl, still circled by his arm, looked up trustingly into his kindly face, as he read a line of verse from the book.

'An orphan's curse would drag to hell a
spirit from on high.'

Lady Carteret felt a surge of blind despair,
and at the same time experienced a chilling
cold. She looked up, and found herself back
in her bedroom, shivering in her thin nightdress. Her nocturnal perambulation among
the ghosts was at an end.

If things continued like this, she would be
overcome by raving madness. It was time to
shake off these craven fears and assert herself
once more. That man, that Jackson, had
evidently declared war on the Carteret family.
Well, it was time to take that war into the
enemy's camp. There were things to do.
Tomorrow, she would begin her counter-
attack by writing a letter.

That girl . . . That daughter of old Paget,
she was another of the brood. Things had
been going very well with respect to her, but
perhaps more drastic methods were needed.
True, she had the Deed of Release safe,
snatched from the dying hand of Maximilian
Paget, but when she had examined it, she had
seen that it was an open deed: if no special
legatee was named, then enquiry had to be
made to seek out the next legitimate heir. She
and Hector had slaughtered their way to a
fortune, and the Forshaw money would stay

where it was. But that girl was a Paget; had she inherited her family's love of wealth? Would she be content with her uncle's meagre legacy? Perhaps.

But then again, perhaps not. There would be copies of the Deed of Release, and the girl, if so inclined, could make a legal challenge to secure the fortune to herself. An open deed allowed for that, but then people would start probing and, like that man Jackson, might find out more than was good for her. So tomorrow, she would write a letter.

That night, she left the candles in her bedroom lit, and contrived to sleep fitfully until the welcome dawn.

★　★　★

The guide employed by Messrs Cook shepherded his little flock of foreign visitors across The Ring, and so out of Hyde Park and into Kensington Gardens. It was early in the morning of the 31 August, and a Friday, so he would not be on duty again until the coming Monday.

'Ladies and gentlemen,' he intoned, 'we have now entered Kensington Gardens, in which is situated Kensington Palace, one of the Royal residences. The building was designed by Sir Christopher Wren, and built between 1689 and 1691.'

'You say it is a palace, yes? The good Queen Victoria dwells there?'

'No, sir. She does not.' Foreigners required not only courtesy but firmness. 'William the Third and Mary the Second, joint sovereigns, both died there, as did Queen Anne, and George the Second. Her Majesty Queen Victoria was born there in 1819.

'Stretching in front of you — '

'And this palace, the citizens can go there, to visit, is it not?'

'No, it is not — no, they don't. But the state rooms are being restored, and it is said that they will be opened to the public in about six years' time. The palace is currently the residence of Her Royal Highness the Princess Louise, and her husband, the Marquess of Lorne.

'Stretching in front of you is the Long Water, which is a continuation of the Serpentine, which we saw in Hyde Park. This waterway leaves the park at Albert Gate, over in that direction, and so joins the London main drainage system. We shall now — '

'And that black object, floating in your Long Water, what is the meaning of that? An old custom, yes? Ach! *Mein Gott*! It is a dead man!'

Foreigners! The French weren't too bad,

251

but these Germans: nothing but questions! Better find out what the fellow was talking about. The guide walked over to the edge of the Long Water.

★　★　★

Inspector Blade and Sergeant Bottomley looked down at the drowned and sodden corpse that had been hauled out of the Long Water. It lay on the well-cut grass of Kensington Gardens, where a canvas screen had been hastily erected to preserve the sight from curious eyes.

The Cook's guide had made a brief statement, and had furnished them with his name and address; he and his volubly excited party had left the gardens by the way that they had come.

'I failed, sir,' said Bottomley. His flushed, homely face regarded the body of the Reverend Walter Hindle with an expression of anguished distress. 'I stayed behind in London when the guvnor went back to Warwick partly to make sure that nothing happened to this poor old gentleman. But they got the better of me in the end.'

'You can't be everywhere at once, Sergeant,' said Blade. 'You were very wisely keeping an eye on that young lady in Saxony

Square. So don't reproach yourself. Ah! At last! Here's the duty police surgeon. He'll take a quick look, and then arrange for the body to be removed to Brompton Road. Doctor McMaster, will you look at this man lying here dead?'

The doctor was a lean, red-headed man with a poker face, and a twinkle in his eye. He looked Inspector Blade up and down before kneeling down beside the body.

'Dead, is he? How do you know that? Since when were you last in medical school?'

'As always, Dr McMaster, you're a model of courtesy. Will you please examine that dead body? You'll be better able than me to say whether it's dead or not.'

The Reverend Walter Hindle's face was that of a man who had quietly fallen asleep. His eyes were closed, and his mouth slightly open. His white hair clung in sodden strands to his forehead. He was wearing the clothes in which Bottomley had last seen him. Herbert Bottomley thought: he's been drugged into unconsciousness, probably with chloral hydrate, then brought out here to be thrown away like so much rubbish . . .

McMaster seized the corpse by its shoulders and turned it on to its left side. A stream of water immediately poured from its mouth. He roughly examined the head for wounds, grasping the corpse by the chin, and moving the head from side to side with a callousness born of long experience as a police surgeon. Then he sat back on his heels and looked up at the two policemen.

'He died by drowning. Brought here from somewhere and put into the water. He may have been drugged first — probably was. I can do a full *post mortem* this afternoon. Do you know who he is?'

'Yes, Doctor, we know who he is. Sergeant Bottomley and I have work to do, so I'll bid you good morning. Come on, Sergeant. Let you and I go now to Barbary Court and beard that hypocrite Morrison in his den.'

★ ★ ★

'I cannot believe it! Cannot. He was here at dinner yesterday evening, wasn't he, Nurse?'

'Yes, sir, and then he retired to bed. He seemed quite happy and contented, poor old man. He didn't come down to breakfast, and we assumed that he had decided to sleep in. He was very old and frail, Inspector.'

'I've sent an orderly to check the doors leading into the alley at the back of the premises,' said Dr Morrison. 'Oh, it's impossible! Are you quite sure that it was the Reverend Walter Hindle that you found?'

'Yes, Doctor,' said Inspector Blade. 'It was him without a doubt. And he's dead. Drowned in the Long Water in Kensington Gardens.'

The door of Morrison's office opened, and a man wearing a short white linen jacket entered the room. To Blade's eyes he looked more like a discharged waiter than a medical attendant.

'Sir,' the man stammered, 'the little door beside the kitchen had been left unlocked. The key's still in the wall-box. That's how Mr Hindle must have contrived to get out. Maybe he wanted to go for a walk, or to catch an omnibus. Half the time he didn't know what he was doing, poor old gentleman.'

'But it was your duty to see that all doors were locked at night, and only opened after breakfast. And now a patient has died. He must have got as far as Kensington, walked through the gardens, felt faint, and fallen into the water. You are to blame, Higgins. You are dismissed. Collect your week's wages from the porter, and go.'

The man, hanging his head in shame, left the room.

★ ★ ★

'A nice little play, Sergeant,' said Blade, when they were out in the street. 'They'd all learned their parts, and delivered them superbly. We'll leave them where they are for a while, and when the time's ripe, we'll sweep up the whole gang.'

'I don't think Mr Hindle was there at all, sir,' said Bottomley. 'I think that after our last visit they got the wind up, and moved him to some other house. It's just a feeling I have.'

'You may well be right, Sergeant Bottomley. I'll look into it. Meanwhile, I suggest you resume your watch over Miss Catherine Paget. I wouldn't like to have another murder done on my patch. She's a brave young lady, but bravery can make people do foolish things. Watch over her.'

13

Catherine's Narrative:
Lady Carteret's Story

On 4 September I received a letter from Lady Carteret. It was only five days since Sergeant Bottomley had called, and told me of his suspicion, shared with his inspector, that this titled lady had murdered Uncle Max.

The envelope was of the best cream-laid paper, with the coat of arms of the Carteret family embossed on the flap. I opened it, and found a page or two of bold writing, signed at the bottom with a fine flourish of penmanship: *Bella Carteret*.

I held the letter unread for quite a minute. Was this woman mad, to write to me? But then, why should she think that I knew anything about her nefarious doings? She had no way of knowing that I was now an intimate of Sergeant Bottomley. My curiosity got the better of me, and I began to read the letter. I have it still, and reproduce it here.

Providence Hall
Upton Carteret

257

Via Monks' Stretton
Warks
31 August

My dear Miss Paget

We have never met, and so you may well be surprised to receive a letter from me. However, there is something that weighs heavily on my mind, and I can no longer sustain it without sharing the burden with you. I believe that absolute frankness is essential. Please read on.

I am the woman who called upon your uncle, Maximilian Paget, on the afternoon that he died. As you will know, he had recently inherited an old property at Mayfield, in this county, and he had been good enough to grant my written request to search in the muniments of that property for a long-lost deed belonging to my family, which had been lodged there by a distant relative many years since, and then forgotten.

Your uncle was successful in securing this document, and wrote to me, inviting me to call at your house in London, both to receive the document, and to have a talk over old times. I had known your uncle well when we were both younger, but had long lost touch with him.

I called, as I think you know, but for family reasons I did not want to be announced, and wore a veil to conceal my features. Your uncle duly gave me the deed, and tea was brought in. It was then that he told me of an atrocious murder that his late brother Hector had committed, a murder of which he had full knowledge, although he had not himself participated in it. He began to talk wildly, and I became frightened.

To calm myself I poured us out another cup of tea, and saw him put some kind of tablet into his. I thought it was medicine of some kind. He drank the tea, and immediately cried aloud and expired. He had committed suicide. I did not know what I was doing at that moment. I picked up the cup, which had fallen from his hand, and put it back on the saucer. I heard a noise in the house, and fled to my waiting carriage.

I told no one of this, and I have since heard from my servants and others that ugly rumours are circulating about me, rumours that could redound to the detriment of my dear husband, Sir Leopold Carteret.

Will you come down to Upton Carteret and talk to me? I will show you the deed that your uncle retrieved, and you will see that it is an innocuous proof of title to some of the fields bordering our demesne. Come and stay for a few days; my husband is very anxious to meet you and, I hope, reassure you. If you feel nervous at the idea of coming to Providence Hall, then by all means bring a friend, who will be welcome too.

There is nothing viler, my dear Miss Paget, than unsubstantiated rumour and suspicion. Do say that you will come. Write to me by the next post.

Ever yours sincerely

Bella Carteret

Suicide? Could this woman be telling the truth? I was in my sitting room overlooking Saxony Square gardens, admiring the steady morning sun, and the attractive architecture of a London square. I enjoy trips to the country, but I am a Londoner at heart.

I remembered everything that Sergeant Bottomley had told me, and was grateful for his warnings; but would it be right to show him Lady Carteret's letter? The assertion that Uncle had committed suicide was basically reasonable: my uncle had been in a very curious, fatalistic mood when I had last seen him, as though he were quite certain of the fate that was awaiting him. He had been anxious that Michael and I should leave him for the theatre — was that anxiety linked to a secret determination to do away with himself?

I would accept Lady Carteret's invitation. Hitherto, she had been nothing but a name. If I saw her in her true role as chatelaine of Providence Hall, the wife of a baronet of ancient noble family, then I would, perhaps, be reassured.

But I would take her advice, and come with a companion. I looked down from my window into the square, and saw Michael crossing the roadway towards my house. He had rather too stridently criticized my receiving Sergeant Bottomley, and interesting myself in the case, and Marguerite had abetted him in a way that bordered on impertinence. But who better than my fiancé to accompany me to Providence Hall?

'No, Catherine,' said Michael, when he had read Lady Carteret's letter. 'I'm very strongly opposed to this. You don't know these people. What if you are walking into some kind of trap? Leave it alone. If I were your husband, I would forbid you to go. As your fiancé, I can only plead with you to show some common sense. Do not reply to that letter.'

Once again, I felt the spirit of rebellion stirring in my soul. What gave these men the right to lord it over women as though they were some kind of inferior creature?

'On the contrary, Michael,' I replied, 'I have every intention of going. You are not my husband yet, and I shall do as I like. Will you come with me or no?'

He flushed, but I detected a secret admiration for my stance. I could see a kind of satisfaction in his eyes. He was not marrying a ninny!

'Very well, Cath. I'll come. But I'm going as a guard, not a guest. I'll leave you now, and get back to the delights of the dissecting room. Will you write today?'

'Yes, and Milsom can post the letter to catch the midday delivery. Thanks for agreeing to come. This lady may be right: I wondered myself at times if Uncle Max would do something of the kind. Remember, in that letter he left for me, he accused himself of complicity in a great moral crime.'

NOTE. Ten years is a long time, but the events of those weeks stay vivid in my memory. I was foolish beyond measure, but I was still only twenty, and very sure of myself. How fortunate I was to have a male friend at Providence Hall! Without that good fortune, I doubt that I would be here today, with my doctor husband, and my two little children. Fate can play strange tricks.

(March 20, 1905)

We set out together for Upton Carteret on the following Thursday. On receipt of my letter, Lady Carteret had sent me travelling instructions by return post. There was a daily train at 10.45 a.m. from Paddington to Copton Vale, in Warwickshire, where we were to change to a local train for Monks' Stretton. A carriage would be waiting for us there.

It was hot and stuffy in the train from Paddington, and once out of the seemingly endless suburbs Michael drew down the window. We had decided to travel first class, and we were the only occupants of the compartment. He had bought himself a copy of the *Morning Post* from the bookstall at Paddington, and gave it a cursory glance before throwing it down on the seat beside him.

'Cath,' he said, 'do you really believe this Lady Carteret's story about witnessing your uncle's suicide? Milsom said that when she found him he was still alive, and in the last stages of toxic spasm. But Lady Carteret said that he was dead when she left the room.'

'Either of them could have been mistaken,'

I said. 'It was a terrifying moment for both of them, and they may have misinterpreted what they saw.'

Michael shook his head dubiously, and was silent for a while. The train's whistle emitted a warning shriek and then plunged into a tunnel. When we emerged into the light, we found ourselves travelling along on the skirts of a vast tract of woodland.

'Milsom said that there was terror in your uncle's eyes. She said he uttered a shriek — '

'I know, Michael,' I said, rather testily, 'but it may be exaggeration on her part. Let us postpone judgement on the matter until we have heard Lady Carteret's side of the story.'

I was all for being fair, you see. I had received an excellent education at a private school for girls, where we had learnt of the merits of examining both sides of a question before rushing to judgement. I have since perceived other ways of tackling issues, both those of an intimate nature, and those that concern the public interest.

Michael, who had resumed the reading of his newspaper, suddenly uttered an exclamation of shocked surprise.

'I say, Cath, look at this! Do you remember telling me about an old clergyman whom Inspector Jackson met in a churchyard? He saw him just a few days ago, in a nursing home somewhere near Pewterers' Hall. Listen to what it says here.

' 'This Friday last, the drowned body of a Dissenting clergyman, given as the Reverend Walter Hindle, was retrieved from the Long Water in Kensington Gardens. Inspector W.P. Blade, 'C' Division, who is in charge of the case, does not think that the unfortunate gentleman's death was an accident. Foul play is suspected, and we are confident that Mr Blade will bring the perpetrator speedily to justice.' What do you think of that?'

I shook my head, but said nothing. This poor old man, I knew, was involved in the whole complex matter of the Forshaw inheritance, but I knew nothing in detail. I was very sorry — no, I was outraged, as I always am when the innocent suffer — but at the same time I thought: well, whoever murdered him, it was not Lady Carteret. No ingenious theory could lay that crime at her door.

★ ★ ★

At last, the train drew up at a long wooden platform, where a notice announced that we were at Monks' Stretton Halt. We alighted, and were met by a liveried coachman, who told us that his name was Andrews. He took

265

us down a short incline and on to a narrow road where a carriage was waiting, its horses both chafing at the bit. Andrews told us that we would be at Providence Hall in just under half an hour.

It was pleasantly cool, sitting in the open carriage, with a light breeze blowing across the ploughed fields lying beneath sheltering tracts of woodland on either side of the road. We came to a village, which Andrews told us was Upton Carteret, but before we came to the main street he turned the carriage away and on to a narrow lane which ran behind an old church. Quite abruptly, we entered a deer park, and a few minutes later we found ourselves coming to a stop on the flagged forecourt of Providence Hall.

I confess that I was for a moment overawed by the grandeur of the ancient Tudor mansion, long and low-roofed, with black and white timbers and diamond-paned windows. Towards the east, the old building abutted on to a Georgian extension in Cotswold stone. I was only a short time on the forecourt, but it was time enough to realize that Providence Hall and its surrounding demesne spoke of wealth and prosperity. For a fleeting moment I recalled the dilapidated and wretched Mayfield Court. These two houses, I mused, belonged to different worlds.

Michael and I were received in the cool, flagged entrance hall of the mansion by a butler who was very obviously part of the established order there. I learnt later that his name was Hopkins, and that he had been in Sir Leopold Carteret's employ for over twenty years.

It was Hopkins who preceded us into the drawing room, a spacious Elizabethan chamber furnished in a mixture of antique pieces contemporary with the house, and comfortable modern furniture and draperies. It was a beautiful, welcoming room.

It was here that I got my first glimpse of Lady Carteret. I had built up a picture in my mind of the woman whom my uncle had called the 'harpy', and had seen her as a kind of sere and yellow hag with a vicious mouth and a dangerous, half-mad voice. I could not have been more mistaken.

I learnt later that she was sixty-five, but she looked many years younger than that. Her beautifully tended hair was still black, and her complexion, innocent of artificial aids, was flawless. She was wearing a morning gown of pale blue crêpe-de-chine, with one of the new halter necks. She had been standing before the great open fireplace of the room, and came forward to greet us as we entered. As we were expected, we were not announced.

'My dear Miss Paget,' said Lady Carteret, 'I am so glad you agreed to visit us. And this young gentleman is your fiancé, you told me in your letter. You are very welcome, Dr Danvers.'

Her voice, that of an educated lady, was both charming and welcoming. It was from this point that I began to think that Sergeant Bottomley and his superior — how odd it was, that I could never remember his name — were mistaken in their belief that this titled county lady was a deranged murderess.

'Hopkins will take you up to your rooms,' said Lady Carteret. 'When you have refreshed yourself, please come down here for coffee. Perhaps I can begin to discuss things with you then. Sir Leopold is visiting one of the farms just now, but he will be back well in time for lunch at one o'clock.'

She motioned to Hopkins, who had stayed in the room, and we followed him back into the entrance hall, where two liveried footmen were standing beside our luggage. We went in procession to our rooms on the first floor; they were at the front of the house, overlooking a formal knot garden.

When we were ready, we met each other on the landing. Michael looked very thoughtful and, as we descended the stairs, he whispered, 'She doesn't look much like a harpy, Cath. I wonder — Well, I wonder whether those two policemen friends of yours could have gone badly wrong.'

I was secretly inclined to agree with him.

* * *

Morning coffee was brought in by a very young and demure maid, who set it out carefully on a low table near the fireplace. She looked timidly at Lady Carteret, who gave her a little nod of approbation, upon which she curtsied and left the room.

'The housekeeper's making a very good little servant out of that girl,' said Lady Carteret. 'It's hard to get decent maids out here in the country. Leah is the daughter of one of our farmers. She was delicate as a little girl, not really fit for farm work. So we were glad to take her on.'

Michael and I were sitting on a sofa, with small tables placed conveniently at hand. Lady Carteret rose, and poured out the coffee.

'How do you like it, Miss Paget?' she asked, and I told her that I liked a small drop of milk but no sugar. Michael was given his cup with sugar and milk. Evidently, mere men were not to be asked!

Lady Carteret sat down in her high-backed

brocade chair, and sipped her coffee in silence for a while. I looked round the tastefully furnished room, noting how its Tudor features — the great stone fireplace, the large expanse of diamond-paned windows, the coffered plaster ceiling — had been complemented by fine modern furniture. Old and new blended admirably. Lady Carteret followed my glances with her own eyes.

'When I first came here, Miss Paget,' she said, apparently reading my thoughts, 'this room was overfilled with ugly, oversized Tudor and Jacobean stuff. Most depressing! Fortunately, my husband readily agreed to my schemes for refurbishment here. Later, perhaps, or maybe tomorrow, you must see what we did in the Regency rooms.'

I looked at Michael, who gave what I will describe as the ghost of a shrug. Like me, he was bewildered. Could this cultured lady possibly be the 'harpy' who had murdered my Uncle Max?

Lady Carteret put down her cup, and gently relaxed in her chair. I noticed how she contrived to sit upright, so that her grace and elegance were not compromised.

'Now, my dear,' she said, 'tell me: is your fiancé completely in your confidence?'

I saw the beginnings of a smile on Michael's face, which he instantly suppressed.

'He is, Lady Carteret,' I replied. 'So if we are to talk family matters, you may safely do so in his presence.'

'Very well. I told you in my letter that I knew your Uncle Maximilian: we had been acquaintances when we were both young, though he was some years my senior. Do you know what is meant by *une amitié amoureuse?* It's a kind of romantic friendship which never goes beyond the bounds of propriety. The French have some wonderful ways of expressing these things. Well, your uncle and I were like that.'

She cupped her chin in her hand, and looked at me without speaking for a while. It was a penetrating, rather unsettling look, but it soon passed, and she continued.

'As you know, my dear, your uncle had a brother, Hector, and it is of him that I wish to speak now. He was a decent man enough, at least initially; but he married a handsome woman who was possessed of a cruel and ruthless personality. He soon fell under her influence, and ended up just as wicked as she was. Her name was Arabella Bancroft. I am talking now of events that happened thirty years ago.

'Arabella had an older sister, Cecily, who married Henry Forshaw, a very rich man who had inherited the family fortune from his

271

brother Edward. Well, this Edward was killed in a railway accident — in 1857, I think it was — and two years later Cecily married a man called John Walsh, a widower with a little girl called Helen.'

I started involuntarily, and Lady Carteret gave me a sympathetic glance.

'Yes, Miss Paget — I know that you have heard the story of little Helen, who was kin of yours in a rather convoluted way. Are you able to follow all this tangle of names?'

'I am, Lady Carteret.'

'Very good, then let us have some more coffee. There are sugar biscuits there, which are made in the house.' Once again, she poured out coffee for us both, and resumed her seat.

'Cecily Bancroft and her first husband, Henry Forshaw, had a son, their only child. His name was Gabriel. He died in 1865, at Bonny, in Africa, and the fortune passed from him to Cecily and her second husband, John Walsh. Then Cecily died. And her husband John Walsh died. They died within days of each other.'

She suddenly rose, and crossed to the window. Her face had grown stern and indignant. She pointed out into the grounds.

'Beyond those gardens,' she said, 'and across the road leading into the village, you will find the ivy-covered ruins of Waterloo House, the former residence of the Forshaw family. There is a man over there, a man called Inspector Jackson, who is engaged in digging into the foundations of that house in search of bodies. He is looking for the body of Gabriel Forshaw, who he thinks was murdered there — and that man, that rural inspector, has convinced himself that *I* am the murderer of that man! He is trying to frighten me, but if he thinks he will succeed, then he will find that he has got the wrong woman.'

Michael gave an almost involuntary cry of protest.

'You, madam, a murderer? I don't believe it!'

Lady Carteret gave him a half-amused smile as she resumed her chair.

'Well, thank you, young man,' she said. 'I only wish that this man Jackson could be persuaded to believe the same. I have no proof — not one shred — but I have always believed that Arabella Bancroft murdered her own sister, and her husband, John Walsh. And so the fortune descended to little Helen. By then, its value had reached one million pounds. You know — you know what happened to Helen, don't you? You went to Mayfield Court with your uncle, and the people there would have told you about it.'

'Yes, Lady Carteret, I know all about it. At

one time I thought that I was being haunted by that poor little child's ghost.'

'Hmm . . . Well, I am to be made the villain of the piece. It is too tiresome. We're having the chief constable here next week, and I'm hoping that my husband will persuade this Inspector Jackson to start looking for Arabella Bancroft, and leave me in peace. I have been lady of the manor here for over twenty years. I come from a good Warwickshire family. I do not deserve to be persecuted in this way — Ah! Sir Leopold has arrived. He will be delighted to see you both.'

⋆ ⋆ ⋆

Sir Leopold Carteret was a slightly-built man in his fifties, clean-shaven, with an unlined face and mild blue eyes. He was dressed in a brown tweed hacking-jacket, and his trousers were tucked into leather riding boots. His voice held a curious caressing quality that put me immediately at ease.

'So you are Miss Catherine Paget, Maximilian's niece? How very nice to meet you. I've been visiting one of the estate farms, so I hope you'll excuse these boots. I shall change presently into something more presentable.'

He crossed the room, and solemnly shook hands with me.

'And you are Dr Michael Danvers, Miss Catherine's fiancé? How very interesting. And do you practise, Dr Danvers? Oh, in a hospital? You must tell me about it, and what it is that you do there.'

That first day at Providence Hall was characterized by this kind of gentle, very normal conversation. Lunch was served in a magnificently opulent dining room, and Sir Leopold regaled us with tales of his family's history, and some of the more eccentric baronets who had given the family an exciting reputation in the last century. We talked about our different occupations and interests, the quiet of the countryside as opposed to the fury and turmoil of London, and the differing strengths of the various City department stores.

When lunch was over, Sir Leopold took Michael off to see the gun room and the stables, while Lady Carteret gave me a personal tour of the great mansion. It was a beautiful, fascinating house, upon which, I realized, much money had been lavished. I had sometimes visited country houses on open-days, and there had always been a kind of endearing shabbiness about some of the furnishings and fabrics. At Providence Hall, everything was in pristine order.

Later that afternoon Michael managed to

have a word with me alone.

'Cath,' he said, 'do you really believe that this nice aristocratic couple can be murderers? It's time for us to bow out gracefully, and get back to London. I was right, you know, and so was Marguerite. You should not have got yourself embroiled with those country police officers. Inspector Blade in London will surely find out who it was who murdered your uncle. We've been involving ourselves in what is, in effect, an appalling and misguided slander.'

For once, I held my tongue.

At dinner that night Sir Leopold told us how delightful it was to have a couple of young people staying in the house.

'Lady Carteret and I, alas! were not blessed with children, and the heirs to this estate are a collateral branch of the family, the Duttons, of High Grange, in Oxfordshire. Very sound people, you know, but they're not Carterets.'

'Leopold,' said Lady Carteret, in gently chiding tones, 'our guests don't want to know about the Duttons. Neither do I, for that matter. We're not dead yet.'

'No, that's true,' her husband replied, with a smile. 'What I wanted to ask, was whether you'd both like to stay for a few more days? Stay for Saturday and Sunday and go back to London on Monday. Make a short holiday of it, you know. Perhaps we could have a little dinner party . . . We could ask Mr and Mrs Bold, and the Rivingtons — they're only young, aren't they? Well, in their thirties, perhaps. What do you think?'

'I think it's an excellent idea. Will you both stay?'

Of course, we both agreed. In true patrician manner, Sir Leopold and Michael remained for port, while Lady Carteret conducted me to her little private sitting room on the first floor. It was a pleasant room, with wallpaper and fabrics which I recognized as having come from Liberty's in London.

'We'll join them for coffee later, in the drawing-room,' said Lady Carteret. 'Meanwhile, I want to revert to that last terrible meeting with your uncle. You don't mind, do you? I know how terrifying the whole thing has been.'

'I'm glad you've brought the matter up again, Lady Carteret,' I said, 'because there is one small point that puzzles me, something that Michael pointed out to me on the journey down. You said that my poor uncle actually died when you were in the room with him. My housekeeper, Mrs Milsom, is convinced that he was still alive when she found him, after your departure.'

Lady Carteret nodded her head vigorously.

'Yes,' she said, 'that's precisely the point that I wanted to clear up. I said that poor Maximilian had died while I was there, but I realize that I could not be absolutely certain of that. He may have lost consciousness for a while, but at the time I was convinced that he was dead, which is why I fled. I am not a young woman, Miss Paget, and the shock of what I witnessed drove me to a kind of . . . palpitating panic, if you can understand what I mean by that. Do you think I should write to the officer in charge of the case, and tell him what I saw? The time for concealment is over.'

'I think that would be a very good idea, Lady Carteret,' I replied. 'I will write down Inspector Blade's details for you, so that you can write to him.'

'Excellent. And now, let me show you the document that your poor uncle gave to me when I met him in Saxony Square — '

'That will be entirely unnecessary, Lady Carteret,' I replied. 'You have no need whatever to justify your actions to me.'

From somewhere below, we both heard the faint tinkling of a hand-bell.

'That means that the gentlemen have gone into the drawing room. Come, my dear, let us go down for coffee.'

It was Thursday, and we had been invited to stay over until Monday morning. Once back in Town, I would write to Sergeant Bottomley, and tell him all about our visit to Providence Hall. Since his first appearance at Mayfield Court I had felt a special affinity with him, and I was anxious for him to distance himself, if that were possible, from his inspector's mistaken hypothesis. I told Michael of my intention, and he reluctantly agreed with my proposed course of action. He still maintained that only Inspector Blade was competent to solve the mystery of my uncle's death.

14

Sergeant Bottomley's Day

Herbert Bottomley stood under the great oak in the gardens of Saxony Square, looking across the carriageway at Miss Catherine Paget's house. Ever since the discovery of poor Mr Hindle's body in Kensington Gardens just a week earlier, he had spent some time watching over the young lady who reminded him so much of his eldest girl back home in Warwickshire. The rest of his time had been taken up with helping Mr Blade at Little Vine Street. He was a good officer, who valued having an extra detective to assist him for a while.

Mr Blade had not forgotten the smooth-talking Dr Morrison. He'd let Bottomley loose on that beauty, and he'd made a few discreet forays to the district where the nursing home was situated. He'd found a friendly little public house, the Pewterers' Arms, where he'd been able to ply a couple of old soaks with gin, and ask them questions.

Yes, they knew that Dr Morrison's place. People were always dying there, and there'd

280

be mortuary hearses arriving, and the doctor and that sour-faced nurse of his would come out on to the steps, weeping, and waving black handkerchiefs.

Visitors? Yes, he had visitors. Tradesmen, mostly, and the occasional relative to see one of the patients — Oh, thanks, guvnor! Villains? Well, it's hard to say what a villain looks like, isn't it? Some of the biggest villains unhung look as though butter wouldn't melt in their mouths.

There was one bloke, though — a nasty piece of work *he* was, who'd come from time to time. Dressed as a gent, and with a big bushy beard. A foreigner, he was. Russian. Pole. Something like that. Come to think of it, he'd called there last week. Here, George! Didn't you bring that foreign, bearded chap to Dr Morrison's last week?

George, who had turned out to be a cabman, had agreed. Yes, he'd brought him to Dr Morrison's. It was 1/5d, and he'd given him two shillings. Take him back? Of course he'd taken him back. He'd told him to wait, hadn't he? Oh, thanks, guv. A glass of bitter would be very acceptable. Yes, he'd taken him back. Number 5, Chatham Court, off Moorgate. Same fare, same tip. Foreigner, he was. German, by the looks of him.

He'd written the address down, and it was

at this moment burning a hole in Bottomley's pocket. When the time was right, he'd pay a call on this Russian Polish German, and ask him a few questions.

* * *

Nothing unusual seemed to have happened in Saxony Square during the week. Most days, he had seen the housekeeper leave by the front door, and walk quickly across the square and into Berlin Street, where there was a row of shops and a genteel public house. By dint of following her discreetly, he had seen where she went, learnt the names of the streets she frequented and the shops that she patronized.

He knew that, when shopping was done, she would nip into the public house, which was called the Albany Arms, and emerge after half an hour with a renewed spring in her step. A measure of gin, perhaps, or a small port.

An elderly police constable was rounding the corner from Berlin Street and into the square. He looked hot and uncomfortable in his heavy blue serge uniform, and he moved steadily but slowly as he made his way across the road and into the gardens. He came across to Bottomley, and stood looking him up and down for a while. He had a stern eye, and a bristling moustache.

'I've had my eye on you all week, my lad,' he said. 'It's Friday now, and you've been hanging around here since Monday, off and on, eyeing them houses more than I like. Now, you can move on, in which case don't come back, or you can give me a reason why I shouldn't take you up for loitering with intent. It's up to you.'

Sergeant Bottomley fumbled in his pocket, and produced his warrant card for the constable to read. The constable looked at it, and handed it back. He didn't apologize. Why should he? He was only doing his duty.

'Mr Blade should tell people what's going on,' the constable grumbled. 'How was I to know you were a detective sergeant? What are you up to here, Sergeant?'

'I'm keeping a discreet watch on number eleven,' said Bottomley. 'Miss Paget's house. It's all connected with a case of murder we're investigating in Warwickshire.'

'Miss Paget?' said the constable. 'You won't find her there, Sergeant. She and a young gentleman left yesterday in a cab. I was passing by at the time on my beat, and heard them give directions. They were going to Paddington Station.'

Bottomley recalled Inspector Blade's words:

'You can't be in two places at once.' He'd lost Miss Paget, but it shouldn't be very difficult for an experienced detective to find her again. He'd start now. Bottomley thanked the constable for his help, and crossed the carriageway to 11, Saxony Square.

*   *   *

Mrs Milsom cast a dubious eye over the big, shambling man who had rung the front-door bell. She left him standing on the step while she read the rather crumpled card that he handed to her.

'Detective Sergeant Bottomley?' she said. 'And you say you've met Miss Paget before? Well, you'd better come in. It's been nothing but police in this house ever since the poor master was murdered by that awful woman. It's not very nice, you know. Miss Paget is away from home for a few days. How can I help you?'

'Well, ma'am,' said Bottomley, 'Miss Paget and I first met at a place called Mayfield Court, in Warwickshire, when she was visiting there with her uncle, the late unfortunate Mr Maximilian Paget. I met her again just a few days ago — on the twenty-ninth, to be precise — and we had a little chat about various matters.'

'The twenty-ninth? I don't recall answering the door to you.'

'That's because you didn't, ma'am, it being a Wednesday, and your day off.'

'And how did you know that, pray?' Really, this clodhopper of a man from the provinces knew more than he had a right to.

'I know a lot about you, Mrs Milsom,' said Bottomley, treating the housekeeper to a rather sinister smile. 'I know that you like to buy your vegetables at Purdy's, and your cheese and bacon at Savidge's, and then, if you're feeling a little fatigued, you like to slip into the Albany Arms for a drop of — '

'Goodness me, Mr Bottomley, who told you all those things? And why did you want to know them? Surely you don't suspect *me* of — What do you mean?'

'Tell me where Miss Paget has gone,' said Bottomley. 'That's all I want to know. For the moment. Tell me that, and I'll bid you good day.'

Mrs Milsom looked quite pale and nervous. Well, it was all to the good. These housekeepers clammed up if you asked them anything about the family. They were worse than butlers, and that was saying a lot.

'Miss Paget left yesterday with her fiancé Dr Danvers. They will be away for a few days. They've gone to stay with a titled gentleman in your part of the world. I forget his name.'

'I never forget anything,' Bottomley replied, 'I remember you going into the Westminster Bank branch in Leipzig Row, and cashing a cheque for four pounds. I remember — '

'They've gone to stay with Sir Leopold and Lady Carteret at a place called Upton Carteret,' said Mrs Milsom, her voice climbing perilously near to a shriek. If only this dreadful man would go! Not a bit like Inspector Blade.

'That's all I want to know, ma'am,' said Bottomley, raising his battered bowler hat. (His hat! She had failed to ask for his hat as he stepped into the hall. Was that why he was raising it? Dreadful man!)

'I'll bid you good day. And young Dr Danvers went with her?'

'Yes.' Mrs Milsom's fear of this man was being rapidly replaced with indignation. 'Yes, Dr Danvers went with her. Why shouldn't he?'

'Why *should* he?' asked Bottomley. Before Mrs Milsom could reply, he had left the house, pulling the front door shut behind him.

★　★　★

Bottomley stood in Chatham Court, and looked round him. He didn't think much of

286

what he saw. The cobbles were strewn with horse droppings, and no one seemed to have bothered to swill them down for days. The livery stable was open, and bales of straw spilled out on to the pavement, but there was no sign of any horses.

The dark, shuttered brick house would have been entirely anonymous but for the brass plate telling all and sundry that it was the residence of Dr Igor Zhdanov, Consultant Physician, who would see you by appointment only.

There was a nameless public house in the court, and Bottomley went in. It was dark and empty, and smelled of stale beer and tobacco smoke. A defeated-looking man in shirtsleeves sat behind the small bar, reading a newspaper. He looked up as Bottomley came in, and put the paper down.

'What'll you have?' he asked.

'Give me a glass of London gin,' said Bottomley. 'You can leave the bottle on the bar.' He downed the gin in one gulp, and immediately poured himself another.

'That house next-but-one to this,' he said, 'there's a foreign doctor lives there.'

'Is there?' said the morose man.

'Yes, there is. Now what I want to ask you, is this: have you ever seen that doctor come out from his house accompanied by an old man? Or have you seen him putting an old man into a carriage?'

Bottomley poured himself out a third gin. His speech began to acquire a kind of slur, but his eyes remained bright and alert.

'What's it to you what the doctor does? He minds his own business, and I mind mine. You'd better drink up and be off with you. Who are you, anyway?'

Bottomley produced his warrant card, and laid it down on the bar counter.

'That's who I am,' he said. 'And that's why you should keep a civil tongue in your head. Did you ever see this foreign doctor bundling an old party into a cab?'

The landlord rescued the gin bottle, and put it on a shelf behind the bar.

'I might have done,' he said, with what he hoped was an air of nonchalance.

Bottomley smiled, rummaged in one of his pockets, and produced a half-crown, which he put down on the bar beside his warrant card. Then he suddenly reached across the counter and pulled the landlord up and over by the lapels of his coat.

'Did you see him? It's murder, friend, and if you don't tell me what you saw, I'll take you up as an accessory. So tell me, and earn yourself two and a tanner. Did you?'

'Yes, guvnor, I did. There's no need for

pugilistics. Strewth! I never seen a man knock back so much gin and stay upright. It's going to cost you one and eight.'

Bottomley slammed down a few more coins on the counter and retrieved his warrant card. 'Tell me,' he said.

The man lowered his voice, and glanced around the empty bar.

'It was last Friday, guv,' he said, 'and no later than half past four in the morning. I have to be up by then, to get this place ready for the market porters who swarm in here at half past five. I saw a cab — well, it may have been a private fly, I'm not sure — draw up outside Dr Zhdanov's house. The door opened, and the doctor appeared. He was with another man, and between them they helped an old gentleman into the cab.'

'How did the old man look?'

'He looked far gone to me, poor old soul. All three got into the cab, and were driven away. It's a kind of nursing home, you see, and that would have been one of the patients. Maybe he was cured, and they were taking him home. He was a clergyman.'

'Was he, now? How did you know that?'

'He was wearing black, and he had a clergyman's collar on. Is that all? Can I be left in peace, now?'

Bottomley walked slowly towards the door,

and there was a slight stagger in his way of walking that told the landlord that he was not quite himself. Not drunk, but not quite himself.

'I'll tell you what, landlord,' said Bottomley, 'coincidence is a wonderful thing. The very morning that your neighbour Dr Zhdanov was taking his old clergyman patient home, having cured him of whatever ailed him — you did say he was taking him home, didn't you?'

'It's what I assumed, Officer. It's not an offence, is it, to assume something like that?'

'No, it's not an offence, I just wanted to make sure that that's what you suggested. Well, here's the coincidence. At the very time, last Friday, that Dr Zhdanov was taking his old clergyman patient home, somebody else was taking an old clergyman into Kensington Gardens, in order to drown him in the Long Water. And guess what? Your old clergyman and the one found drowned in the Long Water were one and the same person. It makes you think, doesn't it? Or are you more stupid than you look? Say nothing about this to anyone. Meanwhile, I'll bid you good day.'

★ ★ ★

'Here, Sergeant, drink this black coffee. You should keep off the bottle when you're on duty. Still, you've done well. I've heard mention of this Dr Zhdanov. Now we can kill two birds with one stone.'

Inspector Blade put an enamel cup of steaming coffee in front of Bottomley, who was sitting on an upright chair near a tall filing cabinet in the inspector's office. He looked suitably contrite. After he had left the public house in Chatham Court, Bottomley had visited two more hostelries before making his way to Little Vine Street. When he got there, he was decidedly unsteady on his feet. He leaned against the filing cabinet, and sipped his coffee.

Inspector Blade left the office, and Bottomley could hear him shouting for someone as he stood in the corridor. Somebody else shouted back, and in a moment Blade returned with a burly uniformed sergeant, a man in his late fifties, who was carrying a bloodstained cricket bat.

'If you'd given me another minute, Mr Blade,' he grumbled, 'I'd have had this offensive weapon properly docketed. Now I've got to carry it around with me until you've done with me — '

'I'll do with you all right, you cheeky man,' said Blade, half laughing. 'Docketing? I'll dock you a day's wages if you don't button your lip. Now, what I want you to do,

Sergeant Humphries, is tell me all you know about Dr Zhdanov of Chatham Court. You tangled with him once, didn't you?'

'I did, sir. It was a couple of years ago, when he lived in Grace Street, just by the Monument. He was a vet — what they call a veterinary surgeon — and he made a living by putting down poor old dogs and cats who'd reached the end of the road.'

Sergeant Humphries glanced questioningly at the recovering drunk slumped against the filing cabinet.

'Sergeant Humphries, meet Sergeant Bottomley, of the Warwickshire Constabulary. So he was a vet? What did he do, besides putting down people's pets?'

'Somebody called at his premises after hours to collect his deceased terrier, sir, in order to give it a Christian burial. This man found the back door unlocked, and went in. There was a smell of chloroform in the air, and he — this man — saw a young woman lying unconscious on a trolley, while this Dr Zhdanov was bending over her with some kind of instrument in his hand.'

'I see. And this man who called for his dog reported the incident?'

'He did, sir. But when we went round to his premises, which we did straight away, the young woman was still there. She was

292

drinking a cup of tea, and Dr Zhdanov was standing beside her, smirking behind his great black beard. The young woman, he said, had called to collect her kitten, but had suddenly been seized with a choking fit. Realizing that she would die if he didn't take action, he had laid her on the trolley, and with the aid of one of his instruments had removed a brazil nut from her throat. He actually showed us the nut in question. The young lady was ever so grateful, she said, and we left. But we knew, sir, what he was doing, and what she'd asked for. Both were criminals, and each covered for the other. A man who will do that, Inspector, will do anything. Now, as to this offensive weapon — '

'Take it away, Sergeant Humphries, and take yourself off with it. Then detail two constables, and have them standing ready. Find PC Roberts, and tell him to run round to Mr Beak in Swallow Street, and get him to sign a warrant of search and arrest.'

'Sergeant Bottomley,' said Inspector Blade, 'we'll cook this Dr Zhdanov's goose by making his co-conspirator, Dr Morrison, confess all. It won't be difficult, if we leave him to conclude that all is known. We'll have to wait a bit for PC Roberts to return from the magistrate's. Meanwhile, you'd better go out to the ablutions, and smarten yourself up.

If you're working with me, you have to be a credit to 'C' Division.'

Blade dropped his half-bantering tone, and looked at Bottomley gravely.

'Today, Sergeant,' he said, 'we should be able to wrap up this murder of poor Mr Walter Hindle. I have the results of the *post mortem* here. He died from drowning, right enough, but traces of chloral hydrate were found both in the stomach and around the lips. He had been rendered semi-conscious, and then deliberately drowned.'

'That landlord, sir,' said Bottomley, rising to his feet, 'he saw Zhdanov and an accomplice dragging Mr Hindle out to a cab, but his evidence is uncorroborated. And our theory as to how the body came to be in the water is just that — a theory. We can't link the drowning definitely to Zhdanov.'

'I know, Sergeant, and that's why we must employ a certain amount of bluff. The genial but shifty-eyed Dr Morrison is the weak link in this chain of deceit and murder. Leave him to me. I'll use Morrison to bring Zhdanov to the gallows.'

★ ★ ★

Inspector Blade had planned a frontal assault, and proceeded to carry it out. The portly Dr

Morrison's ready smile did not survive for more than a few seconds.

'Edward Morrison, I have here a warrant for your arrest, which I intend to execute immediately. The house is surrounded, and it would be fruitless to attempt an escape. I charge you that you did, on Friday, 31 August, 1894, conspire with another unknown to drug and render senseless the Reverend Walter Hindle, and that you did put him into that body of water called the Long Water, in the parish of Kensington; and that you did murder him. Sergeant Bottomley, secure him, and take him out to the van.'

'It's not true!' Dr Morrison, wringing his hands in anguish. 'I told you when you came here: Mr Hindle wandered off, through a door left open by the carelessness of an attendant — '

'It won't do! Your guilt is known. You conveyed your victim away from these premises to number 11, Chatham Court, assumed to be another of your properties, and there you drugged him prior to taking him to Kensington, where you drowned him. Sergeant, take him away.'

'I tell you it wasn't me! I tried to stop it, but I could not. Yes, I lied to you when you came here: but I did not murder Mr Hindle. He was taken away by his nephew, who delivered him into the hands of Dr Zhdanov, a criminal poisoner.'

'Place your hands behind your back,' said Bottomley, and when the wretched man had done so, he slipped a pair of handcuffs over his wrists and locked them.

'We've never heard of any Dr Zhdanov,' said Inspector Blade dismissively. 'You'd better say nothing more until you appear at your trial for murder.'

Dr Morrison cried out in anguish and pulled himself away from Bottomley.

'It's true, I tell you! I'll tell you everything you want to know. What is that shrieking? What is happening?'

'One of my sergeants has just arrested your nurse as an accessory. She's up for murder, too. Come on, Sergeant. Let's get this business over and done with. Take him out.'

'Dr Zhdanov is the killer, not I. Why don't you go and secure him before he bolts? He's the killer, and he lives in Chatham Court. It was Mr Hindle's nephew who came here, and took him away. I knew he was going to entrust him to the tender mercies of Zhdanov, but I was too weak to make a protest.'

'And I suppose this Dr Zhdanov was acting off his own bat, was he? Maybe he just liked drowning aged clergyman? You'll need a better defence, Morrison, than all this bluster.'

'This whole business was brought about by a woman called Lady Carteret. See, look in my desk, the third drawer down: you'll find all the relevant documents there. It was she who committed Mr Hindle to my care. She, and her husband, Sir Leopold Carteret.'

At a nod from Blade, Sergeant Bottomley unlocked the handcuffs, and withdrew them.

'You will be a material witness against this Dr Zhdanov,' said Blade. 'You can remain at liberty for a while, but I warn you that you will be under constant surveillance. You will appear before the magistrates next Monday, where bail and recognisances will be set. Meanwhile, you had better arrange for competent medical supervision of this establishment. That's all.'

* * *

'We'll bring in Dr Zhdanov this afternoon, Sergeant Bottomley,' said Blade, when they left the house. 'This Morrison may escape with a short custodial sentence. He's a shady customer, but I don't really think he's a murderer.'

'I'd like to thank you, sir,' said Bottomley, 'for everything you've done to help me over this case. It's very much appreciated, if I may say so. It's time I returned to Warwick

— there's work for me to do there. I'll catch the eight o'clock evening train from Paddington. It's time for us — the county police, I mean — to bring that woman's depredations to an end.'

Bottomley raised his hat, Inspector Blade saluted, and the two men parted.

Later that afternoon, Inspector Jackson, working on a report in the back room at Warwick Police Office, was handed a telegraph message that had just been received from Charing Cross Telegraph Office in London.

JACKSON, WARWICK PO. HINDLE MURDERED BY AGENTS OF LADY CARTERET. MURDER PROVEN. ARRESTS TO FOLLOW. WILL RETURN TOMORROW. BOTTOMLEY

15

Catherine's Narrative:
An After-Dinner Interlude

The following day, which was a Friday, we spent the morning touring the estate, and its outlying farms. We made the tour partly on foot, and partly in a smart pony and trap, driven by Sir Leopold Carteret himself. Providence Hall stood in extensive grounds, including the deer park, and once again I was impressed by how well tended everything was. The farms were clean and prosperous, and considerable deference was shown to Sir Leopold by the various labourers we encountered.

When Michael and I came down to breakfast that morning, we heard that Lady Carteret had passed a disturbed night, and was breakfasting in her room. So it was Sir Leopold, Michael and myself who ventured out to view the estate, on what proved to be a lovely September morning.

'My wife is often troubled by restless dreams,' Sir Leopold told us. 'They can leave her quite debilitated, you know; but we get by. Yes, we get by.'

Sir Leopold Carteret was a quietly spoken self-effacing gentleman, with an air of courteous enquiry that I found rather endearing. Everything one told him seemed to hold his entire interest. For instance, I happened to mention that I had been educated at Holbrook Girls' Academy in Hampstead.

'Holbrook Girls' Academy?' he had said. 'Really? How very remarkable. And at Hampstead, you say? Well, I find that most interesting. And it was a school solely for girls?'

He had continued his questioning until the subject was exhausted, and yet, on mature consideration, I realized that he had asked no real, pertinent questions at all. All that he had gathered was the name and location of the school; evidently that was enough to satisfy him.

Lady Carteret appeared at luncheon, looking a little pale, but in every other respect her old self. She liked me well enough, I felt, but she had taken a particular liking to Michael. She sat beside him at table, and conversed with him in low tones, while I listened to Sir Leopold telling me about his ancient family, and the part that some of his ancestors had played in great affairs of state.

When lunch was over, I asked whether I could wander through the extensive conservatory that was reached from an elegant Regency music room at the back of the house, and my hostess readily agreed. Sir Leopold declared that he was going to his study to smoke a cigar and read *The Times*. I half expected Michael to accompany me, but he left the dining room deep in conversation with Lady Carteret. It was ridiculous, of course — she was old enough to be Michael's mother — but I felt a twinge of jealous resentment as I watched them walk away together.

It was hot in the conservatory, and the air was perfumed by the many exotic plants growing in brass and china tubs. There was, too, a profusion of ferns, and a number of woven cane basket chairs placed in their shade. I sat down, and within minutes I had fallen fast asleep.

I woke with a start, and rose to my feet. I consulted the watch that I wore about my neck on a silver chain, and realized that I had been asleep for no more than twenty minutes. I could hear voices quite near to me, and, venturing further along the conservatory, I saw that it had another exit into the library of Providence House. It was here that Lady Carteret and Michael had gone, for I could see them standing together at an open desk placed beside one of the tall, carved sets of bookshelves filled with old, calf-bound books and annuals.

'There it is,' said Lady Carteret, holding up a document for Michael to see. 'It was a Deed of Release, right enough, but its contents are more baleful than I could have imagined. True to his honour, he never opened it.'

'Why has it not been destroyed?' asked Michael. 'And what was so baleful about it?'

'What would have been the point of destroying it? A document of that nature will have been copied. I'd not thought of that possibility, but Sir Leopold made enquiries, and it's true enough. And it's baleful, because it makes open provision for descendants of either line — people who were not born when the deed was drafted. It is not a closed deed.'

Evidently Lady Carteret was regaling Michael with some passage in the family's history. I turned to retrace my steps to the dining-room passage, but something that Lady Carteret was saying caused me to linger near the door, still hidden by the forest of ferns.

'And so, dear boy,' she was saying, 'the great enterprise will have to be abandoned. It would have been a most desirable consummation, but there: it cannot be. So, it will have to be the other way.'

Their voices suddenly dropped, and there was something so easy and intimate about their manner that I felt myself blush with vexation. I didn't like that 'My dear boy'.

302

Must Michael concern himself so deeply in his hostess's family history?

I was moving away into the conservatory when I was conscious once again of that mysterious, unheard voice addressing me, desperately trying to pierce the veil between this world and what lay beyond it . . . Whose was that soundless voice, and what was it trying to tell me? And then, as always, it stopped, as though giving up in despair. These things never frightened me — I have always had some psychic awareness — but it was unsettling, nonetheless.

In the afternoon I lay down for an hour, and once more woke abruptly, this time because a certain expression had suddenly obtruded itself on my consciousness. 'Deed of Release.' Surely Uncle Max had mentioned such a document in the anguished letter that he had left for me to read after his death? It was the very document for which he had been searching at Mayfield Court, a document drawn up by Gabriel Forshaw's solicitor all those decades ago. I wondered then whether Uncle Max had obtruded those words into my sleeping mind . . .

I remained very uneasy for the rest of the afternoon, but when Michael reappeared at tea time, I felt reassured. As on the previous day, afternoon tea was served by the little maid in the drawing room. Michael lavished attention upon me, and began to talk about what we would both do after we were married. I thought that he was a little embarrassed at the attention that he had been showing to Lady Carteret, for he virtually ignored her. She, for her part, seemed to be fully engaged with her husband and his affairs. The two of them talked in low tones for a while, and then Lady Carteret turned to speak to Michael and me.

'It's a great nuisance,' she said, 'but Sir Leopold must leave for London immediately after tea. There's some business there that cannot be left to others, as his signature is required on certain documents lodged with our London solicitors.'

'I'm so sorry, Miss Paget, and — er — Dr Danvers,' said Sir Leopold, 'it has been most interesting to have you here as our guests, but I can assure you that Lady Carteret will see that the remaining part of your stay is interesting and enjoyable. Goodbye, Miss Paget. It has been delightful to make your acquaintance. And it was a school for girls, you say? Most interesting.'

Sir Leopold left soon after five, and with his departure a certain stability and normality appeared to have gone with him. Lady Carteret seemed preoccupied, scarcely replying to any questions put to her. She would glance sharply into dim corners of the room, and occasionally shudder. I remembered that she had passed a bad night, and wondered whether she was afflicted, too, in the daylight hours.

Michael, too, seemed to be holding some nebulous but strong emotion in check. I saw him glance at our hostess with something approaching dislike, not unmixed with fear. After the tea things were removed, the three of us sat on in the drawing room, seemingly unable, or unwilling, to get up and pursue some useful occupation.

The fine weather of the morning had given way to a sultry dullness, with a promise of summer thunder in the air. By six o'clock it had darkened perceptibly, and the first great thunder-spots began to fall. I felt a sudden yearning for my own town house in Saxony Square.

We threw off our lethargy when the footmen came in to light the candles. One drew down the great crystal chandelier, and lit the candles nestling among their brilliants before gently pushing it back upward on its pulleys. The other attended to the candle sconces on the panelled walls. The room was flooded with welcome light, and my own personal gloom was dissipated.

That evening, we were joined by the rector,

the Reverend Mr Bold, and his wife, and a cheerful young couple called Rivington, and we enjoyed a very appetizing dinner of pea soup, a delicate sole, and roast rack of lamb, followed by lemon water ices. Michael seemed to be his old self, though at times I saw him glance at Lady Carteret with that look of distaste mingled with fear that I had noticed earlier. I wondered what it meant.

I slept well, and Saturday morning dawned bright and sunny. Lady Carteret had come down to breakfast, though I thought she looked quite ill, and a certain redness about her eyes convinced me that she had been weeping. Michael seemed not to notice.

'My dears,' said Lady Carteret, 'I propose that we go on a picnic today to Bodley Castle ruins. We'll take the small phaeton, and Andrews will drive. Had my husband been here, he would have driven himself. What do you think?'

I thought it sounded a very good idea. It would be a relief to get away from the confines of Providence Hall and out into the fresh air. By ten o'clock, all was ready, and a substantial wicker hamper was put into the carriage before we set off at a brisk pace along the road that wound through the deer park and out on to the village street. We travelled for an hour through pleasant countryside, passing through a number of small hamlets and one substantial village with its own lichen-covered church.

'This is a pretty place,' I observed. 'What is it called?'

'This is Walton Carteret. There are several villages in this part of the county named after my husband's family.'

I heard the pride in Lady Carteret's voice as she said these words.

Eventually we entered a small wood, and in a few minutes emerged into a clearing where we could see the ruins of Bodley Castle rising above us. It was a very pleasant spot, and Andrews the coachman busied himself with setting out the picnic. From the box behind the carriage he produced a set of folding chairs and a table to match. Lady Carteret herself set out the contents of the hamper. There was a great pie, ham and chicken sandwiches, and a selection of pastries. To complement these good things, there were two bottles of white wine, secured in a small ice-box.

While Andrews stood guard, we explored the ruins of the old castle. Lady Carteret told us that it had been slighted during the Civil War, and had subsequently fallen into ruin. It was a romantic spot, conjuring up all kinds of dramatic scenes in my mind, but as I walked through the various rooms, all roofless and with springy turf for flooring, I was jealously conscious of the fact that Michael, my fiancé, walked with Lady Carteret, and not with me.

It was midday when we sat down to enjoy the picnic, and I must confess that, despite my uneasiness of the past day, I thoroughly enjoyed the repast. Eating in this way, *al fresco*, seemed to enhance my appetite, and I sampled a little of everything that was set before me. The coachman had led his vehicle a little apart, and we could see him sitting on an ivy-clad bank, lighting his clay pipe.

The wine was a delicate hock, still well chilled, and I finished my meal with two glasses in succession. I began to feel very charitable to my neighbours, and remembered a warning that my old uncle had once given me: 'If you must drink wine, Catherine, drink it slowly — sip your way to sobriety.' I contemplated a third glass, but a questioning look from Michael restrained me.

It was when we were halfway home that I began to feel strange. I was not inebriated, and I was not feeling sick; but I seemed to be inhabiting a kind of trance-world. Sounds, even the voices of my companions, appeared to be coming from afar, and colours were brighter than I had remembered them. I said nothing, because I was not ill, but it was disquieting, to say the least.

When we returned to Providence Hall, I excused myself, and retired to my room. I lay on the bed, wondering what could have caused this altered state of consciousness. I closed my eyes, and almost immediately fell into a deep sleep.

I dreamed of Uncle Max, alive, and frantically searching through the masses of ancient paper at Mayfield Court; I saw the forlorn little ghost again, dumbly pointing to the bed, and experienced the same frozen fear that I had felt when I had first seen her; curiously, I did not identify her with the little gypsy girl who had shown me how my belief in ghosts had been foolishness. And I dreamed of Sergeant Bottomley, the man who had, I believed, appointed himself my protector.

I had no idea how long I had slept, but at one stage I imagined that the door had quietly opened, and a shadowy figure had crossed the room, temporarily blocking out the light. It may have been so; but when I forced open my eyes for a second, I saw that there was nobody there.

I dreamed that Lady Carteret and Michael came into the room, and stood by the bed. My eyes were closed, and I was still in a kind of lethargic trance, but I imagined that it was they. 'Tonight should see the end of it,' said a voice, and another voice answered, 'Yes. You were right. It will have to be tonight.'

When I awoke, I found it was nearly time for dinner, and the sky was beginning to darken. It had been just on two o'clock when we returned from the picnic; a glance at my watch showed me that it was now nearly six.

The heavy, trance-like state had not left me, and I stumbled about as best I could, changing from day clothes into my evening gown. When the gong sounded, I went down to dinner, clutching the banister to make sure that I did not fall.

The dining room was cheerfully lit, but the candelabra on the table — two great, silver-gilt affairs — seemed to be aslant, and the light they shed was fractured into the many colours of the spectrum. Lady Carteret and Michael seemed not to notice my peculiar state, but a kind of silly, youthful pride prevented my telling them how strange I felt.

I cannot now remember what I ate or drank at that meal, but I was glad when we all rose and retired, not to the drawing room, but to the great, dim library, with its forbidding shelves of calf-bound books and old periodicals. I saw that coffee had already been brought in. I sank gratefully into a leather armchair, and Michael brought me a cup of steaming coffee.

I drank it gratefully, and looked at my

hostess and my fiancé. They sat facing me, but neither seemed to look at me, or, indeed, at each other. I realized that they were waiting for something to happen. Why did they shimmer, and why were they encircled by iridescent haloes? Michael seemed frozen where he sat. Lady Carteret looked affronted by something that I could not fathom.

'I hate this hellish room,' said Lady Carteret to Michael. 'I've had some frightful nightmares connected with it.'

I tried to reach out to place my empty coffee cup on a small table standing beside my chair, but found that I could not move a muscle. Alarmed, I tried to cry out, but realized with horror that I could not move my lips. I was, to all intents and purposes, paralysed.

A door in the panelling opened, and Marguerite, my friend and Michael's sister, came into the room. She merely glanced at me, and then sat down beside Lady Carteret, who gave her a perfunctory kiss on the cheek.

'Mama,' said Marguerite, 'is tonight really going to see the end of it? And after that, can Michael and I start to live ordinary lives?'

'I'd prefer you to live extraordinary lives, if that's possible,' said Lady Carteret. 'But that must be your choice. And yes, this night will see the end of it. Miss Paget is the last of the

Paget clan, and while she's alive, that cursed open clause of the Deed of Release still applies. Her uncle was content to relinquish all interest in the matter — '

'But that didn't prevent you from poisoning him, Mother,' said Michael, 'leaving me to continue dancing attendance on that dreary girl, there.'

'Better safe than sorry,' Michael's mother replied. Marguerite laughed.

I was, of course, drugged almost to the point of death, and one appalling symptom of that particular narcotic, which must have been administered to me in the coffee, was that I accepted all that was happening as though it were normal. I felt some fear, but no indignation, even though that part of my brain that governed understanding still made me aware that it was Michael Danvers — what was his real surname? — who had handed me the poisoned coffee, and described me as a dreary girl.

I accepted, almost without demur, that I had from the very outset been the victim of a coldly planned conspiracy. Michael and Marguerite were the children of the woman now known as Lady Carteret, so that my first meeting with Michael must have been carefully contrived. I recalled that meeting, in the Army and Navy Stores, when Michael had tripped and fallen against me, sending my collection of small parcels to the floor. It had been so easy for him and his sister to lure me into their company. What a little fool I had been!

I made an effort to rise from my chair, but was quite unable to move.

Lady Carteret stood up.

'Well, let's get it over with. I brought her here because we can carry her up to her room from this part of the house without the servants seeing us. My late second husband, Hector — not your dear father — preferred to hire professional assailants to get rid of unwanted people, which is what he did in the matter of Gabriel Forshaw. I prefer poison, followed by suffocation. That's what I did with little Helen. Hector was far too squeamish to murder a child.'

Marguerite tittered. I had sometimes wondered whether she was weak-minded, which would account for her girlishness, which sat ill on a woman in her thirties. Now I knew that I had been right.

'Control yourself, Marguerite,' said her mother, giving her a glance of distaste. 'Come, now, Michael, pick her up, and follow us up to her room. Why are you hesitating? Have you really fallen for her youthful charms? Be careful where you place your feet:

these back stairs behind the panelling are very narrow. We can't afford to drop her. Bruising would look suspicious when she's found dead in bed, tomorrow morning. I'll get Susan to take her hot water up tomorrow. She's not a screamer, so there'll be no fuss.'

Lady Carteret suddenly walked over to me where I sat, paralysed, in my chair. She bent low to look at me, putting her hands on her knees.

'What a silly girl you were, to walk right into my trap! Yes, I killed your uncle, but I would have been content for Michael to marry you if that Deed of Release had not opened the way for you to contest the Forshaw fortune had you suddenly decided to do so. But that would have been the end of my son and me. So, my dear, you must go along that path that little Helen trod, thirty years ago.'

Michael, who was a strong young man, picked me up, though my body was so numb that I could not feel his hands supporting me.

Lady Carteret opened the door in the panelling — and Sergeant Bottomley burst into the room.

'We have heard all,' he said in a low voice, 'and you are condemned out of your own mouth.'

She screamed — an appalling, animal

sound — and ran frantically the length of the library, seeking escape. But when she reached the door that led into the conservatory, her way was blocked by the stolid figure of Inspector Jackson, who was flanked by two uniformed constables. Like me, Lady Carteret had walked into a trap, but it was one from which she would never escape.

She knew, then, that she had failed. I could hear Mr Jackson speaking, and assumed that he was making his formal arrest. Lady Carteret had fallen quiet, and allowed herself to be manacled without making an undignified fuss. Inspector Jackson and the two constables led her away.

The house was stirring, and a few weeping servants had made their appearance in the library, wondering what had happened to disturb the aristocratic tranquillity of Providence Hall.

I watched all this, paralysed and immobile, from the floor, where Michael had unceremoniously dropped me when Mr Bottomley had suddenly appeared. I wondered what Michael would do. He looked down at me, his face as white as parchment.

'I'm sorry, Cath,' he whispered, 'but you must see that I had no choice. Mother was so strong — '

He was given no chance to say more, for

Sergeant Bottomley, his face convulsed with rage, felled him with one blow of his large fist. He roughly turned my unconscious fiancé over, pulled his arms behind him, and secured him with handcuffs. Then he picked me up effortlessly from the floor, and I saw the look of tender concern that dissipated the anger which he had saved up for Michael.

'All will be well, my dear,' said Mr Bottomley, 'asking pardon for being so familiar. They drugged you in that coffee, but the effects will wear off very soon. I'm going to take you right away from here to a place of safety nearby, and you can stay there until you're better.'

I could already feel some sensation returning to my limbs. My rescuer sensed this, and laid me down gently on a *chaise-longue* which stood against one of the walls. He rubbed the sleeve of his coat roughly across his eyes, and said, 'I blame myself for this. I advised you to confide in that villain — that apology for a man — when I met you at Mayfield Court. 'Tell your Michael all about it', I said. And in saying that, I delivered you into the hands of your enemies.'

It was, I think, the tears that sprang to the sergeant's eyes that unloosed my tongue. I managed to whisper, 'It was not your fault, dear Mr Bottomley. You have been my guardian all this time, and now, today, you have delivered me from the jaws of death!'

★ ★ ★

I can still recall with pleasure the feeling of relief when Sergeant Bottomley, accompanied by one of the two constables, conveyed me away from Providence Hall. They had summoned the little maid who had served us tea, and she had packed my things — I was still too weak to do this myself. Then they took me down to the forecourt, where a closed carriage was waiting, its lamps gleaming in the dark. I learned later that it belonged to Mr Bold, the rector of the parish, whom I had met at dinner: Inspector Jackson knew him, and had prevailed upon him to lend his carriage for the occasion.

'Were you in the house all along?' I asked.

'I came into the house this afternoon,' said Mr Bottomley. 'No one saw me, of course, because it's part of my work to get into places unseen. I located the bedroom where you were lying down, and when that precious mother and son came in to look at you, and gloat over what they were going to do, I hid at the side of the wardrobe until they'd gone out again — '

'So it wasn't a dream! I heard you cross the

room, and then thought I'd dreamed of those two talking about me as they leaned over the bed. What did you do then?'

'When they left your room, I followed them without being seen, and heard them plan to take you into the library after dinner, and spirit you away through a staircase behind the panelling. I left them then, searched out that hidden staircase, and took up my position behind the door in the panelling. I heard every word that they spoke.'

'And Inspector Jackson? Was he hiding in the house?'

'Mr Jackson came to the front door, armed with warrants, and demanded entry. And that was the end of thirty years' planning, and plotting, and murder.'

We were driven no more than a quarter of a mile out of the village, along the darkened main road, when we turned left into a carriage drive. I looked out of the window and saw an array of lighted windows defining the front of a modern mock-Tudor house. Two gas globes glowed on either side of the front door.

'Miss Paget,' said Sergeant Bottomley, who was sitting beside me, 'this is Meadowfield School, a very high-class place where people of quality send their daughters to be educated. It was the school to which the child who passed herself off as Helen Paget, your little ghost, was sent.'

'What happened to her?' I asked.

'Well, she proved to be a first-rate pupil, and did very well. In the end, she married a prosperous gentleman who lives in Birmingham, and she has two children of her own, who both go to schools like this.'

He was silent for a moment, and then added, 'She came from the poorest of the poor, Miss Paget, and made a great success of her life. She was only eleven years old, too, when her adventure began, and I'm hoping to keep all mention of her out of the trial, when it takes place.'

I don't know why it was that I suddenly burst into uncontrollable tears at this point. Maybe it was all the talk of marriage and children, and lives fulfilled, and the sad knowledge that poor little Helen had never been given the chance to know these things herself.

Or maybe it was because I knew now how very much alone I was in the world. Not many girls had been engaged to a man who had all along accepted the possibility of her being murdered by his own mother, with his connivance. It was vile. I would never contemplate marriage again. I would live comfortably in my London house, with my housekeeper and servants, until one day I would be known as 'the old maiden lady who lives in Saxony Square'.

The thought brought me little comfort, and I began a fresh bout of despairing tears. Mr Bottomley, throwing etiquette to the winds, put a brawny arm around my shoulders and patted me as though I were a baby. Which in some ways, of course, I was.

The carriage stopped, and I was helped down by the police constable who had driven us from Providence Hall. A pleasant, grey-haired lady stepped forward from the porch to receive me. She was wearing a black evening dress, with a fine cashmere shawl draped over her shoulders.

'Miss Paget?' she asked. 'I am Miss Jellicoe, Principal of Meadowfield School. My friend Mr Bottomley there wants you to stay with me until such time as you feel strong enough to return to London. Come inside out of the night air.'

★　★　★

I stayed in Miss Jellicoe's private quarters in the school for a week, after which time I felt able to return to London. I had very quickly determined not to make enquiry about this wretched Forshaw money that had led to so many deaths. I wanted none of it. My uncle's legacy was sufficient.

During my stay at the school, Mr Bottomley came and sat with me every day, and answered whatever questions came into my mind. He was a very kind, avuncular man — no, not avuncular: he was a fatherly man, with daughters of his own, who knew what a young woman would want to know. I asked him what would become of Lady Carteret.

'Lady Carteret — she had so many names, miss,' Mr Bottomley replied. 'Arabella Bancroft, then Mrs Temperley . . . We found out that she was married first to a decent farmer called Colin Temperley. She had two children by him, Michael, your fiancé, and his sister, Marguerite. Colin was a good man, but his children inherited their mother's bad blood.

'After that, she married your uncle's brother, and became Mrs Hector Paget. Later, after he had died, she married Sir Leopold Carteret. Mr Jackson thinks that she rescued him from certain ruin, and that the Forshaw fortune finally ended up there, at Providence Hall, in Sir Leopold's coffers. That's what he thinks, but we don't know for sure.'

'And how is she?' I persisted. 'I suppose she denied everything.'

'Oh, no, miss,' said Mr Bottomley. 'On the

contrary, she can't stop talking. She's told us just about everything. Her poisons — she liked poisons — were latterly provided by her son Michael, Michael Temperley, to give him his real name. He really was a doctor, you know, his training paid for by Forshaw money, but not the type that I'd like to give *me* a bottle of medicine. Incidentally, it seems quite clear that Sir Leopold Carteret had no idea that Michael was his wife's son by an earlier marriage. He knows more about her wicked ways than he admitted but he didn't know that.'

He had looked at me then with grave concern.

'Do you still love him?' he asked. 'Or did you only think you loved him, because he was the first young man you fell for?'

'I don't love him,' I replied. 'I was willing to venture all to be with him, and all the time he was quite willing to murder me, if his mother told him to! I tell you, I've done with men. Life is much safer without them.'

'Well,' said Mr Bottomley, 'you might be right, but I'm not quite sure about that. Yes, Lady Carteret has talked, and the more she talks the more the police surgeon is convinced that she is sane. Sane and wicked. The souls of her victims cry out for vengeance, and they shall have it. She will hang, Miss Paget, and so will her son, Michael. The daughter, Marguerite, is verging on the simple-minded. She won't figure in our investigations.'

Marguerite . . . She had been my companion in our visits to spiritualists, and I had accounted her as a true friend. She had accompanied Michael and me to the theatre, chatting away like a little girl, too young for her age. Well, let her apply to Sir Leopold Carteret for charity, she would get none from me. She was lucky to have escaped with her life. I am thankful to say that I never saw her again.

'Have you got a young lady friend who can be with you when you return to London?' Mr Bottomley asked. 'Go about with you, I mean? A girl with kindly parents who will keep an eye on you until, well, until you've decided how best you will be an old spinster for the rest of your life?'

'Yes,' I replied, 'I have a nice, uncomplicated friend called Maisie Grossman. And as for becoming an old spinster, well — '

'Oh, I'm sure you'll like it,' said Mr Bottomley, gravely. 'You'll enjoy meeting with other old women of twenty to gossip about the latest scandals. I'll leave you now, but if ever you want help or advice, you have my card, and know where to find me.'

I remained friends with Herbert Bottomley

for many years, and still see him, occasionally. He never became an inspector, because of — well, he was, to use his own words, 'too fond of the bottle'. But that didn't stop him being, in my opinion, one of the best and kindest of nature's gentlemen.

16

The End of Mayfield Court

Sir Leopold Carteret, looking pale and strained, sat in his private study in Providence Hall, waiting for Inspector Jackson to finish his tale. It was a terrible story that he told, and it was essential to listen to it all with the necessary gravity. (He must tell Albert to wind up the clocks; two of them at least were minutes out.)

'And that, Sir Leopold,' Jackson concluded, 'is the whole truth about this case, and about your wife. In the whole of my career, I have never investigated so appalling a catalogue of capital crimes.'

'Appalling!' Sir Leopold agreed. 'I have been married to her for twenty years or more, and have known her only as a loving and dutiful wife. We were never blessed with children, but now you tell me that she had a son by a first marriage. And he, too, was a killer at heart. Will you believe me when I tell you that I knew nothing of all this?'

Yes, Jackson thought, he knows that he has only to persist in that denial, and we can do nothing. His wife sent him up to London to get him out of the way so that he would not be implicated in the death of Miss Paget. In all her endless confession in her cell at Copton Vale Bridewell, she has said not one word that could implicate her husband. She's devoted to him. I can't touch him, and if he has control of the Forshaw inheritance, then it is going to stay with him.

'Sir,' said Jackson, leaving the baronet's question unanswered, 'why did you tell me that you had no knowledge of the Reverend Walter Hindle? He was your wife's brother, and your own brother-in-law.'

Sir Leopold contrived to blush. He shifted uneasily in his chair.

'I admit that I was guilty of deception there, Inspector. It was family pride, you see. Walter was becoming senile, and I could never be sure what indiscretions he was going to commit. To my own shame, I decided to deny all knowledge of him. After all, he was back here, safe in the house; I never did believe your little fiction about him being part of one of your cases!'

Sir Leopold gave Jackson a rueful smile. One up for me, I think.

'Sir,' said Jackson, 'Lady Carteret will face trial at the Warwick Assizes, and I must advise you that her case is hopeless. You must prepare for the worst. Her son, too, must face trial as an accessory to murder, for it was he who furnished his mother with the poison she used to end the life of Mr Maximilian Paget. And for him also there can be no hope.'

Sir Leopold was silent for a moment. He shaded his face with his hand, as though Jackson's terrible words had proved too much for him.

'It is all too monstrous to contemplate,' he said at last. 'I hope I am putting on a brave face here, Inspector, because that's what a gentleman must do. But I am devastated. Desolate. What can I do? My house, my private papers, are all at your disposal. And I will co-operate fully in any subsequent investigation you wish to make. I can do no more. Perhaps you will leave me, now? I must write to Sir William Orpington, QC, so that my wife can have the best counsel available for her coming ordeal. Poor, dear, Bella! Perhaps she was tainted by insanity?'

Saul Jackson made no reply. He bowed perfunctorily to the baronet, and quitted the room, leaving Sir Leopold to his own thoughts. As he left the house, he saw the hostile stares of the butler and the two footmen. Already the lord of the manor and his dependants were coming together as a unified force. Nothing could be done to dislodge this soulless hypocrite from his position of wealth and privilege.

He found Sergeant Bottomley waiting for him in the churchyard. Together they crossed the grass to the Forshaw monuments, and Jackson showed his sergeant the inscription that Hector Paget had composed to cover the murder of Gabriel Forshaw at Waterloo House.

Also Gabriel Forshaw, beloved son of the above Henry, perished of a fever at Bonny, in Nigeria, 7 August, 1865, aged 24 years, and buried there.

'I expect Sir Leopold will have that inscription effaced, and replaced by another,' he said. 'But of course, the Forshaws are no kin of his, so perhaps he'll leave it there, to commemorate a wicked lie, and an equally wicked murder.'

'A telegraph message came through at ten o'clock, sir,' said Bottomley. 'It's from Inspector Blade in London. Doctor Morrison will get three months' hard labour in the House of Correction, and his licence to practise medicine will be revoked.'

'And Doctor Zhdanov? Anything about him?'

'Yes, sir. Mr Blade and his posse went

328

round to his house with an arrest warrant. Zhdanov pretended to yield himself up to them, but suddenly tore away and ran upstairs. He entered a room there, and bolted the door before they could reach it. They were preparing to make a rush and knock it off its hinges when they heard a shot. Zhdanov had chosen suicide rather than the gallows.'

Jackson looked round the old churchyard.

'We're finished here, Sergeant, and there's a lot of work to do before that woman's trial. It's time for us to make our way back to Warwick.'

He opened the gate that gave out on to the public road, and they walked together through the sunlit village of Upton Carteret until they reached the Carteret Arms, where Mr Hardacre had a hired trap waiting to convey them to Monks' Stretton Halt.

★ ★ ★

Sir Leopold was thinking of his future. He had better stay at the Hall until poor Bella's trial was over, and then he would go to the South of France for the winter. Cannes was always pleasant, with lots of interesting company.

He would take Lucas with him, and

possibly leave him there. It seemed that the police had not connected his steward with the abduction of poor Walter, and the ultimate solution of his particular problem. It would be safer for all concerned if he lived abroad. Meanwhile, he could lose himself in London for a few months.

It would take a year at least for the scandal to die down. He would give all his dependants a rise in wages, and the cottars six months' relief from rents. That would ensure their loyalty. And then he would ride across the county to Beauville Castle, and call upon the Honourable Adelaide de Bolter, whom he had known in his younger days. A widow now, with two children of impeccable pedigree, he would try his best to lure her to Providence Hall as his wife. An alliance with the de Bolters would be to both families' advantage. He didn't care to be wifeless, and Adelaide would do very nicely . . .

He was roused from his reverie by Albert, the senior footman, who had come into the room unbidden. The lad's eyes were full of tears.

'Can I get you anything, sir?' he asked. 'Some coffee?'

'Why, Albert, how very considerate of you! Yes, please, I would like a pot of coffee, and some of those little biscuits that we usually have. And perhaps you could wind up the clocks some time today?'

Charm will do it, thought Sir Leopold, when the footman had gone. In a year's time all will be as it was. There had been Carterets at Providence Hall for centuries, and it looked as though they were going to be there far, far into the future.

Catherine's Narrative Concluded

The trials of Lady Carteret and Michael Temperley took place at Warwick Assizes in March, 1894. With an eminent QC appearing for the defence, and an almost rabid Press eager to report every detail, the trial was a sensation. Lady Carteret's plea of insanity, entered by Sir William Orpington, QC, was discredited by expert medical evidence produced by the Crown. Michael attempted a grovelling defence of undue influence, which was effortlessly proved to be a sham. Much sympathy was expressed for the plight of Sir Leopold Carteret, who was seen as a grossly injured party. They were, of course, found guilty, and condemned to death. They suffered the supreme penalty in April of that year.

In the early autumn of 1894 I went to stay with an old schoolfriend of mine, who after leaving the upper form with a special scholarship, went up to Lady Margaret Hall, the college for women at Oxford, established in the 1870s. A brilliant girl, she had been elected a junior fellow of the college, and was in residence when I went to stay with her. I was still only twenty, but my experiences had made me feel much older and wiser: I had experienced things that very few people would have to endure in a whole lifetime.

I will not tell my reader the girl's name, but if you heard it, you would immediately recognize it, for it is a household word now, in the 1900s. Well, it was on this autumn vacation that I met a young man who was studying medicine at Magdalen College. He was my friend's cousin, and such was our mutual attraction, that in the spring of 1895 I married him! My dream of genteel spinsterhood was very effectively shattered.

NOTE. I hope you won't object to appearing in my narrative, dear Robert. If you do, and I really turn this account into a novel, I'll change your name, or even leave you out altogether. But I hope you'll agree to remain. We have now been married ten years, and have two dear children, and your medical practice, with rooms in Harley Street, is thriving. I think we both know that we will always live in the house in

Saxony Square, which we both love. One of the things that attracted me to you, Robert, was the fact that you had visible parents, readily available for inspection, and that they were eminently respectable academics! But there, I must go back into the last century to bring my narrative to a conclusion. I thought a long time about the title, and have decided that, if it is published as a novel, it will be called *The Ghosts of Mayfield Court*.

Catherine Paget, 1905.

Soon after my marriage, I made arrangements to sell Mayfield Court to a charitable body who wished to demolish it, and replace it with a small cottage hospital. I could think of no better use for the site, and readily accepted the £450 that they offered me for it. I went down in midsummer to examine the work in progress.

The house was already half demolished, with only the ground floor rooms remaining, and the garden had been cleared of some of its outbuildings and half of it ploughed up, ready for the laying of the foundations for the new hospital. But the lower end, where the remains of little Helen Paget had been concealed, was still a wilderness of overgrown, rank vegetation.

I walked slowly along the path, where the smell of brick-dust seemed to have replaced the perfumes of the unkempt blooms of yesterday. When I reached the ruins of the washhouse, I vividly recalled the little gypsy girl, pointing mutely to the skeleton that she had discovered, and putting her finger to her lips.

But on that day there was no sign of Hannah Price. True, I did find myself looking across the weeds to the far wall of the wilderness, where I saw another girl child standing. She was wearing a dark, olive-green dress, with lace at the collars and cuff, and I remember thinking that it was a very formal dress for a child wandering in a ruined garden. The little girl looked at me, and a brilliant smile transformed her face into something welcoming and attractive. I turned away for a moment, and when I looked back, the little girl had disappeared.

We do hope that you have enjoyed reading this large print book.

Did you know that all of our titles are available for purchase?

We publish a wide range of high quality large print books including:
Romances, Mysteries, Classics
General Fiction
Non Fiction and Westerns

Special interest titles available in large print are:
The Little Oxford Dictionary
Music Book
Song Book
Hymn Book
Service Book

Also available from us courtesy of Oxford University Press:
Young Readers' Dictionary
(large print edition)
Young Readers' Thesaurus
(large print edition)

For further information or a free brochure, please contact us at:
Ulverscroft Large Print Books Ltd.,
The Green, Bradgate Road, Anstey,
Leicester, LE7 7FU, England.
Tel: (00 44) 0116 236 4325
Fax: (00 44) 0116 234 0205

Other titles published by
The House of Ulverscroft:

THE CALTON PAPERS

Norman Russell

Arthur Waldegrave is the heir to a vast fortune. But when he perishes in a fire, Detective Inspector Saul Jackson and his sergeant, Herbert Bottomley, establish that he was murdered with cyanide. Who would gain from Arthur's death? His brother Lance, in debt and pursued by the girl he's betrayed? Or architect Jeremy Beecham? Arthur had bitterly opposed his engagement to Margaret Waldegrave. Then, following a second murder, Jackson discovers the mysterious Major Pomeroy, owner of the Calton Papers. Jackson brings his investigation to a devastating and unsuspected climax when the papers reveal the underlying motive for Arthur Waldegrave's death . . .

Making Management Simple

'I read *Making Management Simple* and thought it was
excellent . . . I am a great believer in the importance of
getting the simple things right. The book ought to be widely
used as the starting point for any management course and
virtually anyone starting a job of any kind.'

Bruce Lloyd, Professor of Strategic Management,
London South Bank University

'This book is any easy read. It is a management course
in iteself. It should be essential reading for any supervisor
or new manager.'

Martyn Hurd, Company Trustee for ITN Pensions and
Finance Director of the Broadcast Journalism
Training Council (BJTC)

WEST SUFFOLK HOSPITALS
CLINICAL RESOURCE CENTRE
....
.... BURY ST. EDMUNDS
SUFFOLK IP33 2QZ

WEST SUFFOLK HOSPITAL
LIBRARY

T13148

If you want to know how . . .

Resolving Conflict
How to manage disagreements and develop trust and understanding

Offers an understanding of the nature of conflict and structures.
This book enables us to begin to meet our needs and those of the
other person, while maintaining the relationship and resolving our
differences respectfully.

Becoming a Director
Learn the basics and become an effective and successful director

Explains the basic responsibilities and opportunities of
directorship, removing the legal jargon and mystery – not just a
list of rules but a practical guide.

Voices of Experience
The expert's guide on what to say and how to say it

Full of practical advice on presentation skills from those who've
made them work. This book is constructed around the author's
personal interviews with distinguished personalities such as Gary
Lineker, Desmond Morris, Roland Smith and Karan Bilimoria.

For full details, please send for a free copy of the
latest catalogue to:

How To Books
3 Newtec Place, Magdalen Road
Oxford OX4 1RE, United Kingdom
info@howtobooks.co.uk
www.howtobooks.co.uk